#ENTRANGEMENT

Where Colours Don't Bleed

Zizzi Bonah

Published by
She And The Cat's Mother

Published by She And The Cat's Mother 2016
SheAndTheCatsMother.co.uk

Lyrics from the song 'Said the Red Wine to the Water' written by Ida Barker. Copyright 2009 Beatroute Records International. www.IdaBarker.live

A CIP catalogue record for this book is available from the British Library.
Paperback ISBN: 978-0-9935527-2-4
eBook ISBN: 978-0-9935527-3-1

This book is dedicated in two parts:
To my lovely mum, Gwen Hullah – for her dry humour and sound advice and whose reasons are justified by encouraging me to re-group, re-think, re-try. And to my late grandparents, Ida (maiden name Bona) and Tommy Hullah who farmed within Nidderdale. In memory to them, my nom de plume – merging Bona and Hullah into Bonah.

Chapters

SALT

#Salt – *Sensing I am alone now, I open my eyes and confirm there is nothing between myself and the flickering source of candle light, only the book – I reach down and take its edge.*

Moments ago, a prison guard hurled the book into my cell – taunting words followed – according to common wisdom it's unlucky for a prisoner to read their own book of life. The truth is – I am my own woman, and anyone who claims I am not, professes to know a different me!

I lower the book, letting the candlelight shine onto it. The title reads: **Prisoner Of The Past: Salt Delray**. *I open it, but am bedazzled by dancing light and shadows. Only a stir of knowing reaches up from the pages; and I'm transfixed, seemingly recognising the outline of words. The book becomes heavier in my hands as new pages and chapters are added to the volume – it appears to be writing itself.*

I take the candle and move it close to the book. The hot wax drips onto the pages, the liquid runs, spelling out words as it presses and cools to congeal. It has written: **If you sit very still, you can hear the sun move**. *The meaning doesn't resonate to me. Then I gasp, sighting a kiss from the flame to the book's corner. Instantly my fingers fly to knockback the fire, but the book has already changed into charred paper, unravelling wisps drift upwards and out through my prison cell window, towards the setting sola sun.*

Turning my face to the wall, despair escapes me which isn't silent. I only hope my instincts aren't as close as far away. For I have read of a time and a place yet to be lived – the future. If I'm right, and this isn't a cruel deception, then my life will continue.

But if I'm wrong?

The cell door bangs open. I wheel round. A prison guard rasps, "It's time!"

:

(1) PITCH WHITE

:

#WaterHasAMemory – His cold steely eyes reflected only the face that looked into them. Her face.

She barely recognised herself. Her naturally illustrious cinnamon-black hair hung shamefully damp and lank, placing emphasis on white transparent skin, shadowed by bruising. The separation of her shaded breasts just visible, but Salt's amber eyes burnt like glowing embers out of a gaunt face captured in the windows of Judge Helsby's soul.

"Salt Delray," he began. "Under the law of Supreme Munrah, you have been found guilty of murder by drowning Kielter warrior, Rhuand Mezarron. You are therefore sentenced to peremptory death!"

Salt felt like someone who had been struck without warning. Engaging in reflection that gave back dullness and without saying a word, she opened her mouth and let out a silent scream.

Judge Helsby's voice continued to grate like granite across the courtroom. "To prepare leaving the fourth element you are hereby granted a measure of daylight by the shoreline of Lake Gardenia before a poison metal pellet will be administered to you."

Lowering his reflective eyes and with commanding weight, he bought down the gavel. "Guards! Pursue the Metalgant virtue and return *this* Earthlet prisoner to cell block PW4!"

Forcibly, two Metalgant prison guards who had shadowed Salt since her arrest, directed her through an ornate door that led to long darkened corridors.

Devastated, through word of mind, Salt spoke to Rhuand – *The fault didn't lie in the loving, but in the circumstance.*

Her shackled departure echoed loudly down passageway after passageway, but Salt didn't protest. Not now. She knew all too well, no favour would it gain her. Resistance would result in further punishment of the Iron Cage, which she had struggled to endure twice before this prejudicial hearing.

Salt needed time to think –

Could there be a way out?

She recognised there was little food or sympathy from Metalgant prison guards. And less so now she had been convicted of killing a Metalgant – the self-appointed ruling class. She had no alternative. She would have to accept fate was delivering her securely back to the dark, dank cell she had known since her capture. Hope, she perceived was possibly the cruellest word of all.

Bang!

The guards slammed shut the reinforced iron clad door behind her with menacing force, then lifted up the lozenge-shape viewing flap from the outside to scrutinise her.

"Occupancy of prisoner Delray resumed!" jeered prison guard one, the taller of the two men. She closed harassed eyes against all the cruel encumbers, wondering desperately would she ever find herself again –

"Yeah, innocent, eh?" taunted the other. "She may as well plead the rain's snowing fast."

As their dialogue emanated into her cell she realised their hatred against her would only deepen. Yes, it could only escalate now she was deemed a convict who had killed one of their own.

But she knew deep down, no-one could break her emotionally, for she had already been broken. Broken from the death of her beloved Rhuand — there had been something lawless about him that made him dangerously handsome. She had struggled desperately to put the shattered pieces back together again, but the fragments were a jumble she had mentally glued together in the wrong order. She was too broken to break up ever again.

Metalgant guard one's penetrating voice pierced through the viewing hole and into Salt's chain of thought. "Everyone's either a liar or a saint behind these prison walls, and by my reckoning the only saints round here are we, the Metalgant guards."

Salt recoiled further into the depths of the darkened cell as they burst into harsh laughter. She quailed deep inside herself, yet almost completely without self-pity.

"Send your dreams up to heaven, Delray," he continued, "cos these streets aren't meant to be dreamt on!"

And with an unyielding turn of the sterling key, Salt was locked inside.

Incarcerated.

Until the inevitable.

Her death!

:

The rain hammered against the bars of the prison cell window, jolting Salt from disturbed sleep. Its hammering rhythms translated through her ears and into her mind a soliloquy, repeating in an unbroken loop:–

"I didn't know what day it was,

When you walked into my life,

Like the streets where the buildings,

Scrape the sky.

The way some people do,

When they get clouds,

In their eyes..."

Her mind flashed back to the remembrance of Rhuand – those were the last words he said to her before – she turned her mind away. Not wanting to remember as known before – the tragedy.

With a sheep's fleece separating herself from the rusty metal bed springs, painfully she strained to sit upright. Her yellow prison overalls held little resistance to the biting cold. Uncontrollably she shivered, acknowledging her stiffened bones and aching muscles from the unforgiving weather elements her cell was regularly bombarded to – standard prison conditions.

Only Salt wasn't a standard prisoner. She was an Earthlet. Part of the underclass regarding the current element system. Not only had she been found guilty of murder. Worse, murder outside her own element structure.

From her date of arrest, inmates encouraged by Metalgant prison guards had forced her into the realm of outcast. Shunned. Ridiculed. Ridicule she'd willed not to see or hear. Such treatment reinforced her belief not to look up to the ruling Metalgant system; when all that looking up can keep you down.

To her mind, fortune favours affray – but even she had to admit, in the peremptory eyes of law Munrah, her fight was lost. For as sure as rain is right, following Judge Helsby's verdict, her penalty of death was now assured.

Salt stifled the screams raging in her head. The stresses, strains, the torments were all etched on her young face. She grasped at small comfort, at least her parents were not alive to see her in such frightening and dreaded circumstances. Emotionally they would have suffered along with her. And their worry would not have altered the outcome from the trial.

No, worry changes nothing. It only wounded the heart.

Salt had taken a physical downturn following the two Iron Cage punishments shortly after her arrest. By protesting innocent, she was branded defective. Each punishment was issued as a way to instil obedience to Metalgant prison rules. Salt had found both subjections equally harrowing. The process was known by prison guards as: *'being put out to jejune'.*

No water.

No food.

The punishment involved a solitary prisoner entering a metal gridded cage. This would be winched up via a crane high above the prison walls indefinitely. Those prisoners not strong enough would succumb to vicious attacks from the vulturous birds circling the railed cages.

Resolutely, Salt closed her eyes tightly against the horrific recalls she had witnessed and suffered, but there was no way of shielding herself away from the reality. For she would forever be a fugitive to her own memory. Unable to escape the blood curdling screeches of the carnivorous birds, and the screams of those prisoners who scraped the sky, only to barely, or not, make it back to their prison cells. Alive.

Dark circles framed Salt's almond shaped eyes and her skin no longer radiated blossom-like freshness, instead arid and blotchy in colour. Her tortured body and bruised mind against such relenting adversity had left the prisoner nursing the raw feeling of utter destitution churning repeatedly in the pit of her knotted stomach. There was no-one to turn to in her need so dire.

Jadedly she opened harassed eyes and pushed back the lank cinnamon-black hair from her swollen face.

"Last season. The beginning of something wondrous, wouldn't you agree?" The voice appeared to come from outside Salt's window. "Something called – love?"

From a dull haze, Salt's eyes cleared instantly. Was she hearing the very echo of her own soul? "Pardon. What did you say?" She hesitated before rising painfully to her distended feet and sway jaggedly across the stone flagged floor towards the direction of the voice.

"A twisted truth. You do realise, Female Munrah put you in this position? Incarcerating you on account of her own cruel mandate." The voice spoke calmly.

"What have you heard?" Salt's speech quivered. "Who are you? And how can you claim to know such detail?" Nobody had ever suggested Salt's innocence before. Nobody!

"Don't you know water has a memory?"

Salt felt the raindrops touch her face and the crisp outside breeze envelop her fatigued mind and body. And for the first time since her entrapment, she didn't feel alone. While there was no way of reaching the prison cell window high above her, she keenly listened to the mysterious voice. Aiming to gain further insight from each nuance in tone.

The voice carried with concern, "You know, there was a time

when I thought you might drown in your own tears, girl." The voice paused. "Rhuand, from what I've learnt, he was a very important Metalgant."

"Was…" replied Salt distantly.

Rhuand, dear beloved Rhuand. Where could she begin? He was dark, lithe and dangerously handsome. A mercenary! Her body trembled violently at the remembrance of him. His presence. His touch. His warmth of breath. The loss of him she found too expansive for words – her whole being shook to its core. "Rhuand, he meant everything to me." Salt struggled to speak clearly. "Tell me, how do you stop loving someone when they've gone?"

"Love travels to where love exists."

She edged closer beneath the austere iron barred window. A window to a world beyond her confined space. "But where does love go?" she questioned in a manner that would not easily be wrestled from her.

"It finds its way to the intended," the voice replied. "As well you know Salt, Rhuand was one of Female Munrah's Kielters. He helped to keep time in a prolonged state of autumn in order for Female Munrah to preserve the fourth element for as long as possible. Therefore, time itself is slowed down. And as the element metal brings about the onset of winter towards the end of its cycle, so the fifth element will begin, that being water."

"Yes," agreed Salt, "and when this occurs, Female Munrah will lose all power and control. Consequently, it is vital for her well-being and that of the Metalgants to prolong autumn if they are to survive in a state of privilege."

She recollected vividly, Rhuand showing her a puncture wound positioned close to his left chest muscle. He had been one of the three chosen recipients for the Actimm programme, whereby through a medical procedure quartz crystals had been introduced into his bloodstream. Rhuand had further confided in Salt how the crystals oscillated between the beats of his heart. These frequencies were monitored by Metal Fort's Hub Base, allowing them to harness the frequencies and successfully transmit wireless waves into the core of the planet to inhibit its magnetic pull. Result: time itself would be slowed through the process of altering the planet's rotational speed.

Salt upturned her face to the barred cell window, feeling as though she had fallen out of a generous sky. "Why didn't Female Munrah investigate further into Rhuand's death? Surely as he was so important to her..." Her heart rate pounded in her ears. Almost deafening. But then, Rhuand always had a physical effect on her when alive, and it was no different from his death. She'd seen the heart of him not the shadow.

Salt tried to centre herself.

Concentrate.

Breathing in deeply through her nostrils to exhale slowly through a parched mouth, her troubled thoughts found speech, "Why weren't all options looked into instead of blindly arresting me, an Earthlet from the third element?"

No answer came forth.

"Hello? Hello! Answer me! Are you still there?" she pleaded, feeling a sudden separateness.

"Salt, I am a water vis-viva – an energy of water. Known to my friends as Lapis-Lazuli. Wherever water is, so am I. When Rhuand came to pass on Lake Gardenia, I was a witness."

Sudden unsteadiness engulfed Salt's bruised body, her legs

buckled beneath her and ungracefully she shunted down against the metal panelled wall beneath the window. "You... you was there?" She managed with tremendous difficulty to hold onto herself. "You, witnessed the accident?"

"Accident? This was no accident, Salt." He spoke with amiable firmness. "Female Munrah was alerted to Rhuand and yourself during the first encounter you shared together, and thereafter through Rhuand's pulse rate increasing and admonishing a warning of faulty time to the Actimm – such a sustained increase would bring about the fifth element sooner. It is for this very reason love is a condemned luxury for a Kielter. Love is a sin. There is no place for it under Female Munrah's order. It is better for her to be feared than have love jeopardise her tyrannical reign."

It was all she could do to keep up with him. "Are you saying that she, Female Munrah killed Rhuand?"

"Not directly," he replied cautiously. "Female Munrah and her confidant, Skada followed Rhuand on horseback to the lake which had newly frozen over from the onset of winter. Whereupon, the sight of seeing two lovers ice skating into the arms of each other proved to be the biggest betrayal Female Munrah could foresee. A confirmation of her dark suspicion. So with dire hatred within Female Munrah's core, I saw her approach the edge of the frozen lake."

Salt clasped the opening to her prison uniform collar, hunching her shoulders up to her ears. She dreaded the unfolding knowledge the water vis-viva was about to share with her.

He continued to speak, "There, Female Munrah vehemently vowed to destroy you, Salt. For as she saw it, it was you, a mere Earthlet who dared to overturn the balance of autumn by diverting the course of her number one Kielter. I'm sorry to say, you were the intended. You were the target."

There was a shared silence wherein no words were spoken as this new knowledge filtered its way through Salt's mind, body and soul to a resonance. She didn't doubt the unravelling details – her impression from the spoken voice was one of honesty.

Salt confessed, "The attraction between us was just too strong. It was magnetic. Such an immense pull. Nothing either of us had experienced before. We both knew, I being an Earthlet, and Rhuand a Metalgant, fraternising together was forbidden." She began to sob. "Oh Rhuand... he wasn't meant to die. For it should have been me!"

"This isn't easy to hear." Empathy was clear in his voice. "All the same, you should be aware of the truth. Factually."

Instinctively Salt had known from the outset nothing said at her courtroom trial was as it had seemed. She had fought so hard against authority to put her version of events across. After all, this shouldn't have been unreasonable. It was her trial –

The trial of Salt Delray.

Yet, her viewpoint, her evidence had been so quickly discarded from the light and while she was aware sometimes language can get in the way of deliverance, now courtesy of Lapis-Lazuli the truth was proving to be more shocking than she could ever have anticipated.

Lapis-Lazuli's tone became more pensive, "I saw Female Munrah as she ground down into frozen Lake Gardenia with her fierce iron stiletto heel. Such rage. Such intensity. An emanation of all her metal power. The ice, it creaked, then cracked its way with the greatest force of violence and speed." He held a pointed silence as though hiding in plain sight. "And once it found its way to you both, giving way under your skated feet–"

"My Earthlet mother once told me, death starts from the feet up," she reminisced sorrowfully.

"I must assure you, Salt. Rhuand, didn't hesitate. Franticly he searched under the ice bound waters to drag your unconscious body back onto the ice surface."

"Only he couldn't save himself." The words caught the back of her throat. She swallowed her pain.

"Tragically, no. He became trapped under the vast solid planes of ice, unable to surface between the ever moving and closing gaps."

"So Female Munrah, from her vengeful actions killed Rhuand. Then, instigated my arrest for his killing, and now my death. Do you know, Lapis-Lazuli, I wasn't even allowed to attend Rhuand's funeral. She even took that away from me." Her tone sounded faraway even to herself. "Have you ever noticed, the word funeral? It's spelt with the word *fun* at the beginning – how insolent."

Salt was now passed crying. In fact, she was all wrung out. Even reprisal inflicted on Female Munrah following her deathly deeds, Salt conceded would never bring Rhuand back to her. No, instead he would eternally remain at distance, alive only through her memories.

"You escaped death on the lake," Lapis-Lazuli said gravely, "therefore the order of death must be reinstated. Hence, Judge Helsby following Female Munrah's command, sentenced you to death – to avoid a seismic wobble where we would enter real-time."

"How do you mean?" she said sharply.

"Without your death, Female Munrah is unable to enable a new

Kielter to replace Rhuand. You see, it didn't work to plan. And the alternative–"

"Plan? Alternative?" Salt was baffled. Frightened even.

"The quartz crystals removed from Rhuand's dead body continue to emit a signal, causing an imbalance to the remaining Kielter frequencies. He wasn't meant to die. It wasn't written into the Actimm programme. Inadvertently the crystals remember Rhuand through an echo."

Salt tried to assemble the facts. "So if I die, the order will be reinstated, and Rhuand's echo will be depleted? Is that what you're saying?"

"Exactly," reflected the water vis-viva. "This will undoubtedly weaken the remaining Rhuand quartz crystals."

"And if I don't die?"

"Well, this is the alternative! You see, Rhuand still walks the Gardenia Lake."

"Rhuand, is still alive? No… No!" Disbelief took hold of Salt. She felt her face twist with mixed intensity as she clambered to her feet and leaned heavily against the cold iron panelled cell.

"You don't rest just because you're dead."

"How can you make such a prosilient statement?"

"I can because it is the truth, Salt! Rhuand is waiting for you. I've seen him, though you wouldn't recognise or know him as before. He's in limbo between the cycle of elements we live by, and the infinite above. His spirit remains at the lake. You see, as he saved your life, only you can save his death."

"But how can I save Rhuand, I'm locked in here, shortly to receive peremptory death?" she appealed to him with exposed bleakness to her constricted surroundings.

"Where colours don't bleed, there is a gateway. A hidden under-lake arched bridge. Before you receive the poison metal pellet at Lake Gardenia look for the bridge. This will take you into a breath of new dawn. And there you will reunite with Rhuand."

"Why are you helping me?" asked Salt in a voice choking with passion.

"Because Female Munrah believes all five elements are separate. She has gone out of her way to rule over them all and tamper with the natural time of seasons – when each element should lead seamlessly into the next subsequent one. Harmony. One takes nothing away from the next, it merely adds to it. A continuum in the cycle. No beginning, no end. I wish you all the very best, Salt Delray. Be dexterous! Be resilient! Be brave!"

:

Stood iron manacled on the shoreline of Lake Gardenia, Salt frantically cast her gaze across and down through the rippling lake waters. In the distance she could hear a faint rumble of thunder, as the overhead rain clouds began to release their burdening downpour onto the restricted zone cornered off by the prison guards.

"Bring back any memories, Delray before we buttonhole you?" taunted Metalgant guard one.

"Claimed she lost her lover here, eh? Where's the show of tears, then? Where's all the blubbering?" sneered the other.

Salt could not be distracted. She had to be strong. She had a plan!

Unrelenting, guard one continued, "I heard they had a struggle to hack his body free from the frozen ice–"

"Can't imagine a high-ranking Metalgant looking at the likes of her. An Earthlet, can you?"

Their voices resonated across the lake to echo back and forth...

Forcibly, Salt closed her mind to them.

Risk and reward.

There was only a small window of time to locate the underwater bridge before her opportunity would be lost, and she would fatally be made to swallow the poison metal pellet.

But where's the bridge?

It has to be here…

Somewhere…

Chunks of thawing ice bobbed along the water's surface, signalling – Salt noted – the onset of winter had retreated since the devastating event of Rhuand's passing.

She moved away from the prison guards to create a greater distance between herself and them. As long as they could clearly see her it shouldn't arouse their suspicion. After all, there was nowhere to escape to apart from the waters. She stepped closer to the lake edge. "Lapis-Lazuli," she urged to the lake in a hushed tone. "Lapis-Lazuli, are you here? I can't see the bridge you spoke of…"

There was no reply. The silence was steadfast. Salt began to feel anxious. What if the water vis-viva had misled her? Maybe he was a member of Female Munrah's alliance. Could this be a further wicked lie before Salt Delray's end?

Suddenly there was a break in the overspread clouds to the east side of the waters. Blinding bright sunlight permeated through and Salt could just make out a beautifully muted Rainbow extending above the Gardenia Lake. She was mesmerised. Its colours became more and more vivid the longer she concentrated upon them. Her eyes followed its arch until it became apparent to her the Rainbow appeared to continue down into the lake. Two separate arches, creating a complete Rainbow of circle – the over-world and a hidden underworld.

Yes!

It looked like an upside-down bridge under the moving water currents. And it wasn't all that far from her, just off by the jetty.

"What have I to lose?" she said excitedly under her breath. She had to find Rhuand Mezarron. And even if it all went unjustly wrong, it would be better to die a death of drowning at the place so dear to her and her lover than endure the poison metal pellet administered by the law of Female Munrah. She decided to risk it. Make a run for it. Not to be prevented by her weighted prison shackles, Salt Delray gave it her all.

"Halt! Halt, Delray!" shouted guard one, signalling her abandonment to his colleague.

In force of strength both guards launched themselves after the fleeing prisoner who battled with as much speed and sheer might as she could possibly sustain without failing or yielding along the full length of the jetty.

"She's going to jump! She's going to bloody jump!" shouted the second guard. "Do something! Stop her! Stop herrrr!"

Don't look back, you're not going there!

She propelled off the jetty and in mid-air brought her knees up into her chest. Hoping with all her heart and soul she could reach the submerged Rainbow in the rippling waters beneath her. "Rhuand Mezzzzzarrronnnn..." She screamed a scream which reverberated across the Gardenia Lake and back again and again as her contorted body plummeted into the unknown waters, before disappearing out of the Metalgant guards' belligerent sight.

:

(2) BLUE SALUTE

:

#LakeGardenia – The stronghold of fog blanketing Lake Gardenia began to lift for the first time since Rhuand awoke here. Alerting his being from a nebulous dreamlike state to immense urgency as his senses rapidly climbed.

In the distance he could vaguely hear a female calling his name across the lake waters. Heedful, he pulled back the hood to his long slate-coloured overcoat in a desperate attempt to hear the voice more clearly and locate the direction from which it travelled –

West side!

Replacing the hood over his shorn black hair, swiftly he made way along the uneven pebbled lakeside to investigate.

On Rhuand's approach to the jetty, the calling of his name had now stopped. All he could hear was abrasive coughing and choking, followed by deep, irregular gasps for breath. The jetty concealed his view as to who lie on the other side of it. But without hesitation he closed the gap between himself and the protruding barrier.

Suddenly his brilliant green eyes fell on the beseecher, causing an internal shock to reverberate through his mettle – routing him to the very spot.

Salt!

Rhuand cast tentative eyes over the saturated girl crouched on her knees, head bent downwards gasping for breath on the edge of the lake. Her arched body twisted in distress as the lake waters sounded to have entered deep into an empty stomach. Repeatedly, and violently, she wrenched the waters out, clawing frantic fingers over and round pebbles into the shoreline sediment, as a travail of overflowing tears streamed down her chalk-white cheeks.

With unwavering scrutiny Rhuand continued to observe Salt. She appeared to be much closer to bone than he remembered. Angry welts announced themselves around swollen wrists and ankles. Her wet yellow overalls exposed an area to her collar bone and sternum, revealing unforgiving, infected wounds and inflamed patches of bare skin.

He was outraged. Torture wounds indicated only one person could be responsible for ordering such a punishment –

Female Munrah!

Undoubtedly he was familiar to just what abominable lengths she would relish in exceeding and furthermore, the cruel reason behind his ensnared limbo. Only now, Rhuand steadfastly believed forthcoming events surrounding his and Salt's obligatory situations could take a magnificent twist in their favour. He and Salt, reunited. His ardent dream could flourish into a reality – wherein love no longer represented a crime of brutal chastisement.

Rhuand longed to touch Salt's tormented body. To comfort her and make everything better, not bitter. But in spite of this overpowering desire, unmistakably he knew no such thing could happen. The elevated stage to transcend had not yet commenced for him. Instead, Rhuand's physical appearance was transitional, whereby he moved between a state of liquid metal and solid steel. This extraordinary spirit manifestation was the result of his entrapment here in suppressive limbo, unable to move forward into the next level of elements. Vigorously, at will, he had strived to work with his new changeable abilities. Here, an individual would suffer a condition relative to their own born element, known as Iquique.

Many times Rhuand felt dreadfully ungrounded, and so ritualised hiding his eyes under the rimmed hood of his overcoat, in an attempt to feel less exposed to his fearful circumstances.

In all his life as a Metalgant, he had been a ruthless force to be reckoned with. Extraordinarily intelligent, strong in body and resilient of mind. These qualities had been a key factor as to why Female Munrah had specifically chosen him as Head Kielter. He had successfully ascended up through all her torturous training regimes with acquired pain-resistance, proving himself to be indisputably the best candidate for the Actimm programme. But Rhuand's character had been seriously tested by merely existing and not living in this alterative spirit dimension. There was no preparation for this indeterminate state.

Watching Salt's resilience as she fought to stabilise herself to gain a steadier, more even breath, Rhuand was captivated by her. He could see she was very much alive. No, she had not arrived here in spirit-form like he had, thankfully. Salt still possessed all her Earthletness, to shiver, to sob, to feel. Virtues Rhuand had been severely trained to lose in life. Yes, he had denied feelings altogether until he had unexpectedly met and fallen for her – loving the very bones of her.

However, to endure this state of existence he had learnt: if you do not abandon your emotions, you will most certainly lose your sanity. Yet miraculously, here was wholesome minded Salt, only a stone throw away from him. He must not allow himself to truly feel again – emotions could jeopardise everything.

With readiness, she now appeared to gather herself together. Slowly she tilted her head upwards to gaze in the direction of his shielded eyes beneath the rain-hood. Perceptively Rhuand felt as if she read the extreme depths of his anguished soul through her mesmeric amber stare.

"Rhu, Rhuand Mezarron?"

He willed her on through her struggle to talk between new found breaths.

"I'm looking for Rhuand Mezarron. Do you know where I can find him?"

He was jolted to a devastating realisation. The love of his life, failed to recognise him in death!

Fitfully, he began to wrestle unknown answers to his questions.

Will she learn to love me as once before, or will her love be a still-born memory?

Salt cut into his dark thoughts, "Rhuand Mezarron?" She placed extra emphasis on the name. "I was told to follow a hidden arched bridge, to find Rhuand." Concern and doubt tightened her unquiet face and squeezed her voice to sharpness. "The prison guards, they're not here are they? I have made it across to where colours don't bleed, haven't I?"

Feeling duty-bound to reassure her would mean breaking his silence, but he was at a loss as to know where or indeed how to answer.

"I have to see Rhuand!" Her restless eyes appealed through strands of sodden hair while grappling to her trembling feet. "Do you know where he is? I've been told he is waiting for me."

In Rhuand's fantasy Salt had intuitively differentiated who he was from the beginning of their reunion, but the reality was proving to be very different.

He gazed at her fiercely unhappy face.

His mind lingered over her name.

"This place, it can change a person. Camouflage." As he broke his silence the dense curtain of fog continued to steadily lift from the lake, and Salt took her first unsteady steps towards him.

She exclaimed with wild relief, "My prison shackles, they've gone!"

"Courtesy of Gardenia waters," he said in assurance. "You're released. No longer will you be encumbered by past physical restraints." He felt his spirit surge upwards to meet the increasingly unhindered sky as he shared in her enlightenment. Oh, how he'd missed Salt Delray beyond all words and thoughts.

"Can you help me?" She sounded decisive.

"We can help each other." He wanted by some technique of pure presence to convey to her that she was important in her own light.

Without warning, from the west side of the waters a stunningly lucid blue hue progressively swept its way across the lake and surrounding landscape, elevating the biting cold to a brilliant warmth. Everything touched by the proceeding blue hue seemed to instantly radiate an astonishing glow.

"What's happening?" she cried. "Are we standing in a clear sweep of sky?"

Mentally he placed a reassuring arm round her quivering body. "This is it," he confessed. "We have entered the first arc of the Rainbow. The first prismatic colour, blue."

"But I haven't found Rhuand, yet!" she insisted.

And he felt mourning wash over him, not for lost love – for he would never let go of love – but for vanished happiness. "He's within your sight," he uttered, "k. i. s. s." The letters to an acronym, "Keep it sandsomme stone."

"What!" she said. "Only Rhuand would say that to me! Who are you?" she demanded as if the statement itself was deeply compromising, yet it was one he could not reject.

Gradually the corners of his mouth lifted into the shape of a courteous smile. The Salt he had come to know so well in life was clearly still as spirited as ever.

He recalled the meaning of the acronym he and Salt had conjured together. Sandsomme stone meant a species of freestone; a term which resonated for both of them, to be themselves, free from restraints. He had planned to leave the Actimm programme, moves had been made to train the number two Kielter with mind of his ideal replacement, but a future life shared with Salt was not to be. Savagely it was ripped away from them and took the form of his life-demise through drowning in the Gardenia Lake.

Rhuand felt a dark disquiet of slow rage begin to stir from the core of his being. He had learnt to control this rage as a means to give him an extra strength, rather than allowing it to destroy him. For he knew his time must be bided.

"Rhu? Is that – you?" Her hesitant reaction bought him from the depths of reflection as he was reminded of the here and now.

"Yes. Though I know I'm not visually the same as when we were last together. What you now see is my spirit in transition."

"Oh, Rhuand." Awkwardly stepping over the uneven pebbles she stumbled, reaching out to him.

He could sense apprehension from her to his new appearance. "You can't touch me, Salt. I've not yet started transcending into a more constant form – only when I fuse to an unrelated metal can my system neutralise any shock I would otherwise pass onto you." He was unsure as to her reaction from this explanation.

On the face of this, she sounded unperturbed, "Lapis-Lazuli said I'd not know you as before. Not knowing exactly what this meant at the time, but here, I can appreciate he was right." She paused and he felt her spectacular amber eyes study him. "He also stressed the importance of how you saved my life and subsequently only I can save your death." He heard her voice falter with the stirring up of emotions. "So, where do we go from here and out of this dilemma?"

Rhuand was amazed by her pragmatism. He had always been her strength when she was weak and however unsettling it was to him, their roles had turned. In his vulnerability of limbo, Salt was now his strength. His rock. "We must follow the blue hue until we meet the next colour in the Rainbow." He sounded optimistic to his own senses. "In all honesty, we must persist until we reach the seventh Rainbow colour..."

"How do you know this?" Her voice now rang out crystal clear to him.

"Like you, I met Lapis-Lazuli. Explicitly he revealed to me the first colour, blue. In this colour we must follow the lake water downstream to the Gardenia Falls. He insisted we must hurry to give ourselves the best possible chance to succeed. The reason being, a connecting gateway to the dimension we once lived in, exists where the Gardenia Falls merge with three mighty waterfalls. Female Munrah could access this gateway and enter through a Moonbow."

Salt gasped with horror. "You mean to say we're not completely free of her and her ruthlessness? She murdered you, then conceded to end my existence after sentencing me to your extinction of life!"

"Yes!" Avidly he kept up the verbal pace. "Female Munrah cannot enter here through a Rainbow. Her only option is a distortion of this, a Moonbow. The more distance we acquire from Female Munrah the safer we'll both be. We can do this. We can find the end of the Rainbow. We have each other."

He observed Salt as she lifted her face to the sky in thoughtfulness, "I guess it's only natural Female Munrah will follow us, here."

"Undoubtedly, she'll maliciously see it as unfinished business. Her aim will be to prevent us effectively attaining the final colour. Red." It hadn't deserted Rhuand's thoughts, maybe Salt wasn't here owing to the love she had for him. That feeling of love could have died along with her arrest and imprisonment. Maybe she blamed him for her ominous circumstances.

He dwelt on how it could be selfish to ask someone to love you selflessly over a period of absent time. The subjected persecutions Salt had endured within the Irongate prison, Rhuand could only imagine. Lapis-Lazuli simply mentioned Salt's captivity there – no other details. After all, he wouldn't blame her for hating him, neither of them would be in this dire predicament had they never met and had he not accomplished a high ranking position for Female Munrah. But what if Salt was solely here as a means to escape her own authorised death?

"How will we know which route to take towards entering each of the causeway colours?" she asked.

Again, his attention was jolted back into the present with Salt. "We can only take each colour as we find it. All I've learnt from Lapis-Lazuli is the first colour, blue signifies water. The lake. The place of our enforced separation. We must work forward and through this. It is our Rainbow, Salt. Each different hue represents a unique theme to us, our relationship and our survival."

She nodded acceptance to the unfolding detail he presented to her. "Well, as you say, Rhuand it's rather a case of k. i. s. s. There's only two ways to go. Do or be done for!"

:

Rhuand heaved the rowing boat from the wooden boathouse and onto the calm rippling waters of Lake Gardenia, the lush blue hue gracing the landscape had softened to a paler tone.

The lake congregated majestically between treacherous rugged mountains on either side allowing a constant supply of fresh rainwater to generously run down and accumulate resourcefully.

"Salt, come on!" he shouted in a state of urgency. "Bring the oars with you on the way out."

With expertise she pirouetted. "What do you think, serviceable?" She made her entrance wearing a tight turquoise all-in-one body suit.

Rhuand had always admired her long shapely legs. She looked a picture of exquisite optimism. Vivid sunlight accented her cinnamon hair with black strands, jaggedly bobbed framing her elegant features. "It is very you!" he exclaimed jovially. "I hope it's water-resistant for where we're going."

As she stepped onto the boat with the rowing oars he felt a surge of electricity flow through his spirit. Yes, Salt was irrefutably the love of his life. He felt feverously determined he must win her back successfully. He could not bear the thought of being a stranger to her.

Heading south bound he rowed with relentless vigour on the lake waters. "Do you remember the first time we ever met, Salt?" He searched her youthful face.

She inclined a thoughtful smile. "Yes. I was Earthlet dancing at the Alt Grand Festival for Female Munrah's Sterling Anniversary, and you were in the grandiose circle."

Since Female Munrah procured supremacy to reign over all five elements, Earthlets were mandatorily forced into appalling poverty and judged an underclass to be excluded from metal civilisation.

The only legal way they could publicly make a living was though performing their native dance. Metalgant officials had curtailed the original dance and instead advised Earthlets to embellish their presentation, making it more flamboyant to attract tourists. The Metalgant establishment would then approve or disprove a license for each Earthlet dance group. Severe poverty and squalled narrow-boat conditions existed for the majority of this newly labelled underclass.

"I remember your performance intensely. You danced with such wild vibrancy. A truly remarkable showstopper." Casting his mind back, sitting amongst a raucous crowd, he could almost taste the explosive fireworks lingering in the night air and reawaken the startling sensation of seeing Salt for the very first time.

Salt reached a hand over the boat's edge and into the sinuous lake waters they sped through. "Earthlet dance is an expression through movement to portray passions of the heart and soul. The discipline of the dance is to show real abandonment. You can only be steered by the beat of the music, working from the feet up, one has to have lived an emotion before it can be danced out." In sadness she reflected, "Mama always said, *if you embrace your ability to dance well, it may save you from an Earthlet life of acute poverty'*. Oh, how right she was."

Rhuand didn't break into her recollection of mind. He could see she was emotionally at a distance from him. Instead with sensitivity he waited for her to resume speech in her own natural time.

Carefully she seemed to place her thoughts elsewhere. "You never spoke about your parents, Rhu. What were they like?"

"It is a requirement, young Metalgants leave their parents and join education once they begin to think independently. As you know, my element is encouraged to work as a collective rather than have individual thoughts. That way, no more than a few rise to individual status." He continued to row with broad even strokes. "My parents were barely given enough time to say their farewells to me when Metalgant officials arrived unexpectedly, banging on the door demanding my admittance to training school. As I recall, Mother forced a Regard brooch into my resisting hand. Saying, when I found an exceptional girl to hold in high regard, I should present this as a gift to her. I never saw my parents ever again."

"I still have the brooch."

He was stunned by her words and watched closely as she began to unpin the item of jewellery from her clothing.

"Force of habit, I learnt to fasten it facing my skin as a means of concealment from Metalgant prison guards." She held the large glittering brooch in the palm of her hand. It shimmered profusely in the broad daylight.

Rhuand looked at its ornate flower design with nostalgia. Each of the gemstones were secured in solid iron to replicate a flower petal. "I never dreamt you would still have it in your possession."

"Well, it's the only thing I had from you," she smiled. "Remind me of the gemstones that spell out the word: Regard."

"R is a ruby stone; e, emerald; g, garnet; a, would be amethyst;

hmm, r, ruby again; and lastly d for diamond. Will you pin it on, so I can see the full effect?"

He wondered if he had imagined a reluctantly from her to wear the brooch openly. But in brilliant sunlight, it really did sparkle stupendously.

Did it signify a reward or a punishment?

After ardent rowing he stopped momentarily. "Can you hear that, Salt?" he spoke with surety. They both listened to their surroundings. Hearing in the far distance a rumbling noise.

"We must be gaining on the Gardenia Falls," she said as they saw a cloud of dense water-vapour assemble threateningly to hang in the atmosphere.

"We can't be far off the sheer drop of the falls as the water currents are speeding up. I'll row us to the lake shoreline. We'll carry on by foot." Renewed vigour spurred him on to begin rowing again.

"How will we ever make it down the waterfall?" He sensed her fear of the unknown.

"We'll climb down the rock face. Lapis-Lazuli said, after descending the falls we must faithfully track the river downstream until we reach a substantial building made from sandsomme stone, exhibiting pillars on either side of a colossal door. Open this door and enter the next colour in the Rainbow."

A look of shrewdness and indefensible innocence crossed her face. "Sounds too easy for comfort to me."

"Yes," agreed Rhuand, he cast a knowing eye at the sky overhead. "Hopefully we'll make it before moonrise."

:

#PedalToTheMedal – Salt and Rhuand silently observed the river in full moonshine. It had narrowed significantly, and their view became increasingly impaired by overgrow luscious foliage on either side of the waters.

Taking initiative, Rhuand indicated they tread carefully through the ever decreasing shallow waters, but within little time, shockingly, they discovered the riverbed was reduced to a solitary trickle and then an abrupt stop.

Alarmed, Salt turned to him. "Surely the river should continue further on..." She crouched down to examine the drying wide cracks of the exposed riverbed. "How quickly the landscape changes here," she spoke more to herself than to him.

"Well, a change can be as good as a reply."

She wiped off the muddy residue from her clothing with her bare hands as a means of something to do, hoping not to give away her inner turmoil. "Do you think the river's seeped underground?"

"It's possible, there could be a plane of water beneath us." He looked down at the hardened ground to where the river once lie while gently kicking up dust with his heel.

Salt looked around. "There's no sign of a sandsomme stone building in view." She felt panic stricken from the loss of previous loud water to this unyielding silence. "Don't you find the contrast unnerving, rather like hearing a ticking chronometer, one only becomes aware of it once it has stopped."

Rhuand became quiet and watchful. Her instinct was to draw closer to him.

"Come," he said. "We'll continue further on into the overgrowth."

Relentlessly, they walked on in silence as he fought through the barricade of foliage, breaking and snapping with metal strength through the enormous plants blocking their passageway along the dry, dusty riverbed, already starting to dull the shine off all their clothing as they headed into the unknown.

Hot footedly, keen not to lose him from sight, her disquiet mind flashed to earlier when they had descended the precarious rock face adjacent to the Gardenia Falls – there, hovering in the mist above them, a Moonbow. Its image would remain imprinted on her life-code forever and a day.

The Moonbow was unlike a Rainbow, much more discreet in presentation, exhibiting pastel-like shades in a predominately white arc. Yet, its power was in no way diminished. Her heart filled with anxiety and pure dread while reliving the moment she caught brief sighting of a familiar shape there between the gaps of moving mist: Female Munrah.

Her sumptuous purple velvet gown hardly moved against the force whipped up from the water cascade. Standing next to her was no other than, Skada. Darkly loyal and ruthlessly faithful to his mistress.

Yes, Skada took an equal cruel delight in Female Munrah's horrific crimes as much as she did. They were well matched and deserved each other as scheming companions.

Salt had detected two other darkly dangerous figures, but their silhouettes were unrecognisable to her through the moving mist.

"Keep on, keeping on!" Rhuand had commanded to her. Knowing either one of them could easily have lost footing on the treacherous route, together they had bravely continued down the rugged rock face.

Now, brushing aside damp hair from her cold cheeks, all the while inwardly acknowledging the reason Rhuand and she found themselves in this nightmare was because Female Munrah had made it so. Curbing her inner rage and frustration, Salt reminded herself of one valuable lesson taught while incarcerated at the Irongate prison: nurse your anger close, for anger in openness will allow your enemy every possible opportunity to gain advantage over you.

Tensely, she closed harassed eyes against the unknown, at least for now, Female Munrah and company hadn't caught up to them.

Opening her eyes to take in the magnificent blue moonshine, the Earthlet pulled herself up strictly to the challenge set before them. Rhuand had always been orderly with objectives, and this was one of the merits she recognised persisted within him since his Metalgant life.

It was essential to their well-being to reach the Rainbow's end, without this attainment there would be no prospect of working towards reconciliation, in fact there would be no future together or indeed apart.

Even if circumstances failed to draw them together emotionally as a couple, she still desperately loved the previous Rhuand enough to loyally advance him forward by means of saving his death. "Yes," she said, taking a firm grip of herself, endeavouring to study his silhouetted figure in the blue moonlight. "Let's take care of the things that matter to us, even the things we dislike, and regard them as promises to our future."

Steadfastly, Rhuand battled onwards in the overgrowth and she was secretly cheered by this, but when looking at Rhuand in this alternative dimension, Salt no longer saw his living bronzed complexion, with eyes of gold and the full lipped mouth she so delighted in passionately kissing. Instead, his transition of spirit displayed a pale wash of toning, vivid green eyes and less expressive lips, yet his hair remained jet-black.

From the occasional glimpses she caught beneath the rain-hood, his hair was now dramatically shorter, cropped close, in place of his shoulder length. His stature showed muscular echoes from the past, but Salt was in no doubt the attributes of strength he now possessed had increased immeasurably due to Iquique.

Iquique...

Her mind lingered over the word he had used at the Gardenia Falls.

Then, slowly she pronounced it as it sounded, "E-key-kay."

Unexpectedly, on the rowing boat earlier, she had found the Regard brooch to be a poignant obstacle for her, feeling extremely uncomfortable to do as Rhuand asked, to pin it on her outfit in full open display.

The item of jewellery had been an unspoken reminder to herself of the once intimate love shared between them. She hadn't been ready to wear it outwardly after such a lengthy time of hiding it from cruel Metalgant eyes.

In prison the brooch had given her an inner strength. It would take some time to discard learnt survival habits and embrace what was to come –

Rhuand broke into her thoughts, "Pedal to the medal!" he shouted over his shoulder. "I think I've discovered the first sandsomme stone step." He paused, waiting for her to catch up to him.

And in a life-strike, Salt's attention was in the immediate, as there at Rhuand's dust laden footwear she saw an ascent of colossal sandsomme stone steps. "This must lead to the building Lapis-Lazuli mentioned," she cried. "We must be nearly there!"

As they made their way to the top, a considerably large sandsomme stone building stood at a raised height, illuminated by the dazzling moonshine that radiated down from a great height above the wild forest. On either side of the magnificent huge door, a tall rounded pillar – just as Lapis-Lazuli had described.

"What should we do now?" She hesitated. "Try the door?"

"That's the plan."

Cautiously, together, they approached the sandsomme stone door.

"There's no handle." Her spirit plummeted to zero.

"Can you see a bell?" For all Rhuand's strength and bravery and self-assurance, Salt heard a hint of doubt lay beneath his words.

"No." She sounded rushed to her own ears. "Maybe we just, knock!"

"There has to be a way in." He touched the rough contours of the door as if to find a solution written in braille.

"Wait!" said Salt. "It has an inverted shape." They both moved closer to examine the area. "It looks… somewhat… well, familiar, don't you agree?"

He took in a jagged breath before answering her. "It's the same shape, same size as–"

"The Regard brooch!" they shouted, holding each other's surprised gaze, before casting sight down to the glittering brooch still pinned to Salt's turquoise garment.

With impulsive fingers she fought to unfasten the item of jewellery. "Who would have thought?"

"It has to fit!" He sounded adamant.

Suddenly, Salt stood absolutely motionless. Her whole body arrested right in the middle of a hurry, as though she was listening for the repetition of some sound that she had remembered recently. Petrified, she held her own pained silence. It was too much like facing darkness.

As though reading her thoughts, or maybe subconsciously, she felt Rhuand move closer to her, bringing with him his heart and strength. She felt a precious closeness radiate around them as strong as the pull of their previous lives.

Then, an icy atmosphere prevailed that was close to a let-down, replacing her excitement. Salt tried not to listen to the approaching sounds of fierce iron stiletto heels, striking sandsomme stone.

Feeling imminent danger and full of dread, Salt and Rhuand turned to witness Female Munrah, deviously drawing back into the shade of the shadow projected by a rounded pillar.

:

#SuperficialAngellsWithDangerousFaces – "Well, well well! If it isn't the permutation of Rhuand Mezarron. We must surely be on the other side of tomorrow."

Turning towards the melodic voice, Rhuand sighted the sylphlike and elegant swordsman known as Skada-the-Braska.

Swaggeringly dressed in a loose-fitting collarless black tunic, designed to give unrestrictive movement when wielding his infamous Braska sword, he closed in on the escapees in a circle of movement, while assessing with open curiosity his unwilling prey.

Rhuand's first awareness of Skada was at the Ruthenium Foundation; a training school for young Metalgants. They were both admitted in the same semester.

Skada had shown natural promise to rise high from the outset. Intensely still in showing spirit, yet never solemn. His great level of concentration had led him to take up the discipline of the sword. In his formative years he was a tempter, who developed into an irresistible mainline seducer amongst the Metalgants.

Women could not help but fall hopelessly in love with this dangerous snakelike character. Intelligent bright shining eyes and wavy white-blond hair made him a spotlight magnet for female attention.

Rhuand had witnessed the fall-ins and fall-outs of Skada's love affairs numerous times. Often it had occurred to him, long before Metalgants enchanted snakes, snakes were enchanting Metalgants.

The swordsman continued in a softly-softly tone, "You must think you've come so far, when really you've travelled no distance at all." His powerful stare moved with dark intent from Rhuand to Salt, and back again. "Now, don't be ungenerous in your agreement when I say, let's encourage a new wave of thinking in this game of tiger-gets-the-church-mice, hmm. Give in!"

Rhuand's eyes narrowed. Did the sword-master honestly believe all they required was a verbal nudge before falling into despair and surrender, or was he just cruelly toying with them – provoking them into an impulsive reaction, therefore bringing about their own undoing? The former Head Kielter was enraged. "I refuse to explain myself to you of all people, Skada." There was going to be no real dialogue entered into by Rhuand. No. On his part he aimed to keep answers deliberately short, revealing least as possible to the listening, terminating Female Munrah. He knew by bitter experience, when trying to defend oneself through words, one could often give too much away – he had to protect Salt as well as himself. They had come too far to turn back now.

"Indeed," replied Skada triumphantly. "And explanations do take a deal of time. Time which, may I remind you, Rhuand Mezarron you do not have. Long gone are your Actimm programme days when you could extend time."

Rhuand's clenched hands became solid metal fists from the tension of anger he carried against this unwelcome situation. Just when Salt and he had relentlessly strived to reach the sandsomme stone door, they were now prevented from entering through and into the next pending colour by this danger of growing conflict.

He had to think, and think fast to avoid Salt's annihilation from these superficial angells with dangerous faces and ferocious laws.

Acutely he observed them, acutely observing Salt and him. While Female Munrah remained deadly still and darkly quiet in the pillar of shadow, two axe wielding prison guards had taken a fixed position, blocking the way through which each one of them had walked along before arriving at this levelled clearing.

But Rhuand had no intention of retracing their steps back along the river. Their only means of escape was to proceed forward by opening the immense door.

Forcibly, he rejected the thought from his mind that he and Salt were trapped by these unmerciful individuals. For they had a plan set in sandsomme stone. He would not be misdirected away from that positive thought. He must succeed in his approach to help aide Salt unlock the door, believing this would ensure her true trust in him again. A trust that would echo their past life together.

By successfully entering the next colour, surely Salt would know it to be an absolute truth, together they could reach the final causeway colour, red. He must do what had to be done.

Rhuand steeled his mind against the hostile intruders. Now, mentally prepared, he was ready to fight and fight some more.

"Don't be a stranger to an old friend, for you can never escape us." In level calmness Skada turned from Rhuand to face Salt, square on. "Maybe we could help each other, hmm... for you can never have a future while living with the dead. Save yourself, would be my advice. Perhaps we could reach some understanding? After all, you have led us to this... this renegade... this deserter. And for that action alone you should be, well – rewarded. Ask, and who knows, it may be given."

"Rewarded?" she spoke with grave deliberation, then paused. Rhuand could see she was going over in her head what had just been said. "Please do not profess to know me. It comes to something when you claim to know a different me."

"You're an Earthlet. What else is there to possibly know?"

"I know I made the right decision in turning down your amorous advances at the Alt Grand Festival."

"And you continue to stand by that decision?"

"Yes. We all need to stand for something, otherwise we'd fall for anything skin-deep."

"Salt Delray, loyal to the bitter end. Well, everyone knows a woman is entitled to change her mind. Even, on occasion, an Earthlet one."

"I am my own woman and will continue to fight to remain so, that's a promise."

He sighed deeply. "Ah, reduced to a promise. Perhaps it would be wise for you to keep in mind, rather like the weather, nothing remains constant."

"I couldn't have put it better myself," she answered resourcefully. "And yet your mistress, Female Munrah aims to keep the season of autumn constant to maintain her Metalgant supremacy. She should value your perceptive advice, Skada-the-Braska when you clearly state, *'nothing remains constant'*. One day Female Munrah's reign will be at an end!"

Rhuand valued her creative and witty responses. Defending herself admirably against Skada's barrage of verbal putdown. This was personal, but she proved she could hold her own. She was both brave and resilient. She didn't weaken in the face of such adversity. And yet, he had a flash of doubt from Skada's words.

What if Salt had secretly agreed with Female Munrah and subordinates to lead them to him for a reward? A reward of freedom would be an incredibly powerful incentive.

Could she be capable of agreeing to such an arrangement? Is this all an act?

Incarceration at the Irongate prison with a death sentence bearing heavily down on her would leave Salt little room for alternatives. Their once shared love for each other had been neglected due to their forced separation. And anything neglected, he knew, would eventually weaken and possibly die.

Securing a deal to bring an end to him certainly wouldn't be out of Female Munrah's realm. She'd relish a twist in events such as this – *the Earthlet, Rhuand Mezarron gave his life to save, would in turn, betray him* – he couldn't rule out the possibility.

All at once, there was a sinister movement from Female Munrah's position as she began to move to the forefront in the pillar of shadow. Instinctively he knew she'd studied them long enough.

Suspecting she had given signal to Skada to move events

along and initiate a lethal strike, Rhuand's spirit became a magnified receptor, where every subtle movement in his immediate surroundings translated into a heightened noise. Sagaciously he concentrated – yes, he could even hear Skada's heartbeat. Its rate began to increase. The increase had to be from an order of battle.

During the Actimm programme he'd worked alongside the Braska warrior often, and he knew courtesy of Skada's vanity this would be a one-on-one conflict which Female Munrah would respect. No. She would not intervene in his glory – or otherwise.

"Come closer, Salt," coaxed the swordsman. "And show me what you're concealing in the palm of your hand, hmm?" Rhuand could just detect a hint of excitement in his guarded voice.

Had Skada caught sight of the Regard brooch and if so, did he know of its significance to unlock the sandsomme stone door?

"No!" Rhuand said with unwavering force. "You'll have to go through me first." He placed himself in Skada's direct line of view to Salt, becoming her physical barrier from the nefarious warrior.

"Is that an invitation?" he mocked. "Or a cancellation?"

"It's an order!"

"Well, never say I'm a Metalgant who'd turn down an order. Just remember, Rhuand Mezarron you no longer hold the title or skill of a Kielter. You are merely defined by death."

"Death is feared by many. Respected by others." He motioned Salt to stay close to the door, and to remain at distance behind him. He held her gaze momentarily, trying to reflect back to her that he would protect her.

He wanted her to believe in him.

Not doubt his ability.

"Well, as I see it, death is a permanent state that beholds you.

You do not hold it. Maybe you should have given more thought before you decided to betray your fellow Metalgants." In a flash, Skada drew forth the sacred Braska sword from behind his shoulder from where its sheath hung. He kissed the blade, positioned himself in a stance of imminent fight – one foot placed surely in front of the other, knees bent, left arm outstretched to guide balance, Braska in right hand. He was poised. "By the supremacy of Munrah, let the bravest warrior win."

In surety Rhuand moved forward to meet the infamous swordsman, who with a fanatical attack of the blade, struck at his opponent.

Rhuand instinctively raised a strong steel arm to block the sword, causing a violent metal reverberation to travel along the sword and into Skada's hand, arm and shoulder. This was a clash of metal against metal. With each deliberate sweep in attack from the swordsman, repeatedly the Braska sword failed to embed into Rhuand. Skada looked enraged. Rhuand's actions were not meant as a means of protection towards himself. He was merely going through the motions before choosing an opportune time to move in and render him down.

Why not have a little fun?

After all this swordsman was big on words, but here in this alternative dimension the law of Metalgant rules meant little to nothing.

Here Skada held the lower hand, Rhuand a solid metal one. Something a Metalgant of flesh would know absolutely nothing about. How could he. He was alive. He wasn't dead. The qualities of Iquique belonged solely to those in limbo, and they don't travel back to visit the world of the living. No. The dead don't talk unless they are found.

Quickly realising he was cutting no ice with this former Kielter, Skada began to increase the degree of viciousness and brutality, courtesy of the Braska technique. But each and every lunge of the sword aimed at his opponent continued in its failure to slash or even weaken the other.

If anything, Rhuand gained a strength looking into enemy eyes. Only his slate-coloured overcoat showed damage from the Braska sword as it hung in tatters around his now half naked body-in-spirit.

"I believe a change of name is required," he ridiculed. "No longer Skada-the-Braska, more like Skada-the-non-Braska."

The swordsman halted in his bombardment of physical assault and began to flex his wrist and shoulder in pain. "What are you? What have you become?"

"I am what you turned me into."

"Call that an answer? That's no combat answer at all." He narrowed his suspicious eyes while squaring his shoulders. Was he trying to read deep into Rhuand's thoughts and gain further insight?

"That's not the answer you desire, but it's the answer you deserve."

"You placed yourself in this position when you chose an Earthlet over your fellow Metalgants. Jeopardising the future of your own kind."

"And I have paid for that. We, Salt and I have paid for that." He heard his own voice hold a sardonic quality.

"You have merely part-paid for your choice with all your yesterdays. But mark my words, when I say, you will pay in full. Not just by your life, but by your death! I make it my personal duty!"

"Hand over the Braska!" said Rhuand with deadly intention.

"What? It's not yours to have! I earned this military weapon—"

"I demand you hand it over to me."

"Do as he says, Skada. Appease him!" voiced Female Munrah, now with a foot over the pillar of shadow. She sounded impatient to conclude the whole matter. "Hand it over. Amuse me."

With the skill of a war-warrior, Rhuand took the razor-sharp weapon in his metal grip and with a singleness of attention that was so smooth as to be chilling, removed it from the Braska owner. "I'm now entitled to take ownership of this sword. It's my emblem of justice."

"By the law of the Braska, to take the sword from a Metalgant will mean you owe him a claim by virtue of a right. There will be a request of a forfeit!" Female Munrah stepped out of the shadow.

"In the immediate, I'd call it a matter of aesthetics." And in moments, while held in Rhuand's hands, the once beautifully handcrafted Braska sword changed from its original form.

First, it reduced in size, then appeared to absorb into his spirit, only to remerge, transformed into extreme fine metal threads which weaved and intertwined themselves into the fabric of the overcoat, mending the shredded pieces of material that touched where they fell around his half naked spirit, until the clothing took a familiar shape of his hooded long coat.

Rhuand looked down to bear witness to his renewed attire that glinted in the tropical moonlight before carefully removing the coat and placing it round Salt's shoulders. He stood in only his dusty footwear and black combat trousers. "I have one final task to carry out," he said to her in a hushed tone. "When I do, start placing the Regard brooch into the inverted shape in the door. The coat will shield their view as to what you're doing." She inclined her head to signify agreement.

Assured, Rhuand turned back to face his now unarmed opponent, acknowledging to himself, he would owe Skada. But he needed to securely render harm to the once infamous swordsman in order to carry out his next move. A move which would allow Salt and himself to escape through the door and advance more than a handbreadth of distance from Female Munrah and her subordinates.

"I'll not let you forget this. Remember, you owe me, Rhuand Mezarron!" His adversary's cruel laugh chilled the open air.

"Success is not an accident," said Rhuand.

"Oh, I'm really going to relish destroying you. You and the Earthlet." He was now standing so close that Rhuand felt Skada's sour breath upon his spirit face.

"Shake my hand?"

Skada didn't respond to Rhuand's offer.

The once Kielter was not going to ask again and took the other's hand by force. Immediately an intensive metal shock sparked from the contact made between them. Skada had no metal to protect himself from Rhuand's system. He was rutted. The reverberation circulated throughout Skada's body in a perilous unbroken loop of electricity. His spine arched, his head strained backwards grotesquely over his backbone. His face shuddered while in unbelievable sufferance. Rhuand held on to him mercilessly.

Not a word was uttered from Female Munrah or the Metalgant guards. It didn't escape Rhuand's thoughts, they were stunned into silence as they continued to witness this unforeseen turn in events from his new abilities.

Suddenly, the great sandsomme stone door began to grind open and a shaft of brilliant orange light beamed into the tropical clearing. Rhuand's senses jerked from Skada's contorted condition. Instantly he knew Salt had successfully unlocked their barrier into the next causeway colour.

He took his cue. In metal brutality he took a vicelike grip round Skada's upper arms and lifted the nefarious warrior off the ground. Then with ease hurled him backwards through the air, to descend in a twisted contortion close to the booted feet of the prison guards who leapt away from the convulsing Metalgant.

Without hesitation Rhuand joined the Earthlet and together they stepped across the sandsomme stone threshold to find themselves on the other side of a now rapidly closing door.

Waves of vibrations travelled round his spirit from the forceful grating of the enormous door against the stone flooring. Then, as abruptly as the to and fro sensations had begun, they stopped. The door, now safely shut, sealing them from Female Munrah and the tormentors.

To his amazement they had not stepped into an enclosed building, but a ruin. Only the doorway behind them stood undamaged. No roof above their heads, only exposed light. The dilapidated walls on either side of them had crumbled into the vast desert of sand beyond. Within moments, a whirlwind immerged in the brilliant orange hue ahead.

He opened his mouth to shout warning to Salt, but the words were snatched from him and claimed by the fierce sandstorm that engulfed them.

The dry desert winds howled loudly round and about them, deafening to their ears, stinging their eyes, blinding their vision.

It whipped and battered at them, blowing them off their feet, causing disorientation and separating them from each other into the unknown.

:

(3) ORINOKO ORANGE

:

#AsCleanAsCoal? – The ringing of a telephone. Its sound burnt into her head. But the moment Salt opened her eyes – it stopped.

Something in its tone had sounded familiar as she wrestled to make sense of the environment she awoke in. But she didn't force the memory, instead telling herself it would come back to her in its own sweet time.

Uncurling herself from a tight ball of tension, Salt fought to sit upright, then stand in the shifting sands, while pulling Rhuand's overcoat closer round her slight frame. All she could see was a vast landscape of huge sand hills sculptured impressively in the brilliant orange hue.

A light breeze danced round her body and she noticed at her feet the ripples in the sand constantly moving and reshaping – and in that moment she remembered the severity of the sandstorm: how without warning it had engulfed her and Rhuand. With this knowledge came a sudden receptor of stinging pains on her face, hands and legs from the lashing winds of sand.

Hoarsely she called out his name into the isolated desert, but not one of her beseeching calls was answered.

She was alone.

The sandsomme stone ruin through which they had entered was nowhere to be seen. Was it submerged under a colossal sand dune, or had she been propelled far away from the ruined building?

Salt recognised there was no way in knowing as any landmark reference could alter in this unique landscape. And from this stark realisation followed a dreadfulness – *What if Rhuand had become buried under the moving sands and...?*

She jolted herself into reality. No, his fate couldn't possible end like that. He was, after all, in limbo and protected by death. No-one can die twice. Yet knowing all this, she still found it so hard to picture him dead, when he had been so alive in life.

She had to make a choice. A decision as to which direction to travel in her search to find him, and a way out of this eerie sand plain.

What would Rhuand advise?

She hesitated for a moment and a remark he made on their first introduction at the Alt Grand Festival came to the forefront of her troubled mind – *'Without a measure of darkness and shadow, Salt Delray one cannot justly appreciate the strength of light'*, so fair spoken and with such raw honesty in his voice, as though he had gained a startling insight into his own past.

Invigorated, in the here and now, she gazed up into the orange skies above her and by natural impulse chose to follow the light. The direction of the sola sun.

:

The horizon gave no indication as to what lie ahead, now transformed into a blur by the rising desert heat as it collided with the orange light beating down onto the hostile sands.

Gathering all her strength together, Salt persistently zigzagged her way through the sands. This was as much a mental task as it was a physical one. Mental in the sense that the characteristic of the desert forced the traveller to either overcome or succumb to its relentless landscape.

Every muscle in her body felt tender and ached disquietingly from the ferocious sandstorm earlier. She longed to rest but time was precious.

Refusing to allow herself the luxury of idle time, Salt drew on her Irongate prison experiences, wherein it had cruelly taught her that one pain could distract from another.

In times of hardship and isolation, she had learnt to place her mind elsewhere in order to survive and keep herself sane. Salt concentrated into the future sand hills, for the irksome pain she was enduring would be small in comparison to the alternative – not seeing Rhuand again.

Fighting to hold onto her motivation, she spoke to herself – "Learn how to create your own opportunities." Immediately, amongst the conflicting blur a shape appeared.

Narrowing her eyes to gain better focus, her curiosity was only increased by the mystery of who it could be.

Desperately, and with all her might she proceded onwards, until eventually she could detect tracks laid in the sand. She was closing in. Gaining on whoever lie ahead.

Could it be Rhuand?

Oh, she longed It would be –

Or Lapis-Lazuli?

Salt sprinted forth with new vigour, abandoning any feelings of fatigue. She simply had to reach whoever it was. Then, in wild alarm she stilted in her – and *its* tracks.

Adrenaline flooded her system. Her mind turned over and in on itself in terror. This was not the type of opportunity she had wanted to create for herself – pursuing an animal of great savageness. A tiger!

Dizzy with fear, her heart rate pounded in her ears. Usually this only happened when she caught unexpected sight of Rhuand; but the emotions here were not of intense joy and excitement, instead pure fear as she would be made into tiger food.

She willed herself into invisibility, but knowing this impossible, her mind quickly shifted to protection mode. This would be a case of kill or be killed. But with no armour or artillery to defend herself, and with nowhere to hide in this vast desert of sand, she was entirely exposed.

The tiger stopped in its tracks.

In perfect silence she stood perfectly still.

Does it know it's being observed?

Catching painful, shallow breaths she breathed and breathed again, knowing she was very much alive – *But for how much longer?*

A foreboding disquiet raged through her as she knew there was only a matter of moments to decide which line of action to take – *Fight or flight?*

Turning a supple body to face her head on, the carnivorous tiger lowered its majestic head, purposeful in attention to unexpected company.

Salt could see the powerful animal looked in good condition. It didn't appear to be starving, but to cross the territory of a non-hungry tiger's path was no guarantee to this animal resisting the innate instinct to hunt. At the very least she expected to be mauled to death.

Lifting its regal head to sniff the desert air, Salt caught a glimpse of its deadly jaws – *What do I do?*

Rhuand was not here to safeguard her, and his steel threaded overcoat could only give limited protection against a tiger's savage fangs and razor sharp claws. The long coat wouldn't shield the whole of her body. Her face, hands and legs would be unprotected.

She felt chillingly frantic as the beast began to place its padded paws down into the orange sand and prowl its way slowly towards her – the stalk had now begun.

But there was something unspoken about the animal, something – familiar?

The stripes on its fur were strikingly autumnal in colour. The eyes, spectacular and wide apart. It showed its savage teeth to her and snarled in its reply to her scrutiny. Then the wild animal turned slowly and walked away from her.

Dare she believe it had lost interest?

Within a fractured moment it began prowling its way towards her, before padding away again, then proceeding once more – teasing her.

She began to tremble violently under the stress. It could only be a matter of dreaded, torturous time before the animal would strike her down.

This new colour they had entered was turning into a nightmare. A nightmare where there appeared to be no means of escape. Then, on re-hearing the echo of a ringing bell, a telephone, her senses became alerted to a memory, and she remembered – the dream!

The dream that occurred most nights she slept. Disturbing her thoughts. So much so that she had learnt to dread falling asleep.

She had first suffered the dream after Rhuand's death at Lake Gardenia. Here, now, looking at this tiger, could it be?

She took a jagged intake of breath. Yes, this prowling tiger looked exactly like the tiger stalking her dreams.

Swiftly, her mind flashed back, recalling her mother's words, *dreams are the result of your own personal hopes and fears'*.

If her mother was right, then this reasoning could be extended to say: a recurring dream is a message from the unconscious to the conscious – therefore a dream that repeated itself could possibility be the result of the nightmare-sufferer not listening to their inner-self.

Perhaps, if she could resolve the dream, this nightmare she was now in, would stop.

Stop the nightmare.

Stop the tiger here in this orange desert-land.

The tiger began to growl ferociously. Its navy-blue polished eyes which too frequently she noticed, protruded, receded and revealed a commotion within. She forced herself not to give into the feeling of fear, telling herself fear would be a waste of emotion, she would gain nothing from it, only lose.

Remembering the dream from the beginning, she chose to single out the most important factors that struck her mind in the nightmare.

The dream always started with her stood in a glass room.

She closed her eyes to visualise the room, instantly aware of a horrific shuddering starting from her feet, spreading throughout her whole being.

Quickly reopening her eyes, seeing all four walls of the glass room immerging up and out from the depths of the desert sand, she could hardly believe it. She was standing in the exact same dream room.

Visibility faulted. The room darkened. And it took a while before her eyes adjusted to the change, empowering her to define the outline of her hands and fingers.

Glancing out through the glass walls, the landscape was now completely black, so much so, she was unable to see where the stalking tiger prowled. Alone, she could only hear it breathing, panting. Making the nightmare all the more sinister.

She wheeled round in terror, trying in vain to face the direction of the wild animal. For just like in the dream, she knew it would only be a matter of time before the bounding tiger would crash through one of the glass walls to viciously attack and kill her.

She willed herself to continue in dire reflection.

Must concentrate.

Steady oneself.

She began to search for a light switch to help eradicate the dimness in the room. Then she remembered, she could never find it in time. Perhaps she should actively change her behaviour from that in the dream, otherwise surely she would be destined to bring about her own downfall, by ensuring the same outcome as in the nightmare.

Abruptly, she stopped searching. Instead, remembering a classic shaped black telephone on a metal table. In the dream, she could never reach the telephone to dial for help.

However, since meeting Lapis-Lazuli this was where the nightmare had changed slightly – the telephone would constantly ring on the metal table rather than remaining silent.

But it isn't ringing now –

Talking to herself, she singled out the important factors in her nightmare: Firstly, the glass walls; then the tiger; followed by the dimming lights; and lastly the telephone on a metal table.

All these factors must represent things within her life. Perhaps, dreams were metaphors. A picture puzzle in dream-world.

Instinctively aware the tiger was a creature most deadly. An instigator of pure fear. What this animal must represent to her was... was... Female Munrah.

Of course!

Female Munrah had been surveying Salt closely before and during her capture and imprisonment at the Irongate. Therefore the glass walls in the dream were a metaphor for being heavily observed.

Memories remain powerful, thought Salt. To the dimming of the lights – light surely represented energy. A decrease in energy which she was unable to restore to normal levels in the dream. And she realised, the light had meaning to her own personal energy levels. She had been sapped of energy, sapped of strength, drained of love and kindness.

Things were steadily becoming clearer to her as she began to understand the terrorisation of the nightmare, but the intimidation was still on. She could hear the savage panting tiger moving outside the glass walls, pawing and clawing at the glass.

She needed to think faster in order to resolve the true meaning of the dream before the tiger got the better of her and the nightmare turned into a horrendous actuality.

With all her willpower, she focused on the last factor in the dream. The telephone on the metal table.

The telephone meant – connection.

A connection to the outside. Outside of herself. Since meeting Lapis-Lazuli the telephone had constantly rang and reverberated on the wrought iron table. The most important news from Lapis-Lazuli's message was that Rhuand existed through limbo.

That's it!

The telephone represented her connection to Rhuand. Within that immediate thought, the telephone began to loudly ring, she rushed in eagerness to pick up the receiver. "Hello! Hello–"

"Salt!?! Where are you?"

On hearing Rhuand's voice, all four glass walls shattered into white dust round her. There was no middle ground. The dream had forced her to make choices, pass judgement, to take a stand and prove or disprove her devotions. And now she understood, the nightmare didn't seem quite as frightening as she had first thought.

Watchful from all sides, she scanned the hostile environment back in the open orange desert. The threatening tiger was nowhere to be seen. She had successfully taken it by the tail. She almost broke down and cried from intense relief, but she held on. Her connection to Rhuand remained unbroken.

"I'm in the orange desert." She swallowed her tears and fears, knowing in moments of stress, telephones shorten the distance between the speakers, bringing them closer, so they can hear breathing, silences speak as loud as the spoken sentences.

"What's your location?" She perceived a sharp edge to his asking.

"I really can't tell you as I don't know how far I've travelled from the sandsomme stone ruins, but I've been heading in the direction of the sola sun."

"You must continue to keep pace. I'll meet you on route."

"I've just walked through a total nightmare…" After a full disclosure, her trained ear heard what sounded like the revving of an engine transmitted down the telephone wire.

"Yes," he said. "Your mind had been high jacked. In my experience the orange desert propels the unconscious mind to the forefront. Unlocking repeated fears. The burning of the past allows freedom to better understand what the mind and soul is fighting to help us acknowledge, and so create a new beginning from the memory embers..." His words began to pull away from her, fade in and out of transmission, followed by crackling distortion and lost reception. She couldn't help but wonder, what if its deterioration was due to Female Munrah and her subordinates intercepting their communication. If this was the case, they may have overheard which direction she and Rhuand planned to travel.

Moreover, there was too much of an outlaw about Rhuand and that held its own fascination to Salt. Painfully and in the open, she had to make all the running towards him – by following the sola sun.

:

Time passed. The landscape barely seemed to alter, though Salt had begun to notice the subtle beauty of the orange desert.

At first glance it appeared too vast to take in and comprehend. But now she had cause to run, walk, flee, stop, even stroll sometimes, and marvel at its complexities.

The grand sand dunes were mountainous, and the shadows projected from one sand dune onto a lower one were beautiful in colour, reflecting a light violet wash.

If anything this time by herself had given her the inclination to think and listen to her inner-self. It was a gift in espy. Her mind ricocheted back to her earliest memory of Skada at the Alt Grand Festival. Salt had suspected the Braska swordsman was a snake in the grass. Untrustworthy. She had felt uncomfortable in his presence. He was so completely sure of himself and his abilities to spin heads without uttering a word, to have any woman he chose. He seemed to be in love with love, and primarily a love to be lavished exclusively on himself.

She had watched him work the entertainers' room, covertly seeking the admiration of others as a means to see in their eyes how truly remarkable he was, while his large clear eyes only reflected back the face that looked into them – common anxiety was a stranger to Skada. And she remembered thinking, while he and Rhuand both attained high ranking status in the circle of Metalgant supremacy – that was where their brotherhood ended. He was, in no way similar to Rhuand Mezarron's nature or his mentality for integrity.

Now, dwelling on how different Rhuand had become – his new found strength against Skada-the-Braska. And Skada's unwavering confidence to wound and destroy Rhuand by use of the Braska sword – he was truly unprepared as to how events were destined against his Metalgant of flesh skill. A skill with little effect here to a warrior in limbo and the adage backdrop of Rainbow colours.

Her mind shifted back to Rhuand's half naked body-in-spirit, when his overcoat had hung in tatters from him. His steel torso and powerful shoulders had distinctly shimmered when the moonlight caught him. He was truly magnificent. Her heart raced at the thought of him.

She looked down at the metal coat she still wore – while she or Rhuand wore it, she would not receive a fierce metal shock from him. She breathed deeply in sheer relief, for she had longed for that barrier of fear to be lifted.

With importunity her gaze moved and settled on the Regard

brooch pinned to her turquoise bodysuit. The Regard brooch's precious stones were set in iron.

And iron is a metal.

Therefore, the item of jewellery itself would have been a barrier to an electrifying shock.

She blinked rapidly in disbelief.

What could this possibly mean?

She recalled, after showing Rhuand the Regard jewellery he had not moved away from the thought to remain at distance from each other.

Is he simply using me to secure death away from his own imprisonment of limbo?

Shame as much as love prompted a denial.

All the same, Salt felt a sudden hurt which smarted like a deep injury, quickly followed by a stab of anger. Anger as much towards herself as to her former lover. For she had been blinded to the metal element of the brooch by dangers of Female Munrah catching up to them in their brilliant and new surroundings of the causeway colours.

How could I be so… so slow?

What Rhuand must think of me – if anything?

From this moment, Salt steeled herself against showing any burning emotions.

She would become so smooth as to be chilling.

Yes, she would put her love on ice for the time being until Rhuand came clean about this revelation. In the meantime, she hoped against hope on each and every strained heartbeat, his disclosure would not be as clean as coal.

:

#RainingSoup – He still held a print of Salt in his mind.

A blueprint.

Is it foolish to acknowledge such routine?

Especially when he couldn't be sure if she'd thought about him more than occasionally, and if so, under what terms – a yearning love, where every goodbye isn't gone and every eye closed isn't sleep, or a chilling coat colder from the grief born out of condemnation?

But then, isn't grief the price paid for love?

Remembering with intensity, Salt's eyes, lovely, deep and liquid, expressing tender sensitivity.

However, since their reunion at Lake Gardenia he'd caught sight of a guarded expression – he'd suspected it was against the fear of recrimination.

He must resist the insistence of her coming to live in his heart again, when he felt vulnerable to the possibility she may reject him in his state of limbo – handing her his ultimate terror.

For he was not the Metalgant she had fallen in love with.

He had become someone else.

And moreover, in this vast orange desert he recognised a change stirring deep within himself. He had begun to feel unlike himself. His cast of mind not as it once was, as though it had a corner missing.

He must figure out exactly what was happening – he had been a Metalgant who scrutinised facts before jumping to conclusions, this need in him remained deeply embedded. Long experience had taught him the play of imagination was usually the root of misunderstanding.

Since giving heed to his own thoughts here in this isolated

desert, Rhuand had found answers to old questions, but in turn new questions had surfaced.

It flashed across his mind, Lapis was a constant spring of guidance who proved invaluable and he deserved to be cheered to the echo of truth. He would seek him out, but not before locating Salt.

:

Once spotted it was impossible to lose sight of her. He felt so happy he didn't know how to express it and hardly dared to for fear of it passing away.

But she was plain there – trekking across the hostile desert on the brink of collapse, clearly weakened and borderline hallucinatory from the effects of dehydration and sunstroke.

He had to prioritise and get her back to being animated like a child. It was one of the things that had attracted him to her. She had always been dancing, laughing and chatting to others. He could not tune her out.

When Salt eventually came to face him, there was no overbearing welcome between them. He could see she was holding onto herself. Kind words, he felt, would break her. "I knew you'd make it." His voice sounded perfectly controlled to his own ears. "The Regard brooch is magnetic to the sola fields, and intangible like everything that comes from the soul."

Arid of emotions, Salt stood immobile before him. Scorched faced, unable to even lift her eyes from the baking sand – then slowly – so slowly, she raised her head, opened her mouth, and screamed!

:

Accessing their surroundings he stood on the peak of a

mountainous sand-ridge. The blazing sun highlighted his magnificent gleaming body of steel against an expansive orange sky, and his black combat trousers caught the rise and fall of warm breezes.

No longer did he feel the need to hide beneath the hood and overcoat. The condition of Iquique had triumphed in saving him and Salt from the darkly destructive Female Munrah and her followers, he would no longer deny himself who he had become.

What physicality he would take in the future he did not know, but anything easy and agreeable stirred dark mistrust in him, and anyone abating in severity were, he felt, usually less likely to give notice to others.

Swiftly he mounted the quadripartite machine. "Salt, put your arms round me. You don't have the strength to balance yourself. Not after what you've been through."

Sensing indifference from her to comply with his instruction, she sat fatigued on the backseat of the four wheeled machine. "I'm fine." Her voice sounded stretched and strained with anguish. "Just feel a little disoriented. I'm sure it'll blow over."

Turning to face her, he caught a glimpse of the independent and self-assured dancer he met at the Alt Grand Festival. So much had been experienced together and apart since that one crowded measure of happiness, but it was worth an age without a name. For, as far as he was concerned, she was to remain the only woman to ever touch his mind – to ever – kiss his mind. Though he sometimes found her stubbornness infuriating, still he wouldn't change a thing about her. Curious how difficult it was to put his emotions into speech. Simple enough when he held a dialogue in his own mind.

Her lips moved spontaneously, "The loneliness was like an

absence following…" Her words trailed off and she opened her eyes as if to escape the internal darkness.

"Salt, you're far from the line of fine. You urgently need to gain strength and resolve. I've sighted a herd of Ory Garzelleons. They'll be heading for localised water."

The herd of animals he had spotted from the high outlook were a rare breed of antelope with distinguished markings of white and blue on their faces, and their purple body colouring camouflaged them against the sand dune shadows. "We'll do best by following their tracks to nature's reservoir, whereby we'll find medicinal herbs containing healing properties which will restore you back to being hale and healthy before searching for the next sandsomme stone building."

Salt shifted uncomfortably on the fixed seating. "Can we discard the metal coat? I don't see why it should come between us any longer." Weakly she struggled to take off the overcoat.

"Salt, you're making no sense."

"No sense?" Her voice was small but tentative. "How do you mean? Sense out of meaning, or perhaps no sensation from a feeling?"

He felt she was testing him. Testing his answers.

Is she being plain difficult for the pleasure of it or is it a reaction from suffering dehydration?

In silent frustration he leaned to one side and helped her back into the coat of entwined metal and fabric. "If you remove the coat you'll expose yourself to further sunstroke. You really must shield away from the scorching desert sun as it can have detrimental consequences."

He watched as she gave up the struggle, and appeared to

empty herself into blankness with an awareness she was still somehow present.

"I've seen what the orange desert can do, and it takes nothing away from the cat's meow." Her voice sounded displaced.

"Yes," he countered quickly, not amused by Salt's abstract thinking. "But it too can be a source for misunderstanding. Let's just say, if it was raining soup, I'm sure you'd carry a fork." He placed the hood on her resisting head, then turned the ignition on and revved the quadripartite machine causing the revolution of the engine to resound loudly and vibrate underneath them. "It's time to move!" He felt her place an unsteady hold on his body-in-spirit. Instinctively he knew it was a slackening grip – she was holding on, barely.

Aware that he knew all shades of her touch so well in life. He could tell what mood she was in just by her touch – excited, sad, loving, wearied, frightened – he recalled, as known before, until a thought came into his remembrance – *How it is never easy to hold back from loss?*

Abruptly he turned the thought away as it would surely undo his mind. The importance of taking her to the sanctuary of water was what matter right now.

In the pursuit of the animal herd, he drove at high speed and together they motored dangerously up and down the sand banks. The robust wheels spinning out great volumes of parched sand as he swerved and sped onwards until reaching levelled compacted sand tracks without elevations and depressions.

Glancing down at the now dulled and dusty, once shiny black quadripartite, his mind rapidly flashed back in time to how he'd come across the riding machine –

The result of his recurring nightmare.

:

Rhuand stopped the quadripartite and switched off the bike's engine. The two front wheels were half submerged in a pool of clear water. His right hand still protectively placed over Salt's weak hands round him.

"We've made it!" he announced, while saying a silent *thank you* to the Ory Garzelleons. For without them he possibly wouldn't have found a water source in time to prevent Salt deteriorating any further.

He released her hands and demounted the machine. She slumped forward with a weary groan and he felt a fearful chill, he couldn't lose her now – or ever.

"Salt, stay with me," he said rigorously in an attempt to jolt her mind from the sickening state she had sunk into. "Come on now, Salt. Wake up." Within these horrifying moments he realised, no-one could frighten him like Salt Delray. Dead-on, the thought of losing her would rub his soul raw.

Supporting her to sit upright on the machine seat, he cupped a metal hand and reached into the beautiful cool water. "Try to steady yourself. Take a sip." Weakly, she did as he asked. "It's best to take little and often sips to start with, otherwise the cold water can chill the body and cause fatality in this scorching heat."

Painstakingly, she raised her head and mumbled inaudible words to his beseeched warning.

"Take your time." He didn't know how much of this she would remember, but he wanted her to feel safe and allow her the time it would take for her mind and body to recover naturally before they battled on through the next series of causeway colours.

Vigilantly, he helped her off the seat, and together they slowly walked through the medicinal water and onto the orange sands until they reached a casting cool shadow from a prevalent sand dune.

Languidly, she laid down. He moved her onto her side, tucking her arm beneath her head to support herself, then carefully rearranged the hood of the metal coat up and over to protect her features from the desert breeze.

Rhuand had always been a Metalgant who held his own counsel, but when it came to the welfare of Salt he really had to hold onto himself, knowing if he wasn't careful he'd be no help to either of them.

He had to remain persistent. Practical. He could not be distracted by despair, otherwise they'd end up swinging from a tree or imprisoned down in a torture cell at the mercy of sardonic Female Munrah and her subdivision of order.

Fighting off the block of fog in his head – a major lassitude of spirit and mind, something he could well do without right now. It was like wrestling an internal thunder. "You're going to be fine. Do you hear me?" He was talking just as much to himself as to fretful Salt.

"I do believe she'll recover splendidly. In fact, I'd venture as far to say, she'll be tickerteeboo in the length of time of a night owl's flight."

Rhuand moved his fixed gaze from Salt and slowly turned to face the pool-water behind him. "Lapis! My friend. Am I pleased to see you in this desert-land?"

Lapis-Lazuli smiled generously. "What's given to a friend, isn't lost. The water here contains every healing mineral possible. I should know, I concocted the herbivorous solution myself. Although, I will confess the antelopes did take some budging. In the end I had to drain their previous watering-hole to encourage them to seek out this new one."

He felt an indulgence of happiness as he shook the other's hand. "It's no exaggeration to say, Lapis, I need your careful advice and worthy silences–"

"There's something you should know." And together they followed the edge of water. "How are you feeling within your spirit self?"

"Different. As if a miscellaneous block is restricting my mind and I'm fighting through thick, heavy fog. All the time I'm willing myself and my judgement to be faster. I can only perceive the transcendent process has begun–"

"No. This isn't part of your transcendent stage, Rhuand. It would never take away, it only adds. It elevates the spirit, there is no suppression in the process. That would simply go against advancement."

"Then how would you explain my condition? Is it an effect from the power of the desert?"

There was a perceptible pause for thought before Lapis-Lazuli answered. "While the orange desert presents the unconsciousness to an individual for solution, once the mind riddle has been solved it no longer holds you to ransom."

"To my mind, I've interpreted my recurring nightmare."

"So talk me through it."

"I chalked it down to the process known as living and the aftermath of dying. My nightmare started with a raging black bull charging at me – representing my past catching up to me and my inability to let it go. A metal blockade separated myself from the beast and divided the field – this being a clear metaphor for two different routes, my skilled working life as a Kielter with the Metalgants, and a new fertile field with Salt, who I planned to share my life with before drowning in Lake Gardenia. The quadripartite machine is the dream version of my Iquique, allowing me the means to drive out the past and leave it where it firmly belongs, in the past. And lastly–" He paused briefly, "the yellow signal between the handle bars of the machine connected me to Salt, via airwaves, showing our connection is still alive and while we were forcibly broken up, we never broke away from each other. Yellow, being the element colour that represents Earthlets."

"Does Salt know anything of your nightmare analysis?"

"No. She was in such a volatile state when I found her."

They had walked half way round the pool edge with Salt clearly still in their view, though she had not looked to have moved a muscle since he and Lapis-Lazuli began their talk. "Are you sure she'll be fine, Lapis? She still looks so... fatigued. I see no improvement as yet."

"Be patient," he replied. "You have been driving for the length of eight and a half light shows, and the clock has advanced less than two since you drove-off."

Rhuand cast his sight down to the sand packed surface – where they had walked – no footprints. "Some things are too important to cry over," he said with a stirring up of mixed emotion, fighting hard to hold back memories that remained so powerful.

Lapis-Lazuli smiled, but the smile didn't impact his eyes. It was as though he was running reflective thoughts over a rough edge. "Salt holds up half the sky to your way of thinking, doesn't she, Rhuand?"

The warrior nodded in reply, "She was the only woman I ever

felt my own." Then something caught his eye. The sand close to the pool edge ahead of them looked murky. Obscure – turning dark. Clearly something had happened here. "Lapis, have you seen this?" He indicated towards the disturbed waters.

"Yes, this is the point I was coming to." With cold precision they surveyed the area. "Female Munrah and her assistant Skada... hazardous sinking sand... no warning signs... and these sort of waters can be, well, treacherous... I must have accidentally encouraged too much water flow beneath this section of sand... imbalance... looks like they had a mighty tussle to free themselves, wouldn't you say?" It was the way the water vis-viva beamed, inviting one to join in the mischievous fun...

"You mean to say they're ahead of us?"

"As you know, water holds a memory. While you battled to find Salt in this desert, they advanced as far as this point. I heard them discussing the fact they had sent two unprincipled prison guards back in order to bring reinforcement to capture you both."

"From which point did they turn back?"

"The guards never crossed into this orange desert. Only Female Munrah and Skada ventured into this sandscape."

"Did you hear what type of reinforcement they plan to unleash on us?"

"Female Munrah plans to use a magnet."

"But she of all Metalgants should know a magnet can never impair precious metals. And my system is primarily made up of such metals."

"True. But after seeing the skills you used against Skada she believes while a magnet cannot outright stop you, she's wagering you may have elements of other factors in your spirit, such as iron, and iron is dangerously attracted to a magnet. Even the smallest of traces in your system could affect you, by dulling your skills. This is why you've been feeling so different recently. Not from the beginning stages of transcendence, but because the magnet has the potential to cause a debilitating pull."

"And the two Metalgant guards may already be here in this optic orange desert – since I'm feeling the effects."

"More than likely. The worse you feel, the closer to the magnet you are. Plus, there is another disadvantage."

"Go on, Lapis. We are already conspirators. We have been defeated and yet we are controlling together what we have been defeated by."

"The magnet could prove destructive in a separate way. The Regard brooch. You see, when you saved Salt from drowning in Lake Gardenia, water became trapped within the brooch and formed solid ice crystals."

"I was unaware of this."

"Well, I sensed it as soon as I spoke to Salt at the Irongate prison. The thing is, if a sudden violent impact is inflicted on the brooch, let's say, for instance, the brooch is propelled towards the magnet from a great enough distance, these ice crystals could rupture and cause a catastrophic backlash to any living person in close vicinity. Only those in limbo would be unaffected."

There was a silence.

A silence so loud that it seemed to amplify what he had just learnt. And Rhuand knew, until the second and third grace no longer followed the first, he would never give up the fight to protect Salt.

Regardless of the consequences.

#TemporarilyTheTruth – Under the baking sun a beautiful scent of orange blossom filtered through Salt's senses, and for the first time in what seemed to be an age, she felt sparklingly refreshed and clear headed.

Free from being shackled to pain and discomfort, she embraced a wakefulness to freedom as every savage prison wound and recent throbbing ache had miraculously healed.

It was a marvel and the sense of relief was too immense for words. The only comparison she had to feeling this brilliantly alive, was during her courtship with Rhuand.

Brimming with renewed energy she quickly rose and brushed the particles of sand off herself before taking in a deep breath of dry desert heat, but quite unusually the intake of breath didn't catch the back of her throat, instead it enhanced her awareness in this harsh environment to view the edge of shifting orange sands.

Casting a shrewd Earthlet gaze across the pool of still water, she sighted Rhuand and an individual walking on the other side. They had their heads together, close in conversation.

The individual was transparent in appearance: hologram-like. Wearing nothing but a skirt made from reed stalks. Flamboyantly he tossed his long wavy hair with an air of satisfaction at seeing her. Instinctively she knew he must be Lapis-Lazuli, and this alerted a huge response within her – *The worse form of extravagance, is how you waste your chances.*

And she thought she really mustn't waste an opportunity to hold onto life. Life was too fragile, too precious, mindful it could be taken away so easily, too easily, Salt Delray had become her own best friend – secretive and withdrawn, considering the extremes she had recently endured, narrowly cheating death in this unforgiving desert-land by successfully fathoming out her terrorising nightmare.

Yes, escaping her own self-made entrapment of the unconscious, and now feeling in the best condition she had for an extended length of time, could only boost their chances to advance. And as if Rhuand had shared her walk in thoughts, the warrior in spirit glanced up to catch and reflect back to her a look of understanding.

In that precise moment she thought her heart would turn over – a sudden heightening heat circulated through her body causing her to tingle and prickle with a burning desire, forcing the levelled calm she had recouped to completely desert her.

There was no denying she felt an overwhelming attraction to him, more than ever before in his state of limbo, so much so in fact that drawing comparisons to his old self didn't seem to be as important anymore.

Yes, she would be lying to herself if she didn't acknowledge the strong pull of magnetism towards him now. Furthermore, she knew if she concentrated on the feeling much longer, there was a danger his previous self would pale from her knowing – the thought alone was all too disturbing, but then, perhaps she shouldn't hold back from herself.

Falling in love with the living Rhuand had felt so right, so natural. How could she have not been able to resist him?

Now, however, she never quite knew the depths of him. To her, he shrouded himself in mystery and had become a true enigma.

The closer she got to him the further away he appeared to be, but she had to admit, being kept on her toes like this did prove to be exhilarating. So exhilarating that she could not help herself from performing a whirling swan-like pirouette – again and again – until quite giddy and breathless.

She remembered how he used to say, *'I love you'*, on a Metalgant calendar morning, giving her something to hold onto for the rest of the day.

Was that side of him lost forever or could it be reignited in the future? She longed it would be – but upon hearing those words again, he would no doubt sound like a different person – certainly not his previous self – dark, lithe, dangerously handsome and in addition both sulky and shy. His shark-like instincts were always perfectly concealed by a deceptive mildness.

Furthermore, his voice would sound different, only the pattern of breath between the words would be the same – rather like a fingerprint – but more a print of the soul, ingrained, she believed, remaining part of an individual's makeup.

Visuals may alter, but the soul cannot be taken or replaced. It remains an echo to the conscious, to belong only to the subject regardless of which element they are born from. Salt Delray knew this and more besides.

From activated childhood memories of unlimited Earthlet readings, taught with such relentless and hypnotic persuasion – enough for now to coax out of her mind – perilous and painful circumstances, her thoughts found speech, "Wood – Saplinn; fire – Blazonard; earth – Earthlet; metal – Metalgant; water – Aquala."

Each of the five elements she had learnt, were responsible for creating balance and imbalance within the complete and unbroken cycle, whereby each element led into the next one seamlessly.

The first element, the springtime of wood nourishes fire, and from the ashes of fire, the late summertime of earth is created.

Earth moves the season to autumn and nurtures metal in her veins, and metal then brings forth the onset of winter by allowing water to seep down through and into the ground water-plain, and the cycle is then started all over again as from water, wood is allowed to blossom and flourish.

Then again, she had to remind herself, Rhuand was no longer a Metalgant Kielter, he was... he was... *spirit*. Even thinking the word sounded illusive and completely out of reach to an Earthlet of flesh. Was she wanting something completely unobtainable, something he could not possibly give her even if he so wished? Perhaps she should be grateful they shared a short life of love, destined to never be repeated – merely a memory. And her greatest gift to him would be aiding him to reach salvation of the soul.

Each thought led into another –

Could she settle for that, returning the favour of being saved from drowning beneath the ice at Lake Gardenia, or would she always crave more?

More time to be with him?

Would more be enough – could it satisfy her wants – her needs?

In her stricken heart Salt knew, she would only settle for always. Where love and a compliment went further. So much further.

With these chastising thoughts, she forced the questions away. She must maintain the new way of thinking promised to herself earlier in the desert, to put her love on ice for the time being.

Besides, love held no guarantee to a happy ending, but it was certainly a distraction which could easily take up a great deal of time.

She must find a way to be resilient of mind as it was the only way she could then ask Rhuand the troublesome questions she harboured. She needed to be stronger than strong and in the right frame of mind before asking, as there would be a massive degree of pain to learning some things she may not want to hear.

By holding onto love, she placed herself in a precarious situation. As Salt saw it, to love someone too much, meant putting oneself at risk of losing them. Emotionally she wasn't in that strengthened, safe place of hearing the truth in case it all went against her heart. If the balance of love between them was to be confirmed as unequal, just learning that could sabotage them both.

A sudden sense of urgency took over her disquiet thoughts. Recalling to mind the chilling feeling she'd felt after suspecting Female Munrah had infiltrated the dialogue she and Rhuand shared via the telephone connection. Shading her eyes she raised an arm and signalled a greeting to Rhuand and Lapis-Lazuli.

"Yello, Salt Delray. You look truly resplendent!" His voice matched the voice she'd heard through her prison cell window all that time ago. He is so playful she thought as she walked towards them, feeling her hips and waist were fluid and gently mobile.

"Lapis-Lazuli." She smoothed her hair and felt bountiful. "If I look anything like I physically feel, it's really unexplainable. No pain now. I've never felt more like myself."

Catching Rhuand's eyes as she always did, coming closer, Salt couldn't help noticing his demeanour seemed somehow different, his reactions slower. "Is something, wrong?" Her eyes waited on him in mild expectation and concern. "You look washed out."

"I think my mind has been high-wrought." His voice carried uncertainties.

"Are you sure?" She reached out a hand to touch his steely arm, but he was too preoccupied to notice. Instinctively she felt fearful for them both.

He gave out a brittle, sour laugh. "Nothing I can't handle." Rhuand turned from them. He seemed able to escape the oppression of his persona, as he never could do head-on.

"Are you turning a deaf ear to me or just speaking ahead of your time?" She heard her voice stretched and strained with anguish.

"Neither, in a manner of speaking."

"Well, we may as well argue about what shapes and patterns we see in a burning desert," said Lapis-Lazuli, blinking rapidly in the hot sunshine.

Sensitive to Rhuand not wanting to be pressed on the imperfect subject she moved the conversation on, "I don't think we should hang round here too long, I had an unnerving feeling earlier. A distinct impression Female Munrah was already one step ahead of us." Salt felt a sick feeling begin to churn in the pit of her stomach.

"We believe Female Munrah and Skada are lying in wait for us," Rhuand said.

For an instance, Salt's murderous fury returned, but she denied it by smiling. "And the Metalgant prison guards, where are they?"

"They retraced tracks under strict orders to... to..." It was unusual for the warrior in limbo to struggle to find the right words.

Impatiently she prompted him, "To do what?"

"This is a conflict fought only by professional soldiers who choose to join the Metalgant establishment – who would much prefer to be in the thick of a battle – our battle, than acting as peacemakers."

"So we're between a metal and a hard place?" A silence prevailed and it flew in the face of everything she held dear.

"The situation is more unstable than we realised," said Lapis-Lazuli.

"I don't need protection from knowledge. Surely to be forewarned is to be forearmed. Don't forget we're all in this together." She felt her eyes blaze bright with purpose.

"Yes. I don't need to be reminded of those details." Rhuand responded tersely. "I'm beginning to feel high on feeling low."

He moved in closer to her and she could feel a static current run over her body, she willed herself not to become unfocused by the physical attraction she was so nearly overcome by. Her eyes fixed on his lips as they moved independently.

"It isn't as clear cut as it may first seem, Salt."

"Rarely is!" She tensely swallowed while searching his enigmatic eyes and brooding profile.

"Lapis overheard an unsettling conversation here at the pool earlier between Female Munrah and Skada. The out-shot being, the two guards are under orders to re-enter this series of colours accompanied by reinforcement–"

"Reinforcement?"

"A magnetised weapon." Lapis-Lazuli broke his own silence. "Phenomenon."

Rhuand picked up the lead. "The magnet isn't simply a device. It is a warrior. A magnetico-electrico warrior by the name of Tervanous. The nearer he draws to me through the causeway colours, the greater the effect placed on my spirit energy levels. We anticipate, while I'll not completely be debilitated, I will be slowed down by his power of attraction."

"So what do you suggest?" She felt her mouth tighten. "There must be a way to immobilise him."

"That's certainly one option," said Lapis-Lazuli optimistically. "Tervanous has peculiar qualities of inherent properties that attract elementary metal, whereby he is able to attract or repel."

She turned back to Rhuand appealing with her eyes for an answer.

He looked unsettled. "Inconclusive at this moment in time," he pronounced the words with some difficulty.

"Surely the quadripartite machine will create a greater distance between him and us over ground, won't it?" Her voice wavered into uncertainty.

"Partly," replied Lapis-Lazuli. "But anything gained through visualisation is limited to the colour it was projected in. Once you've crossed over the threshold of the next sandsomme stone building, the vehicle will disintegrate into white dust."

"And meanwhile we're waiting for a solution to strike us in its own sweet time?" she said bitterly.

Rhuand continued to brood, knowing he was as unhappy as she was made the situation tolerable.

Then his eyes fell on the vibrant Regard brooch – still pinned to her turquoise bodysuit. He seemed lost in a thought for the space of a moment. His reaction to her and the brooch immediately sparked an inquisitive feeling from her – *Does he regret ever setting eyes on me?*

If so, she was aware when the time came he could say goodbye like an absent hello.

:

The outside of the next sandsomme stone building looked similar to the first, only larger, with an additional column on either side of its majestic doorway.

Disembarking from the riding machine, Salt repeated the same method of unlocking the door by inserting the Regard brooch into the perfect replicated shape in the indented stone. And as she and Rhuand entered through the doorway; just as Lapis-Lazuli had told them, the quadripartite machine disintegrated into a rapid sweeping whirlwind of white dust to be lost in the prevailing atmosphere.

Once inside the building they were pleasantly surprised to see the interior had four walls and looked much less like a ruin than the other. It had immense glassless windows through which they could distinctly see a spectacular purple hue.

"Do you think each sandsomme building will become more complete in structure, more opulent?" Her restless eyes settled on him. They had, she felt, too little time. The Metalgant elite were shadowing them, and the pressure to keep them at bay was all-consuming.

"The indications are all here. Building upwards from the foundations, I believe."

"I'm sorry, Lapis couldn't be here to see this with us. Conversation with him is always a pleasure, however brief. I guess the major downside to being a water vis-viva is he can only exist where there is water-form."

"Heaven alone knows what is in store for us this time. Lapis gave no further indication." He led the way towards an open archway at the opposite side from their doorway of entry. She followed in haste, feeling – would he ever be able to get out from his shell-of-self?

"Well," she said, "the first colour blue reflected the place of our forced separation, in the second, orange bought our unconscious to the forefront–"

"And now purple."

She studied his slowing swagger. Then taking off the steel threaded overcoat draped round her shoulders, offered it back to him. In turn he took it silently from her. This was her way of reaching out to him. Little comfort she knew, but it was the best she could do while not knowing what the future held for them. She hoped with all her heart he would recognise this went somewhere near – not nowhere – "I hate to see you like this." She could have wept, but she held out.

"Like what?"

"Disadvantage."

"Salt," he raised his voice as he spoke to her, "you learn so much more from being at a disadvantage than ever you do from a success. The challenge is to never place yourself at the same disadvantage again. That is the only failing, to allow oneself to fall into a cycle of repeat."

"You always did show a talent for joined-up thinking." She smiled deep into his eyes.

His voice, harsh to her ears, "All the training and obeying orders, fighting to win wars; being honoured and only a step behind Female Munrah, I was never taught how to live – or die, for that matter."

"Are you in great pain?" She had to know.

"No. Just a dulling to my senses. I can still see you're as memorable as a rose in an arid desert."

She let out an unprepared laugh, not knowing quite how to respond to his last comment. It did sound like a compliment, but it had been so long since she had heard anything remotely like this from him. Fleetingly her mind went blank – then just as quickly, she regained her sanity.

She had been so use to the harshness in life; facts, deceptions, orders, extremes, fighting for survival that suddenly she recognised an act, or a word of kindness could so easily break her in a split moment of time. She began to feel rising anger surge up through her body.

How dare he!

How dare he be so –

Kind?

Don't mistake him for a warrior that cares, she thought, for he may well have his own agenda.

And an old memory darted into her turbulent thoughts: something her Earthlet mother once told her, *'remember, Salt, some guys don't fall in love in case they lose their identity'.*

Rhuand certainly had a new identity emerging, from life to limbo and then the beyond. The unknown. Telling herself she could and would get over the darkly dangerous warrior if a future together wasn't destined – and she'd live a solution, not a problem.

As she contemplated those internal words, they became temporarily the truth.

Not trusting herself to respond immediately, she gave him a delayed reply, "Any Earthlet who never changed their mind, never changed anything."

He turned to study her facial expression and she felt exposed.

Could he read her thoughts, her hidden depths of turmoil? She willed him not.

She would nurse these feelings for as long as possible – they belonged to her. No, she wouldn't be wrestled away from them just yet, knowing anger was just as powerful an emotion as love – each could singularly propel an individual forward by creating extreme energy, a manic motivation to battle onwards.

For now, there was more reliability in holding onto her anger, than there was to her love.

:

(4) PURPLE TOXIKA'SHON

:

#HostToWar – Stepping out into the intangible purple hue took them both aback. It was like walking into a shimmering purple ocean. The fresh cool breeze seemed to invite them to stroll amongst the landscape of fruit trees planted for as far as the eye could see, with all the variations in colour of purpled blossoms and ripe purple fruits giving out a delicious depth in aroma – which strictly brought his thoughts back to her abrupt comment – change!

On occasion her words could strike more than they stroked. "It's good to know some things never change, would you not agree?" His aim, to push her on and explain her choice of words.

"I won't be drawn on the sentiment any further."

"Why?"

"Some things are better left unsaid. I believe words should be chosen with care, as once one has spoken them, even wild horses cannot bring them back."

He looked into her spectacular eyes and knew that no-one could remain unresponsive to this attractive Earthlet. Her power to attract and captivate he found both mystifying and disquieting. "Generally, as a rule I speak as I find."

"Well, I speak as I feel. Language is one of the most powerful tools we Earthlets have to express ourselves with." A mixture of shrewdness, self-indulgencies and indefensible innocence crossed her face.

"You shouldn't disregard action. That can be equally as powerful," he responded with cold precision.

"From the point of view of an Earthlet female I will talk thoughts out loud, whenever it suits me, whereas you would appear to stop talking to find yourself."

"I'm sorry." The smile he knew did not reach his eyes. "I often live in silence trying to hear who I really am–"

"How dare you patronise me." Her eyes were hot with accusation, triumphant almost. "In my performance days, I provoked spirited forays between the public and the stage platform. You should relinquish stubborn conformism, Rhuand Mezarron and trust a female Earthlet's judgement a little more."

He knew she wouldn't be pushed further on the matter. Still, even wrangling her was a delight he had missed. To get under her skin and agitate, and she would free her rejoinder thoughts in protest. He hadn't forgotten her little quirks. Her complete resistance artillery amounted to the odd spoken rebuttal, usually followed by a reluctant giggle, a sigh and surrender.

"Do you think we should taste the fruits?" She lifted her voice, sounding not at all bothered by their spat. "There must be thousands."

"There's millions." He moved alongside her. "Don't see why not." Ever since they had been reunited, he had noticed she was much closer to the bone than he remembered.

"Could they be poisonous?" Her voice held a slight sardonic quality which didn't escape him.

"No, just look at the vastness of these fertile fields. These fruit bearing trees are encouraged to grow for cultivation reasons, to be harvested for consumption, but by who?" he added, watchful from all sides, ready for action. For she showed a resourceful attribute that had always set her apart from more pedestrian females. This aura gave her a sensitivity, which made him want to fall over himself to try and take care of her.

Following his first brief conversation with this beauty at the Alt Grand Festival, he had instantly felt he could share his dynamism with her and give her a helping hand towards her ambitions. Not only was she truly gifted as a dancer, she held a self-effacing ability to understand him intuitively, like nobody else before or since.

He had never met someone he could be so in-tune with, he never allowed anyone that close, never felt the need to share a life. But she had such an enhanced femaleness about her, and her heart and her ego where both squarely in a just place that without warning – he was susceptible to following her anywhere she chose to go. However, within the limited boundaries of marked limbo, *anywhere* had become restricted.

"Let's eat," he said positively. And she did. And he found he was unable to take his eyes off her as she placed sumptuous lips round the ripe fruit to take a generous bite.

Her lips were pronounced, seeming to have an effortless outline as though she had applied colouring, even when she had not. He felt a compelling hunger within himself, to lean forward and make contact with her moist, moving mouth, and... his mind lingered over the thought.

"Try one," she said with a playfulness that he knew she reserved for special occasions. "Hmm, I can testify they are truly sublime." She placed an elegant hand across her bottom lip, and irresistibly wiped away the ripe juice escaping her mouth.

She laughed in amusement.

He laughed, beguiled. Longing to kiss her: taste her: embrace her: and...

She picked more from the laden trees. "They look like Servon plums." She passed a handful to him. "I'm sure they'll be to your liking..."

He was more interested in looking at her. From his perspective there was a definite change taking place within Salt since her full recovery beside the orange desert pool. Lapis-Lazuli was clearly right when he stated she was 'resplendent'.

She is radiant!

Radiant with a blossoming confidence now free from battling against physical pain. She was slowly becoming unhindered. And he was generously reminded of the Earthlet girl he met all those sola suns ago before life was taken from him. Seeing Salt in this beautiful orchard of fruit trees, it was hard not to enjoy her enjoying herself.

They'd had slim time to act like their old selves together, without the pressing trepidation of Female Munrah and subordinates crashing into their mental and physical space. While that constant pressure was always with him, he hoped the strong need for each other in life would draw them closer in the absence of others.

"Take a bite," she said with a charm and singleness of attention that sometimes could set his mind on edge. This time it pleased him.

"It's more important you gain the minerals and nutrients from the orchard. Now you've acquired better health and well-being from the desert pool, it's all about maintaining that level. We can't afford even minor illnesses."

"Surely you can't live off fresh air alone?" Her voice carried anxious overtones.

"Another benefit of being in limbo."

"But you'll miss out all the same."

"No, I just get to enjoy them in a different way, through you. It doesn't make it any less important or real."

"I guess I'll have to remind myself more often that we're on opposite sides of life, each having different limits to the other."

There was a silence. She had spoken a truth. He was struggling with the reality just as much as he suspected she was. All his dealings had been with himself and that larger self of family – the Metalgants. From the way her amber eyes shone, yet couldn't hold his, suggested to him she was in search of the unobtainable… "And that should work for us, not against us. Your weakness is my strength, and vice versa." He did not want to question their being, or see or think what they were doing beyond the now.

"That's one way of looking at it." She seemed to brighten up under his attention. Her eyes met his.

"Wait here." He began to climb one of the trees, causing the ripest of fruits to shake free from the branches and bounce onto the thick ground of purple bell-like flowers beneath the trees. Salt laughed good-naturedly as she dodged the falling fruit. He had forgotten what it was like to laugh whole-heartedly with her until stomach muscles hurt and faces ached. There had been a time when that was all they'd seemed to do.

He took a few vigilant moments to survey the scenery amidst

the glistening purple hue, and what he saw caused him to stop laughing immediately.

"What is it, what can you see?" she called excitedly. Her voice filtered up between the lustrous foliage.

"A huge complex – many great cylindrical shaped buildings." His voice sounded arbitrary to his own senses.

"What would be the reasoning behind that?" she countered quickly. Too quickly.

"Maybe housing the fruits from this orchard and processing it–"

"Like a distillery."

"Anything's possible. We'll take a closer look."

Moving purposefully, they left clear tracks through the covering of purple bells, imprinting, as if on dark snow, and in the great distance a black raven wheeled and dived, crowing harshly – informing or alerting, defending or accusing, the warrior in limbo could not ascertain at this moment. But nevertheless, approached with guarded attention.

Upon reaching the huge complex, there appeared to be hundreds of cylindrical shaped wooden buildings, all designed without variation standing many storeys high. Round the edge of each building was a wooden stairway that curved its way from ground level to rooftop.

Salt stopped at the foot of the first building's stairway. An inscription was carved into a wooden placard and nailed at head-height onto the building. She read the words out loud. *"PRODUCTION OF MONTROSE STONE FRUIT. SEASON DATE OF HARVEST: AUTUMN SOLA SUN MARK-TWO-FIVE-THOUSAND.* So it is a wine processing complex. Say, let's find the building dated when we first met." Not waiting for his response and with unabated enthusiasm she was on the lookout. "Come on, Rhuand, it can't be all that far from here. We're looking for mark-one-eight-thousand."

Ever the optimist, he thought feeling pensive. Once she had set her mind on something, she wouldn't be moved. She was an individual, an independent thinking female, who through the adversity of being born an Earthlet had successfully carved out a career, reaching the level of principal member within the dynamic dance group, Amharik.

Unlike other females he knew, she had an extra quality which immediately resonated with his own inner vibration. She knew what it was to devote one's time to a career, not particularly though choice, more so through a need, a determination to better oneself. She was not apologetic about being headstrong. She simply, was. He had instantly recognised something of himself within her character and was intrigued to know more, and had remained fascinated by her ever since.

While he had actively searched for the ideal woman to partner himself, he had become exacerbated by the whole dating procedure. He had never been able to find that special spark. And so from the disappointment of it all, he had thrown himself, with even more vigour into his life work to becoming a Kielter of great distinction. He knew that was something he could depend on. Something that wouldn't let him down.

Shortly after his introduction to Salt, he had realised, while placing all his dedication and energy into an advancing career, the career would never love him back. This was the turning point. Never before in all his Metalgant years had his career not taken total priority.

Instead he had found his mind deviating to her – fantasising what she was doing, where she was going, and how she was fairing. He just wanted to be with her. The sensation was completely overpowering like no emotion he had ever experienced before.

Initially he didn't know how to deal with these fantastical, bizarre feelings that led to involuntary heart spasms, light-headedness, and perspiring outbreaks. He had thought there was something wrong with him, he must be ill, or at least coming down with something feverish. It was unfathomable to his intelligence.

His ability to keep a clear head and calm heart rate in tested situations was legendary. He had acquired such techniques from rigour and harsh training. In the company of Salt, his programming deserted him, unbalancing his whole system, leaving him breathless with – something without a name – could it be happiness?

His commanders at the Actimm programme swiftly detected his sudden change and promptly confronted him. While he recognised he could jeopardise the programme he had willingly signed to be a part of, and helped to bring into existence, he still couldn't carry out their severe order: to give her up. And so he made the decision to break regulation by continuing to pursue her. She had become his virtue of passion – and –

"Over here!" She broke into his deliberation. Her words echoed off the cylindrical buildings, "Rhuand I've found *the* one!"

"Where are you, exactly?" he shouted from amongst the maze of buildings.

"Just follow the succession of dated placards..."

He could feel a sudden strengthening pull on his spirit. He knew it could only be from the Tervanous effect. Being surrounded in a closely built wooden complex was making him more susceptible to the magnetised opponent – with very little metal in this environment to divert and weaken the pull away from him. He was being homed in on.

Mentally he fought the trepidation away.

I control my thoughts and my thoughts control me…

The only resolution was to find Salt, pursue a way out of here and chance the next sandsomme stone building would lead them into a place whereby diverting the magnetism away, or at least lessening its strength of pull.

When out of the purple, he heard her let out a heart rendering scream and as he fiercely strived to reach her, a sickening feeling overcame him – dreading with all his being what circumstances he may find her in.

He shouted her name, hoping she would answer back and help him focus the whereabouts of her location. Instead he heard muffled, indistinct dull noises and grating.

Rounding another wooden building, his vivid green eyes caught sight of Skada forcibly dragging Salt by her hair up a wooden stairway of a cylindrical building. In his left hand, his choice of weapon in place of the Braska sword – a lethal prison guard axe.

"SKADA!" he shouted, causing his adversary to halt marching footsteps, to then turn, unyielding, and look triumphantly down the stairwell at him.

With a show of contempt he curled up a corner of his mouth. "Rhuand Mezarron!"

The infamous snake-like Metalgant held Salt some distance from where Rhuand stood at ground level. He knew all too well, whatever action he might plan in using against his antagonist, he must remember, Salt was in a precarious position of height, high above the purple ground.

As he estimated and evaluated his chances of reaching her before Skada did anything unmerciful, a familiar fragrance of wild erco flowers, mixed with cold fortified steel began to envelop him, telling his senses of a foreboding presence close behind him.

"Remarkable, how predictable an Earthlet can be." Rhuand turned to face the low, throaty, hushed voice behind him.

Female Munrah!

Her abundant reddish-oxide coloured hair was arranged into a coiffure design to frame her triangular face. Her elongated navy-blue eyes stared back at him, to bore into his and test his strength of will with loaded penetration.

Through his eyes, Female Munrah looked unscathed, untarnished considering the sinking sand incident earlier. But he knew all too well, it was the clearing-up that mattered the most to her.

What was it she'd once said...? 'Perception is everything. The skill is making it the truth.'

Standing in front of her now, he could see she was determinedly in control of her appearance and composure, showing not a glimmer sign of being perturbed.

"I have been proved right in suspecting the Earthlet would seek out the wine dated in the season of your – your – unity. I guess those who are easily duped might call it an expression of love. Whereas I would call it an expression of weakness."

"Love is as love does. It is an emotion only mocked by those who cannot attain it." He knew his aversion to the past was as strong as ever since meeting Salt, and his earlier Metalgant life was now the past.

"Save your poetry for her," she snapped. "Love is a choice, and I'm made of much stronger stuff than that." Her fingers were tipped by long nails carefully buffed to an elegant sheen which caught the purple light every time she relaxed, then re-tensed her capable grasp round the other prison guard axe. She held the weapon possessively close across her firm body.

Rhuand was very much aware the longer he stood and listened to Female Munrah, the further away Salt was being led from him. The urgency to keep her in plain sight was vital. It was imperative. "Let's move," he said abruptly, while glancing up to Skada who had released his strong grip from her hair, and now with both hands round the axe staff, violently pushed the side length of the shaft across Salt's back – forcibly moving her up the stairway.

"My thoughts exactly," said Female Munrah. "The waste of time has been much." Her voice then took on a different tone, almost seductive, "But, dear Rhuand, I must say, if you decide to have second thoughts about this, this – troublesome Earthlet, and instead decide to co-operate with us, I may allow you a place back within my supremacy."

"What do you mean, troublesome Earthlet?" Her words against Salt reverberated in his mind.

"The Actimm programme has been scuppered because of her!" she spoke through a small rebellious mouth.

"It just goes to prove the Actimm programme was built with a fault." He was cautious not to pick up speed when ascending the stairway, pacing himself carefully as well as the words he spoke. He didn't want to speed up the planned proceedings of his adversaries.

If he acted outwardly calm, so might they instinctively, and without knowing, follow his pace – the more time he had, the more time there was to anticipate their devious plan. *Some things should not be rushed into when you can't see what is coming at you*, he thought coldly, mechanically.

"You can't surely think she was worth all this agro. She has been the sheer downfall of you. To end up in this dismal place of surrealism which the home planet does well not to acknowledge."

"I wouldn't say, acknowledge. This place you call surrealism is out of bounds to most–"

"You'd do well to remember," she said with murderous fury, "I made you into who you were, recommended you reach a potential by giving you the opportunity to prove yourself as a favoured Kielter. And this is how you repay me? By throwing away the Metalgant vision of self-preservation, and all for an Earthlet!"

Rhuand didn't trust himself to answer. He had to compartmentalise his mind from her and to what was happening with Salt. How he should best intervene to remove her from Skada's imminent dark deeds.

Everywhere he looked the building and its attachments were crafted out of the element of wood, not metal. He had no ability to bend wood to his way of thinking.

Female Munrah appeared quick to take his silence as acceptance to her statements as she continued in conversation, sounding almost reasonable while maintaining two steps behind him at all times. "The skills you now seem to be in possession of, could, would, advance the Metalgant vision."

"You are saying, you'd concede a place for me within Metalgant ranking, again?" He had now lost sight of Salt and Skada as they rounded the building high above him.

"It's a possibility you shouldn't overlook, Rhuand Mezarron.

After all our technological possibilities could advance through you. You would be at the very heart of a new, ore inspiring project. This would make your name legendary across all five elements. Your reputation would live on forever and a day." Hearing the excited undertones in her voice brought out the mercenary within him – the host to war.

"What are your plans for Salt?"

Up ahead, a loud bang of a door slammed shut, and he felt a separation, so strong, it shook his soul.

"Whichever way you look at it, she must be killed in order to prevent further upset regarding the Actimm programme. Only then can we move on and eradicate errors built into the system. There needs to be a complete overhaul."

"Reprogramming from the benefit of Salt's death?"

"She need be no concern of yours. Your only concern should be what you want for yourself – to remain here with no future, or to come back with us and gain a future beyond possibilities."

They had now climbed half way up the spiral stairway and reached the door through which Salt and Skada had entered moments ago. He paused momentarily to collect his diminishing thoughts and fight off the persisting pull on his spirit – dampening his reaction to move swift of mind and spirit.

He couldn't give in to its influence.

He must battle on.

He had someone who needed him desperately.

Preparing himself for whatever may lay on the other side of the lacquered wooden door. His eyes read the carved placard:

AUTHORISED PERSONNEL ONLY

Pressing down on the latch handle to pull the door open, a prevailing force of air rushed passed him. Forcing his coat of entwined steel to billow out from round him as he peered into the dimly lit building, searching for a reassuring glimpse of the invincible Earthlet.

:

#Badbye – "Halt, Earthlet!" shouted Skada. She did as he commanded.

He had marched her to the middle of a long creaking wooden bridge, suspended high above a wooden vat which covered more than two-thirds of the building's ground space, with an amalgamation of many pipes and taps leading away from the structure.

Salt looked along the bridge walkway, noticing a trapdoor with faded sign-writing painted on it in cadmium yellow:

Her heart plummeted like lead in her chest. And with a tighter grip on the wooden railings she tried to stabilise herself as an unquiet surged through her blood making her light-headed and dizzy.

How could she escape such a terrifying ordeal against her? The outcome looked so shocking. So horrifying. Trapped inside this dimly lit cylindrical building, frantically she searched in her mind for a way to freedom.

From the door through which they had entered, a balcony ran the full extent of the building's inner wall linking it to the wooden bridge beneath her stricken feet.

"Only time stands between now and the final disposal of you." Skada's rasping words did not disguise his perverse pleasure as he waited on her to respond.

She had no intention of keeping him waiting too long. "Time…" she said shakily. "There was a time when all I ever wanted was to be a renowned dancer, performing at the Imperia Hall."

For her, evasion and omission were the preferred methods of dissimulation. She could and would embellish a terrible truth, and if those tactics didn't work, she would use another, and invent a second truth which she hoped would throw powder in the eyes of the first, real one.

He laughed, "From the looks of it, I would say, Rhuand Mezarron is about to join the Metalgant way of thinking once again."

She turned and faced him straight on, and for the first time she noticed each eye was a different colour. Dark like siliceous stone. One reflected gold, the other silver. A shiver ran down the length of her spine, but her spirit was not broken. "You're lying!" she defied him. "I learnt through bitter experience in prison that lying takes the form of pathology, a tool which assists others to slalom their way out, or their way to the top."

He curled his lip in contempt. "Contrary to law. We are lawless. We regulate our punishment to fit the disorder." His eyes shone like metallic stone. "As we speak and breathe, Female Munrah is informing Rhuand about the great advantages he'll reap by re-joining his fellow comrades. It won't take much persuasion before he recognises he'll be better off with his own kind. You are an outsider, a bad influence. We have to dispose of the likes of you."

Out of the dullness, an outstanding shaft of brilliant purple light beamed into the building from the narrow door she had only moments ago entered. Her amber eyes pinpointed the silhouettes of Rhuand and Female Munrah.

She observed their body language, determining if anything Skada had announced could be true. Was he merely taunting her for his own twisted pleasure? He certainly had the character to play vicious and deceitful games without a twinge of remorse.

"As sure as meat is meat, you've been thrown to the wolves. Aaa-whooo!" he howled again and again in beastly tones, scaring her. And the pleasure was his. And it showed.

She felt her bottom lip quiver uncontrollably as she watched the warrior in limbo take direction from Female Munrah to walk along the balcony and into the fortified windowed control room, where they would have an improved view to the full length of the wooden bridge she and Skada stood on.

"Little Earthlet, have you any departing words you wish to speak before we move proceedings on?" asked Female Munrah. Her metallic voice transmitted through an intercom and into Salt's brain.

She raised her head slowly to signal she was an Earthlet of personal integrity and proud with it, while still trying desperately to gain a better understanding of the new and terrifying situation in sight. Polished eyed, she appealed for some response from Rhuand; he reflected nothing back to her.

A low humming interference noise passed through the intercom system as the microphone remained switched on in the control room. Fragmented speech between the Metalgant of spirit and the darkly commanding Female Munrah began to filter into the vast wooden building, signalling her worst fear.

"… place behind us…"

"… unexpected…

"… welcome back…"

"… the Fort…"

"… correct decision…"

Like rain falling in the night, love had always seemed to pass her by; until she had met Rhuand Mezarron. Now it appeared to have come full circle as she realised love was not a permanent emotion, it could be fleeting.

After all the hard work, meeting him, winning him, then losing him, and finally finding him once again – for it all to now fall apart just before the fun should start in a life and a death together was beyond understanding. The strain and pain she knew was beginning to show across her features.

"One must not hold back from loss," Skada mocked. "You should embrace it. Celebrate it like a hypercritical Earthlet!"

"And what would you know about loss?" She must not allow this realisation to crush her. She stood alone. All unease and fear was lost in the luxury of self-absorption. She had come too far to give in. Knowing she was on her own to get out of this deathly tight situation, meant she was free to acknowledge her options lay only through herself. She would not be beaten. She would come out fighting – *There has to be a way out.*

"Atten'shon! Prepare action one!" instructed Female Munrah through the intercom system.

He grabbed Salt tightly by her resisting arm, pulling her along six, then seven paces. She fantasised about kicking him on the shins, or kneeing him in the groin, even grabbing the axe from his hands, to somehow backtrack the length of the bridge and run down the external wooden stairway. Instinctually she knew there was only one shot at something like this, for if she did surprise him like that and was then recaptured, there would be no possible way of repeating such an action again. He would be more than ready for her next time – on heighten alert.

A plan of escape was a choice between life and death. She must take the opportunity without hesitation when it arose.

She watched as Skada hung the axe by its head from the bridge handrail, then assiduously, he began to unlock a large wooden box hinged to the overpass structure.

Now was the chance she had been searching for, to grab the weapon and run.

Rushing forward, she managed to make contact with the weapon, but he was too fast for her, and promptly grabbed it clean away from her hold. Their faces were now only inches apart from each other. Her stomach turned over as she breathed in the Shalimar cologne mixed with his hot acetic sweat and sweet tobacco.

"Steady now, Earthlet," he taunted. "Don't be having grand ideas you can't possibly follow through." He held her eyes, and she felt she was looking into the hooded eyes of a venomous cobra. She took a measured step away from him to create distance.

"Oh, no!" he hissed, "I'll not be taking my eyes of you again, Salt Delray. Not for one milli-moment. I can assure you, you have my full attention." He drew in a long, deep, satisfactory breath. "But then, isn't that what you've always wanted, secretly? I've seen the way you've looked at me. You felt the lightening tension between us." With nostrils flared, he leaned into her, breathing her in. Slowly, in deliberation, he licked the side of her face, from the jaw-line and up her left cheek, stopping just below her eye.

She didn't move a muscle.

Neither did she flinch.

He swallowed gutturally, savouring the moment, "Hmmm, I taste a hint of sweet Servon plum." He smiled a loathsome smile while backing off from her. And again, placed his hand into the wooden box, his eyes never once leaving hers. He felt round, then pulled out a tyrian-purple gas mask. "Sorry! Only one. Looks like you're going without."

"Sorry means you'll never do it again."

"And I plan not to–"

"Atten'shon! Action two," interrupted Female Munrah. Suddenly the wooden roof on the vat below the bridge began to creak and automatically slide open. The bridging began to shudder beneath their feet from the vibrations of movement. And a gradual purple vapour began to rise up towards the wooden bridge from the processing fruit contained in the enormous vat below.

"What a crying shame. The wine of your unity will be forever spoilt. Never to be tasted at its true potential. My commiserations, Earthlet, but when all has been said and done, you shall experience the next best thing. All that's left to do is add the final ingredient to the fermenting wine below. You!"

"Do you always carry out Female Munrah's orders? Don't you ever have a mind of your own?" Her thoughts were rapidly ticking over as she tried to think more clearly how to defend herself from what was about to happen.

"Oh, believe me, I don't lose my sense of freedom. This is all about your termination."

"Freedom? A freedom that's given to you within guided boundaries. I'm sure if you had a mind, there would be something in it for you to be your own Metalgant."

"I won't say *goodbye*, Earthlet. Instead, I'll say *badbye*." He pulled the gas mask onto his head and over his face, then signalled with a dismissive arm gesture across to the control room. Desperately, she saw Rhuand stood my Female Munrah's side. He appeared imperious to her fearful situation.

"Atten'shon! Action three." The trapdoor on the bridge swung open with a loud clang. Female Munrah gave a slow, meaningful nod of order to Skada, her appointed masked partner to inflict the capital punishment on the condemned Earthlet.

Salt could hear his breathing filtering through the metallic protective facial-wear. It was unnerving. But it urged her on to maintain shallow, slow, even breaths, with the aim to breathe less of the toxic fumes which continued to rise up through the gaps in the wooden bridge.

The question crossed her mind, what might she suffer first: drunkenness from the potent fumes, or exhaustion from fighting to stay afloat in the vat of stone fruit wine?

She looked again across to Rhuand in the control room for one last time. He looked vague, vacant even – in some kind of trance. "If you're not the one for me, then who are you?" she said under her breath, turning away from the control room in both sight and then body.

She blocked any further thoughts away.

She knew what she had to do.

There was to be no exceptions.

"Hand the brooch over, Earthlet!" ordered Skada.

She felt her eyes stinging, over-brimming with tears from the toxic fumes and suppressed emotions. "Never!"

Skada lurched forward to grab her. She ran with pure fear in her heart. There was nothing else for it. She couldn't out run him that she knew. But there was one skill she had over him. Salt Delray was a professional Earthlet dancer.

As she came up to the large open trapdoor, she gave a wholehearted leap, extending her supple, youthful, long legs in the turquoise body suit while pointing her toes within the prison-issued plimsolls.

Expertly, she cut through the smog of toxic fumes above the death-hole and without looking down, she soon felt the ball of her leading foot make contact with the wooden bridge, sensing her heel overhung the pitfall for a split moment until the balance of her trained dancer's body whirled her forward. She had made it!

From this elation, came the skill for ingenuity.

How to break Rhuand's trance-like state!

Without a moment's thought she took off her rubber plimsolls and hurled one after the other, high above her into the bridge rigging. The first one missed its target but the second smacked the corner of the intercom speaker, causing it to dislodge and swing out and round the bridge while still attached to its cable of connection, creating a loud piercing screech of feedback. The ear penetrating sound began to increase both in pitch and volume.

Before she could assess the effect of her impulsive action, intuitively, Salt glanced behind her, to witness Skada's sudden descent as he fell short of her distance of jump. She heard a heavy strike of noise.

Gathering up the courage, she stepped closer to the edge of the trapdoor to see him suspended from his axe handle. He had managed to drive the axe blade deep into the swinging wooden door, and was now hanging grimly from its handle.

Stifling sufferable coughing, Salt covered her mouth with a trembling hand, her chest began to feel restricted and tight as she involuntary breathed in the toxic fumes while peering down into the void.

Repeatedly his hands slid down the length of the axe handle as he tried frantically to pull himself up, abruptly stopping at its rubberised end. A metallic yell of frustration filtered through the gas mask, "Help me..." he feigned to her smarting amber eyes.

"Help you?" she shouted through the raucous noise of feedback, "to kill me!"

"Please! I wasn't going to kill you – just frighten you..."

Slowly she bent down onto her knees on the bridge walkway, extending an arm towards him. She paused. Self-preservation jutted into her mind.

Seeing him, seeing her faltering, he mouthed, "Bloody hurry! Can't you see, I can't hold for much longer?"

She clenched her jaw, lengthened her reach and wrenched free the gas mask from him.

"What have you done?" His face was distorted with hatred and his voice guttural. "You–"

"I'm taking a page out of your book, Skada. Badbye." Urgently she pulled the protective mask over her dishevelled cinnamon-black hair and positioned the mask comfortably over her hot, swollen face, while taking short painful catches of breath. She knew only too well she wouldn't make it back to the exit door of the building without this protective facial-wear, and already she felt sick, instinctively fearful of the outcome.

Without a backward glance at Skada, Salt retrieved her plimsolls from the bridge walkway, catching sight of Rhuand through the toxic fumes. She could just distinguish him barricading the control room door by laying an axe within the door brackets, trapping Female Munrah inside.

The feedback worked!

She watched as he reached upwards to rip away two pipes and over connected them.

Instantly Salt knew what he must be doing; connecting the toxic pipe to the clean air pipe which entered the sealed room Female Munrah was in.

She couldn't help noticing his movements were slow, more laboured than his usual self. A rush of concern struck her cold. Infiltrating her being.

Taking a grip of herself, Salt suddenly became aware that there was a dull silence from the transmissible noise she had come to know. Female Munrah must have disengaged the output speakers from the console desk.

Running fast along the bridge to re-join the balcony pathway round the building's interior wall, the Earthlet met the warrior in limbo and lifted her mask. "You took your time. You'd rather be late than wrong, Rhuand Mezarron. I was genuinely on my own over there."

He stared at Salt with a wariness she had not seen before. "The lack of metal in this environment's making me more susceptible to the Tervanous effect." His resonant voice was unsteady. "I yielded to it, only managing to find a break in the suppression once I heard that sphere-piercing screech of feedback. The moment was so arresting."

"What can I say, those who shout the loudest tend to get their own way. I saw no other alternative to bring you out of the trance." Salt Delray smiled congruously, and a thought surfaced across her hot face. "Perhaps this colour is all about temptation. And whether or not to give in to it, or–"

"Temptation?"

"It's a test!" She spasmodically coughed, and quickly brought the mask up to her face briefly to take in a few welcomed deep breaths before lowering it again. "Mine was the temptation of finding the fruit wine dated in our life unity."

"And my temptation?"

"The promise of flattery and notoriety through re-joining Female Munrah and the Metalgants." She passed him the gas mask. "We'll share it, as neither of us will survive without it."

"No. You keep it. The toxic fumes are without consequence to me. Only magnetism can influence my system, not temperature or toxicity." He paused in speech as they heard a prolonged agonising yell from the bridge – which sounded to her unhinged.

"Skada!" said Rhuand. "We must do one thing before leaving here." He placed his arm across her shoulders for extra stability. Eagerly, she responded to him as they moved along the bridge to the open trapdoor.

But on closer approach, Salt held back. "What are we doing? Shouldn't we leave him to his fate? He had no pity on me."

"No. Fate doesn't always favour those who place trust in it." He bent down to kneel on the walkway and reached down into the gap of concentrated purple mist and to her disbelieving eyes, Rhuand pulled up and out, a now drunken Skada, who rolled lewdly onto the wooden bridge.

"Fink yew can tweat me like vis?" he slurred drunkenly between loud gasps for air and irregular spasms of coughing. "Well, hive got somefing to zay to yew, Roo-han Mezzzzzz-arron–"

"Skada!" His higher in rank of command spoke harshly, "I want you to know the debt has now been cleared. I do not owe you anything from attaining your Braska sword. In place, I have saved you from your own death. Understand? Debt annulled!"

The lower in rank didn't answer. Instead he wiped his smarting eyes on his sleeve cuff and began to stagger to his feet.

"Let's go," said Rhuand, and she moved courageously while fighting down a bout of nausea.

Female Munrah banged on the control room's unbreakable window. "I've not finished with you!" Her voice was muted through the division. "I'll find you both, wherever to go. There's no place to hide from me. I've been round, but never turned, unlike you, Rhuand Mezarrron!"

Ignoring the threat, Rhuand threw open the large exit door and a burst of sharp fresh air hit them, revitalising her senses as they descended the winding stairway that hugged the exterior of the cylindrical building.

It was a welcoming sight to see the soft purple hue outside. Salt took off the gas mask and glanced up at Rhuand, seeing his steel overcoat flapping in the cool breeze. "What was the reason in saving Skada when he intended to viciously kill me?"

"Believe me, Salt when I say, he would have been more trouble to us if he had died here in a place of limbo."

"In what possible way?" She failed to see his reasoning.

"He would have gained tremendous strength and skill from a death here, and pair that together with Female Munrah's mind and mental power the outcome would be truly deadly."

"Are you saying – Skada would have become like you – a spirit with Iquique?"

"Nothing more certain. And there's no room for two of the same kind!"

Rhuand looked even more beautiful to her eyes than he had ever done before. His metallic profile held its own mystery as he glowed in the shimmering purple mist. She became aware of a tenderness hidden under this harsh exterior.

Her perception of him was now different, because she was beginning to change by allowing herself to trust in him.

Now her arms ached from the near loss of him. She wanted to rap her arms round him, cupping the back of his neck with the palms of her hands and passionately kiss his honourable moving mouth.

These feelings intoxicated her.

Resourcefully, she pulled back from acting out the impulsive want, for what would he think of her if he knew the imperfect thoughts and reservations she had placed against him while she stood alone on that treacherous bridge earlier?

Would he be disappointed in her?

See her in a different light?

Or would he see passed all of that, and instead she would find herself still written in the palm of his hand?

As he was.

In hers.

:

(5) GREEN EN ENEMIES

:

#HellsInHello – In spite of Rhuand's metal-drive to overcome Tervanous's magnetico-electrico impulses invading his mind-set, he knew these influences were threatening, weakening his resistance.

Deliberately, he avoided Salt's fearful gaze as they relentlessly crushed the soft stems and purple flower heads beneath their footsteps.

"I know how you must be feeling," she said, "cos I feel I've stretched my mind and body, and fear I'll never be able to get back to normal."

Rhuand pretended not to hear her sympathetic tones. He felt an irritating nag of unfavourable comparison. "Calculation, once we find the cylindrical building with the earliest dated placard, we'll see the borderline of purple hue. We are not on safe ground, yet. We have too little time to waste." He fought to blink away the disturbing blankness settling behind his eyes.

"The first buildings we walked passed contained fruit wine much older than those round us now–" she spoke with a continued thread of urgency that hastened him onwards to fight against the gravitating, rhythmic pull of invisible magnetic waves from the impeding Tervanous.

"I suspect all the buildings display a placard significant to something that happened in one or other's life," he said. "Something from which the importance could be snatched away."

"So, this complex holds a record of events that took place in our lives on the home planet?" She appeared to brighten up under his knowledge.

"Yes. Creating a temptation every which way we look!" He

diverted his mind to the way the dancer moved gracefully through the complex, which spurred him on to follow her. He had no excuse for increasing her misery by keeping her waiting unnecessarily. "Cleverly, and sagaciously, Female Munrah was ahead of us on this one, and it showed."

"And my curiosity was a downfall."

"Perfection is not all about control, but of letting go."

"Are you trying to make me feel better about the deadly situation?"

"Does it go anywhere there?"

She thought for a moment. Pausing between her hurry. "Somewhere there – I can't help thinking, to leave Skada in a drunken state on the wooden bridge – well, isn't there a distinct possibility he may not recover from the inhalation effects in his system and die!"

"Highly unlikely."

"How can you be so sure?"

"My reasoning for swapping over the connecting pipes next to the control room was so the pipe emitting clean air would eventually dilute the toxic fumes inside the building. He will, as a consequence, recover, and he will then free a progressively inebriated Female Munrah."

"Now that's something I'd like to see." He was again surprised to hear a slight sadistic tone to her voice. "I can't imagine how obscure and hostile she'd be in such an intoxicated state – and Skada as her babysitter, well..."

Returning a smile seemed easy now, but there was a time when he couldn't remember how to laugh. "I must say, Salt you really were extraordinary the way you leapt across the wine vat terminal earlier on the bridge."

"Resourcefulness doesn't leave a female Earthlet when she faces adversity."

"Indeed. But the way you negotiated that trapdoor–"

"A dancer is always a dancer to the bitter end. I suppose, the rigors of training becomes embedded into one's psyche and never leaves you. In the competitive and theatrical dance world there is no place for a weakened constitution, and with such stealth the unobtainable becomes available."

He could understand her reasoning, although it was far removed from his secret physical and mentally challenging training, received before even being affiliated into the higher ranks of Metalgant regime. Yes, while their experiences had been completely different, the essence was similar. "I just want you to know, you'll never go unnoticed."

She raised an eyebrow. "Once Tervanous's magnetico-electrico effect began to take its toll on you, I felt unnoticed. If I'm honest, I thought you'd abandoned the causeway colours and–" She hesitated, then swallowed hard, as though the memory was painful. "I'm glad you came back to your senses." He heard an edge to her voice of suppressed emotion, and he felt she wanted to say so much more, but held back from him.

"Praise to your outstanding simplicity in creating feedback, I was jolted back into realising what was important to me. I lost clarity."

"And I, nearly lost you."

The Metalgant of limbo would have begun to address the balance of his unspoken words, but he knew now was not the time. They had to advance immediately and without failure into the next causeway colour.

Each antagonised encounter was proving more difficult to bounce back from, and while Female Munrah and Skada were encumbered in the immediate time-frame, the two prison guards accompanied by Tervanous would be merciless in the hunt for Salt and himself.

His mind flickered back – yes, Rhuand knew all too well the part he played in helping to design and programme the personified Tervanous DMS6, and without a shadow of doubt this weapon would be unrelenting in its task to carry out an instruction. There would be no moment of remorse. No empathy. Feelings were programmed redundant. Tervanous was the perfect defence to serve under Female Munrah's supremacy. It would never weaken, unlike life-beings on the home planet.

No, its only possible weakness would be a programmed oversight from a Metalgant of flesh who, part of a collective, designed the machine. That's what he had to focus on, for if they could not out-run Tervanous, his objective must be to discover a flaw, a defect in the system, for both Salt and his sakes.

:

As Rhuand and Salt reached the edge of purple hue they stopped short at the welcomed sight of another sandsomme stone building.

Again, bigger in size from the last with yet an additional column either side of a colossal door.

She removed the item of shimmering jewellery from her turquoise bodysuit, and he noticed for the first time she must not be wearing anything underneath it. His admiring eyes lingered over her taut figure. He could see no line of clothing – an instant heat radiated within his being of seclusion.

"Are you alright?" she asked. "You look, somewhat, challenged."

Challenged was the right word. How accurate she was without knowing the full extent. He clenched his jaw, furious with himself for that disclosure – to give himself away. But then, that was exactly what he wished to do, give himself away to her. He couldn't, mustn't let his mind wonder. They urgently needed to press onwards and into the next causeway colour. There was no room for self-indulgence, and arresting thoughts could cause a fatal distraction.

Forcibly he blocked out mindful images from the past of her moving, naked body – her glowing apricot coloured skin, her tender but firm touch and –

"There's something I'd like to ask you–"

"Anything." He jumped at the invitation of a diversion.

She paused for a few precious moments. Her expression became serious, almost conservative as she regarded him in a covert manner.

"Ask me the first thing that just entered your mind."

She shifted her weight from one foot to the other, and there was a certain look on her face, which he recognised and particularly resented. It came as a result from something that pleased her and was being kept from him.

Then her facial expression changed again, to a brighter self. As though she had changed her mind and decided to ask something else, avoiding a loaded question or reply.

"If, as you say, those who are alive, die here in this alternative dimension, causing their spirit to suffer limbo and subsequently acquire Iquique–"

"Yes. But that's not the question you initially planned to ask, is it?" He knew from her body language it wasn't. She would always bite down on her bottom lip – that was her tell – her tell-tale sign she gave away without knowing.

She ignored his accusation. "Then wouldn't that be an advantage?"

He picked up the cue, hoping his honesty would encourage her to speak as she first thought next time, without edit. "You're speaking with reference to yourself?"

"Surely we'd be stronger here, together and–"

"No! No, Salt! Don't even allow such thoughts to cross your mind ever again. Promise me!"

"Why not?" Her eyes, he perceived, looked remote, unsmiling, as if contemplating some unique destiny.

"Because you cannot join me in that sense. Those in limbo remain in limbo. They are unable to move forward into the light, or even back into their life of past. They are suspended for eternity unless a living being agrees to walk with them."

"But what happens to the living being once salvation is attained for the bearer of limbo?" She turned away and placed the Regard brooch into the groove in the sandsomme stone door. Moving little in a long time the door began to grate open with a sound they had become familiar to. A sound that was becoming a reliable link with their state of being.

Rhuand felt claustrophobic about the questioning as they walked through the building. "They don't pull on the same handrails of the past." His words carried them through the exit doorway and into an illuminated forest of tall Ranhatty trees growing in an evergreen mist of green hue. "I meant to tell you. I didn't know how."

She inclined her head in beautiful understanding, but the

moment was lost by the sinister warning of a black territorial crow perched high above their heads in the darkened tree branches, just visible by the eye, as the dusk began to settle around them. Before they could absorb this new magnificence they were whooshed off their feet!

Gathered upwards –

High into the canopy of trees –

Their bodies unable to escape each other's grasp.

"Booby trap!" Rhuand shouted, trying desperately not to acknowledge the fact that her firm body was pressed tightly against his. With every unsteady struggle and wiggle in movement to gain a separation from each other, the closer and more intimate they became. The intensity increased beyond expectation as their body of entrapment continued to sway precariously in the dusky air, making the motion and movement between them all the more sensual.

"Anger is a brief madness!" She breathed, to his mind, promiscuously into his ear.

At such relentless hypnotic persuasion, Rhuand faltered. Almost. "Nosce teipsum – know thyself," he uttered, aware that her moods were as changeable as the moods in the never-ending day of a child. Her willingness, to his eyes, made her brilliant.

Salt laughed and placed her hands round the back of his neck. In such close quarters and dimming light he could clearly see the outline of her body. Her voice was beguiling which somehow made her almond shaped eyes appear to him as though brightly polished, carrying a promise of tenderness and infinite sensuality, which would turn even the most metal-hearted of warriors.

Then all at once, as though a switch had been flicked, his

regimental rule of mind kicked it. "An element-trap! We've been ambushed!" He jutted his head to examine the restriction that had entrapped them, while grabbing and curling his steel fingers through the resisting netting. "We fell into this with our eyes closed. By the feel of it, the netting's made of tree roots and leaves." He was talking as though he was alone, his concise words commenting on the obvious to help aide a new levelled calmness.

"It can't be Female Munrah's doing, can it?" Salt's lovely face puckered up into a collection of expressions. "She's surely not caught up with us so soon?"

"No! And Tervanous isn't in close radius yet as my energy system would be pulling away from me to a much stronger degree, and–"

"Yallo, yallay!" a voice called from the forest ground. Alerted they peered in a quizzical manner through the gaps in the intricate netting.

"Hello! Hello? We're up here – stranded!" cried Salt seemingly overwhelmed and not recognising a pedantic voice. "Will you kindly release us at once?"

With juddering and shuddering movements they began an uneven stop-start descent. Until finally, they were feet first back onto dry land, struggling their way out from the net and faced with a group of strange faces staring directly back at them.

"I'm really not so sure," said Rhuand under his breath to Salt. "Who are this tribe?"

Cautiously, the group of seven individuals all dressed alike in camouflage suits of jocund green, took closer steps towards the dishevelled couple.

"We may have been safer staying skyward," she whispered

uneasily as they straightened up from an undignified crouching position, and strewed the netting free from themselves while keeping a watchful look-out –

The taller captor of the group walked towards them, supporting his weight by a carved Ranhatty cane. He then stopped and hooked it over his forearm. "You must be the notorious Rhuand Mezarron, and you." He pointed a finger at Salt, "the resilient Earthlet, Salt Delray."

"Yes!" she answered, her eyes bright with purpose and her young face radiating a wholesomeness that was not lost on Rhuand, acknowledging through her he had lost the quality of wholesomeness along the tortuous way of rising to the position of Head Kielter.

She could be so trusting and open faced about things. Whereas he always took a cynical and sadistic stance as a form of protection against the unknown. Always assessed the situation before jumping in feet first. Built by the known, bolstered by the unknown, which had held him in good solute.

Though he greatly admired her for taking things on face value, and had hoped this might transfer to him, but he realised from an earlier stage of knowing her, his training was too engrained in his being. While his edges may have blunted a little, the core was very much unchanged.

During life as a Metalgant Kielter, he had been severely reprimanded shortly after refusing to end his courtship with her. The establishment at Metal Fort's Hub Base had observed a continuing change taking place within him, and Salt's influence of freethinking and freehandedness was not advisable to his honoured position.

He was then instructed to assassinate her!

The matter was none negotiable – *'Adhere to the order or suffer the consequences'.*

He had chosen the latter.

Consequences!

Remembering back to their very last meeting in life – at their usual meeting place, Lake Gardenia – before he could warn her of the severe threat against them both, circumstances outside his control took over and forcibly stepped in. And now they were here – fighting through one colour to another for a chance at salvation.

His inner thoughts jerked back to the present as the speaker of the group continued to talk in an unusually mellow voice, and, he noted sagely, whose eyes were startlingly bright with intelligence and curiosity. "Our mutual friend, Lapis-Lazuli gave a good description of you both. You two will join us in our festival of Candha, before carrying on with your profound journey to–"

"Thank you for the kind invitation," Salt interrupted, her voice choking with passion. "We don't mean to be unsporting, but we really must make headway while we still can."

"This is not an invite, more an insistence!" His tone was firm, indicating he would not be swayed away from an answer agreeable to his arranged social gathering.

Rhuand looked at the captor astutely, the statement itself was deeply compromising, yet it was one he could not reject. "I don't think we should refuse hospitality, Salt – and with reference to Lapis, we should accept this generous offer."

"But what about Tervanous? We can't take the risk."

He laughed harshly. "I'll sense him before he gets too close. You mark my words."

"Isn't that downright dangerous. We only have one shot at this.

"Trust in me." He formulated his eyes to shine dangerously in the veiling greenness of time.

"Trust is a small word that holds big expectations." She smiled thinly. "And sometimes it has a conveniently selective memory."

He turned back to the speaker of the group. "If you're a friend of Lapis, then you're a friend of ours. But tell me, by means of introduction, you know who we are, yet we don't know who you are."

The speaker was slight of build, tall, but not muscular, high forehead, aquiline nose, handsome with an air of gentlemanly about him. "We are Woodlians, from the element of wood. Generated from the family line of Saplinn on the home planet. Our festival of Candha celebrates two equal forces in the wood element, rage and honesty, finding a balance between them creates the beginning of new life through the onset of springtime."

"You originate from the first element?" Salt's tone struggled to be friendly.

"Yes. I am Arkade. My forefathers originate from the Ark of the Constituent. Whereby they founded and helped to preserve transcripts setting out the laws of the five elements. Female Munrah is well known to us. She takes from elements, without giving anything significant back in benefit. She has acquired the ability to suspend and inhibit the continuum of elements in cycled time."

"Are you saying, your people have been effected badly?" The steel warrior in limbo stepped closer. He was intrigued to learn more by nature and by inclination.

"Yes. In our personal battle with her many sola suns' ago on the home planet, we were defeated by her murderous army and found ourselves in a spiritual limbo. Here. She took the Ark of the

Okarpi from us, with a mind to bury it from sight and mind of all five elements, believing in time its existence would be forgotten, allowing her Metalgant supremacy to rein unchallenged indefinitely."

"You mean to say you're people of limbo, just like Rhuand?" Salt looked up at the spirited Metalgant, her amber eyes, heavy and solemn shadowed with strain of behaving well, appealed into his, as if asking him to confirm she had heard right.

"We are. As is our mutual friend, Lapis-Lazuli."

"Lapis too? Oh that explains so much," she said in delayed thought.

"Describe the Ark of the Okarpi to me!" Rhuand's suspicions suddenly came to the forefront of his demandable mind.

"The Okarpi transcripts are carved into five Ranhatty wooden tablets and contained within a large chest which depicts symbols relating to the five elements–"

"Your description rings true to me," he interrupted. "I believe I've caught sight of it in the vaults of Metal Fort."

"Good heavens above!" said Arkade with asperity. "We feared it may have been destroyed – so it still exists?" He looked astonished by the news. "Limbo is the direct result from the current unbalance between the five elements. Our existence here would not be possible if the Ark of the Okarpi was reinstated into the light of knowledge on the home planet – allowing salvation for all limbo-suffers. The wooden tablets are to benefit all elements, and support us to all live alongside one another in harmony, not a twisted variation of this." He spread his arms wide to embrace the moving green mist. "Where one dominant force actively keeps all others suppressed."

"Without jeopardising our plans, is there any way we can help you?" asked Salt.

"There could be." For the time being Arkade held the precious thoughts close to himself. "And in exchange you have my word, you will be escorted safely to the next sandsomme stone building."

"We would both appreciate that greatly," Rhuand nodded, "one good turn deserves another."

"Lapis-Lazuli stressed, we'd know again as once before, from a Metalgant of limbo who was there when white horses left the shore." His tone was solicitous. "And I'm now beginning to see just what he meant."

Taking heed, the group of Woodlians led them happily into a clearing, deep within the woodland. The dark branches and leaves shone white and silver in the cloudless moonlight. A small group began to sway and dance round an established fire burning in the centre, while their spokesman, Arkade signalled to Rhuand and Salt, encouraging them to join him and the others as they feasted on roasted nuts, ripe exotic fruits and succulent vegetal plants, while drinking refreshing herbal perfumed waters that filled the dusky air with the sweet smell of promise.

It was a welcomed release for Rhuand, he began to allow himself to relax for the first time in a long time, seeing Salt's youthful glow and spontaneity as she joined in with the festive Woodlians, to Candha dance round the excessive flaming fire.

He watched her till the crowd pressed round her, reminding him of a time when life was simpler. When it was just her and him. When he could block out all other influences and just be in the time of their lives, sharing moments of sublime happiness.

Salt waved him across to join her. He shook his head in reply. The comfort of the smooth wooden benches were enough for now.

"Come on, Rhu it'll be fun – you can't be any worse at dancing than you were in life," she baited him cheerfully.

He laughed. "In my defence, I did have new shoes on at the time you are referring to. And whoever claims dancing is easy, must have been out in the blazing sun too long."

She danced gracefully up to him, and smiled into his heart. How could he resist her? He simply couldn't. It was impossible.

Salt took his hand in hers. She tugged a little and he responded reluctantly to stand in front of her. "Okay. But I'm not promising any special moves, Earthlet. What you see is what you get."

"I wouldn't accept anything less. You always were special to me."

"Special, hmmm. Special needs, perhaps." And they laughed, unadulterated.

Looking into those delicate but generous features he could see what a beautiful Earthlet she remained to be, with clear sparkling eyes that told a story of sensual secrets only shared between them. He was prepared to fall in love with her all over again. Any male would.

How could they not?

She should be appreciated and adored.

But he'd destroyed her life as she had once known it by the action of seeking her introduction. And the guilt and burden was overwhelming.

If she'd met a different male to him her life would have been so much different. It certainly couldn't be any worse. To his mind, he was at fault and didn't deserved her kindness when he'd ruined every aspect of their once pledged love.

As though reading his thoughts, Salt pulled him across to the fire and effortlessly danced round him.

He took her lead, and together they began to move rhythmically to the beat of the wooden drums. He was entranced by her, and couldn't take his eyes off her cinnamon-black hair as it feathered round her face and teased her supple neck while she moved her head in the freedom of the warming breeze.

"Why don't we take it in turn saying the first word that enters our mind?" she said with a playful laugh.

He knew he'd do anything, all she had to do was ask.

"Fire," she said.

"Heat."

"Passion."

"Kiss."

"Love."

"Torment."

She paused. "Separation."

"Guilt," he said heavily, and intuitively they stopped dancing.

"Guilt?" she said. "What is there to be guilty about?"

"If you'd never met me, but someone else, you wouldn't be living this life of – this life of living hell. I played my part in our undoing. And until now, I never realised hell could be in hello." He couldn't stop his thoughts from finding speech, in this moment, they just spilled out.

"Rhuand, you cannot blame yourself. Others played a demonstrable part."

"When it mattered the most, I didn't protect you."

"You couldn't have protected me any greater than saving me from drowning. Had you not taken that brave decision at Lake Gardenia, we wouldn't be together now."

"I was unable to save myself, and prevent the aftermath which led to your imprisonment at the Irongate."

She stepped back from him and he felt immediately colder. She brought a warmth with her that no other female could. He moved forward to close the gap between them.

"Thinking back, we were not blind to the prospect of an unsettlement against our union." Her eyes glistened in the fire light. "It was just, at the time we found our love all consuming, and so didn't see or even expect the swiftness of Female Munrah's active hatred."

"I was selfish to think I'd find a way round the conflict, and that guilt shall remain with me. It belongs to me and has become part of me." He heard his own voice falter like the crackling fire.

"You choose to feel the way you do for your own reasons. I can only say, I don't see it the same way. To me, yes, we met at the right time for us, but it was the wrong time for others, who, then took it upon themselves to intervene. Some things cannot be planned for. They just are."

The words she spoke were right, so completely and utterly right, he had not realised until now how different their opinions could be from a shared experience of suffered consequence.

"When we think of others, we hand them power." The beat of drumming stopped abruptly. And he heard his last words echo into the opaque midnight atmosphere along with the keen rising flames that licked and followed the breath of breeze.

:

#SaidTheRedWineToTheWater – Arkade stepped forward from amongst the pencil line shadows cast in the illuminating moonlight. Camouflaged in a leafed robe of brilliant jocund green. "As night dwells, we now reach *The Word*. As we know, Female Munrah takes it on her own authority to inhibit each element by unbalancing its Okarpi – the question, and the answer." He paused, eagle-eyed, as if looking for any weakness in the listening assembly. "Until it either becomes too concentrated that it poisons itself, or too weakened that it becomes subservient to her." His gaze fell keenly upon Salt and Rhuand who joined the other seated Woodlians round the open fire that had begun to sink and scorch the ground.

Salt watched its embers glowing in response to the light breeze – and thought – the Candha celebration had indeed bought out emotions which had been keeping their secrets. It had lowered their personal boundaries against each other – Rhuand had given her a rare glimpse into his psyche, and she had learnt he *did* care – in fact, he cared an awful lot and had tormented himself with a guilt she formidably believed he had no reason to own.

Despite all her tactile wording to wrestle the guilt away from him, persistently he'd held onto it, like it had become part of him, part of his identity, using the emotions as a constant flagellation against himself. Leaving her with a distinct feeling this self-torment motivated, or disciplined him to make bad, better.

Salt started to visualise the roots from their past creating branches into their future. Surely, while Female Munrah continued the dark and deadly pursuit of Rhuand and her through the causeway colours, she was leaving the home planet without direct leadership. If the Ark of the Okarpi was reinstated to the elements within this window of time, Female Munrah would lose all stronghold of power to her already unstable position. While the broader consequences were unknown, Salt suspected they would be more favourable to attaining Rhuand's salvation in-spite or maybe because of the volatile situation –

With a sudden jolt, she found herself roused out of her ponderable thoughts to a state of being present.

Arkade continued, "I do believe, together, we will make a great difference by revealing the Okarpi for all element benefit–"

"Yes!" Rhuand interrupted, appearing to marshal his thoughts. "With your help, Arkade I have already begun to formulate a plan of action." His deep melodic tone resonated into the midnight air like a roll of drum beats ensign to kingship. The Earthlet could sense his answer had a dangerous, cruel streak of rewarding retribution – outside the law of what he had been trained to follow and adhere to within the Metalgant establishment. This was personal, as well as element inclusive.

"Then let us alight this night of Candha and hear the transcript from the tablet of the water element in honour of our mutual friend who brought us together, Lapis-Lazuli..." Saliently Arkade raked his Ranhatty cane through the dying embers, igniting fire sparks that travelled upwards in the channelling air from the dampening smoke. "Amunda-ado. Amunda-amay. Amunda-ado. Amunda-amay..." he softly chanted. A stillness of their collective presence settled round them all as they sat patiently and waited – foretasting something to take place – willing nature's strength, her power of continuity and renewal.

Eventually, far-off sounds magnified within anticipation, Salt heard a soft rustle traversing through the leaves of the evergreen Ranhatty trees. The open fire began to crackle rapidly, making snapping noises that carried into the sharpening night air, until two flames began to surge upwards. One was a stunning dark red which almost hurt Salt's eyes – the other flame, a brilliant cerulean blue, very nearly mesmerised her, as they gazed on the flickering, hypnotic movements…

Arkade stopped chanting the tribal mantra, and the two flames of equal height, each appeared to form features of a shining, lucid face.

The stunning dark red flame began to hiss and then to their astonishment, recite a eulogy:–

"Said the red wine to the water,
I have kept the company,
Of many a wise man,
Including King and Queen.

"I have taken men in my grasp,
And from a great height,
I have dropped them on the rocks,
If they should try to fight.

"Said the red wine to the water,
Under my influence,
I have given grand illusions,
Taken away judgement.

"Some come to me for comfort,
Others for a good time,
I will reject no-one,
He who seeks he will find.

"Said the red wine to the water,

I can change a man's mood,
I am all powerful,
Tell me what can you do?"

There was a measured time pause as they served the lucid-one a penetrating silence, giving the strong impression to Salt, as she momentarily glanced from one Woodlian to another, as though they were each compelled to follow the red flame in their minds.

And with a spit and a raging crackle, forcing Salt to look directly at Rhuand next to her – he was sat obscurely in the shadows as the flickering fire lights danced across his shimmering silhouette to spiral dangerously. She followed his concentrated stare into the fire, holding her breath, waiting impatiently for a response from the brilliant cerulean blue flame, which rapidly adhered to the assembly of expectancy:–

"Said the water to the red wine,
I am not one to brag,
About my involvement,
But as you ask.

"I can change many forms,
From ice, liquid to steam,
I was here in the beginning,
Do you not remember me?

"Said the water to the red wine,
My, oh my, how you forgot,
I helped give you life,

In the vineyard of Montrose.

"I have carried the weight of ships,
Turned the wheels of progress,
Quenched the thirst of fire,
And still, you had to ask.
"Said the water to the red wine,
Nothing lives without me,
I rise into the air,
Fall from sky into the sea."

The two flames entwined and in unison spoke:–

"We remain at opposing sides,
A distortion of each other,
One is named red wine,
The other, water."

Before flickering downwards until they disappeared from all sight into the depths of the charred ashes.

A stillness stayed with the observers for some time while they took in the message and meaning behind the words. Salt turned to once again face Rhuand, appealing for a shared sacredness between them. They had just witnessed something that had been hidden away from the majority of element-kind for such a lengthy time that it had been forgotten by many, and so nearly lost forever.

Rhuand locked into her sight. "All sounds die into silence, Salt." His tone of voice led her to suspect he was speaking ahead of their time.

Whatever plan he was formulating she could see his vivid green eyes held a knowing of knowledge and mystery

"I can tell you're not a Metalgant who shoots the crow," said the cane bearer as he joined Rhuand and Salt on the wood-cut bench.

"What do you mean?" said the Earthlet, emotionally in the red of danger.

"I mean to say, he's not a Metalgant who breaks his word by abandoning his calling."

"Recently, I find some things to be so obvious, they have been hidden in plain sight, overlooked and misunderstood," replied the Metalgant in limbo. "When Female Munrah began her pursuit to conquer leadership over all elements, there was no-one to rival her in the collective. Metalgants had been so used to sharing responsibilities, as like all other elements, and this allowed her to violate the guidelines by stepping forward and doing more for them under a guise of caring. But slowly, so slowly that no-one even noticed, her care, turned into total control."

"And the line drawn between being cared for, and being completely controlled can be too fine to distinguish." Salt cringed. "It can be how the recipient chooses to see it–"

"Until it is too late," intercepted Arkade. "And events cannot go back to the way they once were, having gone too far."

"Female Munrah made sure of it." Rhuand nodded his head. "And I played my part in strengthening her violation of truth, her hand-grip. I was an asset to her. Excellent at my job, and I reasoned with myself I could find a degree of freedom thinking and power within her authoritative structure. When really, the independence was a falsehood, with deceitful intentions sold to me like all other Metalgants who made it to the elite inner circle. One is independent, so long as you guard and preserve and lengthen her ruling monopoly. You are dependent on her for your boundary of freedom."

"And then you jeopardised her supreme power to rule, whereas we challenged it." Arkade smiled bitterly.

"Yes. Both acts mean you are never to be trusted again in her eyes, and subsequently you become what's known as a bound marker. She has few enemies as she destroys any movement against her by carrying out assassination plans with immediate results. She never grants a reprieve without detrimental cost to the targeted individual."

"We've been so privileged to hear the transcript from the dancing fire flames," offered Salt. "It is our bound duty to make good and re-establish *The Word* from the tablets."

"I agree with you full heartedly, Earthlet, but it shouldn't have to be a privilege. It should be a given right for all elements to know the history of our varied origins and maintain a balance of love, harmony and respect," said Arkade with deceptive clemency. "But for now, we shall take stock and rest, for at dawn break the birth of springtime will begin, the first shoots of new buds will appear. That is the time for scheduling ground work and planning with dexterity against Female Munrah and her allies."

:

The time of daylight found Salt collecting berries and seeds from the now abundant new forest of growth in the dawn of springtime. She was not alone. Her assigned female escort, Beeche, a slim, vigorous Woodlian who, Salt noted stood tall in a proud manner. Her forehead was high, her cheekbones prominent and her mouth, while thin was well bowed, not severe. Her long hair reflected the colour of rich mahogany which she'd ornately plaited to one side of her noble head. There was a show of beguiling candour in her eyes, surely, Salt thought, by virtue of her cheerful youthfulness.

"Has Arkade always been a comprehensive and magnanimous leader among the Woodlians?" asked the Earthlet as she filled a small container made from pliable twigs.

"Yes." Beeche moved to the next fruit bush and continued fruit picking. "His mission has always been to serve and protect, to watch and warn us of danger and treachery." Her lucid eyes began to mist over as she further reminisced. "He is considerate and liberal. Never once taking what isn't his. Occasionally he may make a cutting remark, but aside from that, he is a straight-arrow."

"Arkade and you are involved, together? You can't hide that. It would be a travesty."

The other smiled. "He loves with an intensity and has no small talk."

"Was that always the way?"

"You mean before we both entered limbo?"

"Yes. Is your intensity the same or different than life on the home planet?" She had to know. Any female would want to know.

"I will not lie. At first everything was different. We were seventh strangers by all accounts, visually unrecognisable to ourselves let alone each other. Following a degree of time and patience, we found each other again, and our connection has increased in strength."

"It's easier to judge my own existence, harder to live it. I'm afraid you have the advantage over me." Salt swallowed her anguish.

"An individual's limbo appearance is the result of the life they once led. We Woodlians were lucky in the respect that most of us arrived here together, whereas by my understanding, Rhuand arrived in isolation. Each experience is different to another, and of course the element one's born into plays an extraordinary part. Under a different appearance you have the opportunity to start again, while not truly living, one is still existing and that should never be disregarded."

"Are you saying, it can be far better to have the right kind of nothing, than the wrong kind of something?"

The Woodlian female nodded in thoughtfulness, and raised an eyebrow. "I couldn't have put it better myself."

Salt took a closer, more furtive look at her elected companion. "And you arrived here through Female Munrah's warfare actions?"

"Yes, she was planning to authorise restrictions against wood, we being the first element. We staunchly fought, but she won the battle. We were defeated." Salt heard the strain in Beeche's voice and her heart reached out to her.

"As an Earthlet, I can sympathise with you. My element had become socially outcast by the movement led by Female Munrah."

"There is a world outside the one we have all been born into," she spoke tentatively.

"I can't help thinking, Rhuand and myself don't have the luxury of time to enjoy your hospitality as much as we would like. With every breath I take, Tervanous must be edging ever closer to us." She felt close to a breakout of tears.

As an Earthlet she was bought up to believe a show of emotions displayed weakness within, only to be seen, if at all, by someone extremely close to her. But Beeche wasn't just anyone. She was in unique circumstances also. Salt was beginning to find relief from opening up to another female of sound mind and judgement.

"You and Rhuand Mezarron are safe here. We have built an intricate root system beneath this woodland to detect any unfamiliar movement across the forest, even subtle shifts in balance cause a heightened alert call. Before Tervanous or Female Munrah and her subordinates gain a foothold in this environment, they will be detected, and held against their will. Even if they successfully escape each and every snare and root entanglement, they shall be slowed down dramatically, giving you both a generous amount of time to progress into the next causeway colour."

Salt smiled. "You don't know what a comfort that is." It made her extremely happy to say this and she even considered repeating it. Just for the sake of it.

"Be assured, when they enter here, they will not go unobserved. The forest never sleeps."

"From which we have personally experienced upon entering your land." They both let out a hearty laugh, and Salt's fundamental good nature was out in the open. She felt like dancing.

"Yes, without doubt. The aspect of surprise often catches an enemy off guard. That's how wars are won."

There was a perceptible pause for thought before Salt spoke again. "Do you expect many enemies through here?"

"No. But from our forced limbo here, we aim to uphold the motto of, *'Preparation is a safeguard'*. Although, I can't think of any female who wouldn't wish to be surprised by Rhuand." She looked long and hard in Salt's eyes. "My guess is, one would have to be disciplined, devoted, single-minded and impervious to his darker side. He is a mercenary. A warrior, in disguise. As deep and cold as

Gardenia Lake, so don't lose sight of that reality, Salt. It could mean life for a life…" The voice held a sapient quality, which was not lost to the Earthlet's sound hearing. "There's something about a handsome, powerful male that attracts ambitious females. I'll bet you've been kept on your toes in more ways than dancing."

Salt hadn't expected such an open declaration regarding his demeanour; this put her on guard at once. But every word Beeche had spoken was true to how she had known him and recently began to picture him. And now hearing this from a voice outside her own thoughts made these unsettling comments all the more meaningful. He was a beautiful, shimmering Metalgant of limbo. Furthermore, she was well aware, he could switch off from making her the centre of his attention one moment, then all of a sudden, she'd cease to exist.

This skilled aptitude she could not practice on him. The outlaw about him held its own magnet to her – she shivered, and shivered again – then nodded in reluctant agreement, without saying a word. Words would only express an impression of how she felt, and she wasn't ready to totally open up about her feelings until she knew his limbo-self better.

Besides, she consoled herself, there was so much going on right now. It wasn't just about them, but also the Ark of the Okarpi.

As she and Beeche strolled into the forest clearing, Salt was glad to let the conversation drop. They parted on friendly terms. Salt decided to join Rhuand, Arkade and two other Woodlians, she could see they were conspiring – ready to move forward – planning. Rhuand had sketched detailed drawings, from which the Woodlians where chipping and carving out intricate shapes from a stock pile of logs close by.

They seemed unperturbed as a large black raven strutted with dignity round the designed wooden blocks assembled at their feet. The inquisitive bird placed its head intelligently to one side surveying the carvings, then slowly, methodically, in grandeur style, the raven dismantled the arrangement to finally retrieve a fat, wriggling, hairy caterpillar-like grub. Then in a sublime manner, it gobbled it down sumptuously.

To Salt's mind, no-one else appeared to be monitoring the raven's behaviour. She held her silence, hearing Rhuand explaining, "We're creating an imitation of the vault door's mechanism that I witnessed being unlocked."

She could see he was gifted with a memento mind and intense intrinsic energy. His excellence shone through even with the impending Tervanous close on their trail – his spirit refused to be damned. Somewhere in the depths of his soul, Rhuand had found an enduring state of mind with the air of imminent force that borrowed a mood of restlessness. Not only did he give the impression to be heading in many directions at one go – he was!

"Who will open the vault door at the Fort, once this procedure to unlocking has been learnt from your memory?" questioned Salt.

"A trusted volunteer," answered Arkade. "As well we know, the abridgement between the state of limbo and the home planet can only be crossed through an illuminating bridge of bow."

"Seems to me, we've come a long distance since I entered through an upside-down Rainbow in the waters of Lake Gardenia," the Earthlet said slowly, yet firmly.

Rhuand nodded with grave deliberation. "And Female Munrah and subordinates, entered through a Moonbow at the Gardenia Falls. A very unsettling experience to say the least." His perpetual smile showed an internal struggle. She suspected this was a way to appear affable and control his harboured aggression within.

"But no-one can enter more than one type of bridge-bow. The route is significant to the individual," voiced Arkade. "And it's worth bearing in mind, bridge-bows don't occur all that frequently, they must be aided by water."

"There is the option of an Icebow," said Rhuand after a perceptible pause, and while everyone exchanged meaningful glances, she looked back at him to find his lucid green eyes settle on the Regard brooch pinned to her figure-hugging turquoise bodysuit. She smiled a little, taken aback by the sparseness of the response.

"An Icebow..." she repeated his words to help give herself time to let her mind catch up to itself, and as it did, a feeling of uneasiness spread through her bone marrow. The feeling didn't belong to her, she felt, but instead from the spiritual essence she was picking up from him. It was in the way he held himself.

"It's possible, but I caution the risks are great." He continued to spin the locking mechanism in his hands of steel, then proceeded to pull out the long replica pin from the wooden model, before replacing it intact.

Then putting it onto the ground, as though a last offer, or a final result and the shiny black raven again strutted inquisitively forward and began to curiously investigate the device.

To their amazement the bird began to copy his first part in the sequence of order. Rhuand looked impressed. "Would you credit it?" He looked expansively from one to the other, and another.

Catching his eye, she gave a little laugh then a spontaneous smile which hid her pure will. A will-power born out of poverty and overcoming adversity.

"After my experience within the prison Iron Cage, I can confirm the fact that ravens are characterised by their mimicry." She swallowed hard to the taste of silence as she unwillingly absorbed the torments within her imprisonment, but she carried no self-pity. "The raven! We could train this raven with rewards of berries and seeds to carry out each stage to unlock the vault. Each reward of food would be hidden within a sequence of the locking device." The proposal was so compelling that no-one denied it was conceivable.

Arkade was the first to break the silence, "And no Metalgant guard would see that coming. The raven could gain access into Metal Fort's Hub Base without so much of a hoo-hah. No controversy. No confrontation. Until it is too late!"

"But no raven can fly the Ark of the Okarpi from Metal Fort's premises." Beeche showed clearly she was in a different frame of mind as she joined them. Then catching Salt's eye said generously. "Or could it?"

They all looked conspiratorially at the bird of prey, who in grandeur style, appeared to be studying the locking device. And as they talked it over for a long while, the silver moon between the vapour clouds sharpened the lines of evergreens that led to the woods.

"There's no denying," Rhuand concluded. "We all know someone, a true friend who has effortless fluidity – and who would willingly assist where the raven left off from–"

"Lapis?" intercepted the Woodlians happily.

Salt was in agreement. "He's certainly a water vis-viva who can flamboyantly moonlight by the grace of day."

:

#SavageSalute – Rhuand lay on the herbal bedding under a canopy of evergreens, dreaming of sleep as he drifted in and out on the tide of returning senses. Restlessly, feeling something done or not done. The raven came squawking harshly, pecking in the holes of his ears with persistency to his waking.

Progress was being made fast. The handcrafted wooden models of the vault locking mechanism had been completed, and the visiting raven had been named Rafe. True to Rafe's brilliant mimicry abilities he had imitated all of Salt's repetitive, yet patient, miming teachings through the encouragement of edible rewards received after each separate procedure to unlocking the intricate device. Now they were ready, at last, to test the extent of Rafe's datum memory.

The Woodlians and Rhuand gathered in the forest clearing to observe Rafe. The vault mechanism was shielded under a covering made from thin, pliable shreds of interwoven wood.

Salt set Rafe down on a hand-carved Ranhatty perch-pole that stood to the edge of the clearing. The majestic black raven gave out a haunting screech in response as she briskly walked away from him to find a viewing seat next to Rhuand.

Salt smiled conscientiously. "I do feel Rafe has a carbon-copy memory." She leaned closely into him. He felt her eyes softly beseeching the contours of his face waiting on his response.

He looked at the lingual squawking raven perched in a laudable manner on the Ranhatty pole. "The skill lies in objective interpretation. Rafe holds the potential to start the change of element structure back to the times of the Okarpi. If successful, I'm sure the elements will join together and present an award to him, even create a title, such as Honorary Flight Hero."

"Imagine that." Salt laughed.

"He could even out-title me." Rhuand nodded, perhaps a little too fast. And the Woodlians reacted favourably.

"There's a lot resting on his inborn skills," agreed Beeche, now taking a seat next to Salt. "Once we catch up to Lapis then we'll know for sure whether this radical plan has legs to run with all the way or not."

"Do you know if anyone has been in touch with Lapis-Lazuli?" enquired Salt prudently. "Each time we've come across him, he's just appeared on his own accord, often before he is wanted but always when he is needed. We've never sent for him—"

"I've already checked the rainwater," offered Rhuand. "It has sunk passed ground level and entered deep into the rock channels below us, reaching such a depth that it is even difficult for the root systems of the forest to locate him. Our only option at this moment is to travel to the border of the forest and find a location plentiful with the element of water – that failing, we must seek Lapis in the next causeway colour."

Masterfully, Arkade pulled back the hood from his camouflage robe, and a display of mid-length dark hair, with coloured wooden beads and jewels woven into his many plaits caught the light as he strode up to the group seated in a half circle. "Comrade Woodlians, and most welcomed guests," he began. "We are gathered here to witness the progression of our honorary friend, the raven. Soon we shall learn the extent of Rafe's memorised training, courtesy of the wonderfully patient Earthlet, Salt Delray."

"Here, here!" called out Rhuand and Beeche.

Whoop-whooping and whistles quickly followed from the other Woodlians. Her cheeks blushed uncontrollably from the unexpected praise, or perhaps, Rhuand suspected, because she had no shield of defence – dance.

Arkade smiled in a praiseworthy manner as he hooked the Ranhatty cane over one arm and moved lithely to lift the interwoven covering away, revealing the locked mechanism. He called to Rafe in a relating bird-like tone to gain the bird's attention while taking several steps backwards.

They watched, and patiently waited as the raven haughtily tilted its head engagingly to one side, then flirtatiously it gave a flicker, then another of its handsome shaped tail feathers. They sat transfixed. Not batting an eyelid between them as the black raven gave out a clear answering call before soaring from the Ranhatty pole, and flying low to swoop abruptly onto the handcrafted wooden model.

"That's the difficult part over with," Rhuand said in a cynical tone. He had been watching the raven, fixedly, since its arrival, with an eye that perceived more than artful movements.

Salt gave him a half smile. "I really hope this works." He could hear the tension in her voice.

"It has to work!" he said. "There's no other way we can proceed–"

"It will work," interrupted Beeche. "Think positive. I know I am." She folded her arms about herself.

Collectively they willed Rafe on as he began to re-enact the first procedure on the wooden dial-plate – sometimes he made loud squawking exclamations, like someone expatiating in their sleep, and sometimes he paused and looked upwards, as though asking himself a question, or, was he looking for exodus?

Occasionally, Rafe swallowed down cries of lamentation and

other times he had a healthy, feudal attitude to pecking and turning the screws on the apparatus – and when the rapacious raven pecked out the concealed ripe fruit, his reward, from behind the first sequence part of the spinning system – the bird of prey looked neither puzzled nor cheated.

To Rhuand's senses the collective tenseness was electrifying as they all held back from a silence breaker, but before anyone could suffer from the immense satisfaction it gave them, the ground beneath them began to move with a low disturbing rumble, accompanied by a violent shudder. Salt grabbed his arm and squeeze it hard. "What's happening?" A look of fear shone from her eyes.

"I believe the forest may have switched to defence mode." He needed to reassure her, but nothing, he felt, could be assured in these threatening times of recent terminal happenings.

"Comrades!" shouted Arkade waving his Ranhatty cane. "We have company. Take up your positions. Immediately!"

"Where should we go?" Salt, turning to Beeche who had sprung to her feet in readiness.

"The root system beneath the forest has detected a breach," she informed her quickly. "It's vital we move you both from this clearing and enter the staunch depths of the forest for your safe-keeping."

"What about Rafe, and the demonstration?"

"There's no time to continue, Salt. The exercise must be abandoned without delay. Follow me!" The female Woodlian led the way.

Swiftly Arkade came across to them. "Take Rafe with you. We must hope he has learnt all he needs to know for all our sakes."

"And what about yourself, are you not travelling with us?" asked the warrior of steel.

"I'll meet with you shortly at the monitor-hide. We must ascertain who and how many individuals have become trapped in the root system. How long we are able to contain them will depend on their resources."

"Thank you for receiving us with shelter and hospitality. You are an exceptional Woodlian, Arkade. Someone I'm proud to call a true friend." Rhuand was keyed-up, motivated.

"Your flattery is received as necessary as breath, and it will get you everywhere, comrade." He reached out and shook the hand of the Metalgant in limbo. "Now go! It's imperative. Time is short." The Woodlian leader then turned to face Beeche. "I'll see you soon." They shared a short but passionate embrace. "Shol alkia."

"Shol alkia," she repeated back to him bravely.

The Earthlet called to Rafe. Immediately the bird of prey flew to her, resting on her shoulder with its head haughtily turned against the vibrations, while its tail feathers fluttered coquettishly in the rippling sensation – "What does shol alkia mean?" she asked.

"It means, until next time. Woodlians don't believe in saying goodbye. To them it sounds too final, believing the word alone can carry bad luck." Rhuand scarcely allowed a smile to crease his face, feeling in a moment both ruthless and jubilant.

Salt went silent.

Suddenly there was another violent movement from the underground.

"Come, we must move!" Urgency was strong in Beeche's voice as she beckoned, leading the way, while with sharp attention the other Woodlians took a different route with their leader, Arkade.

The greenish transparent light from the skies above filtered its way through the dense canopy of the evergreen Ranhatty trees, shadowing the path of their escape. Yet the misty green hue emitted a strength of glow and luminosity that captured Rhuand's mind. It was so beautiful to the eye, and held its own strength of secrecy like a natural code.

As if instinctually picking up his mood, Salt turned her head to look back at him and involuntarily imitated the same expression he wore. And in that split-timing he remembered something once forgotten – something – that in the time leading up to his death at Lake Gardenia had occurred to him, and it had held a certain resonance from a lifework of reaching the select position of Head Kielter: the honour of war doesn't survive the reality of destruction.

Rafe let out a haunting cry that lingered amongst Rhuand's stark memories. The raven then took flight from Salt's shoulder and flew ahead into the forest, stopping to perch within the branches high above, waiting until they caught up to him, before flying off once more and repeating the pattern.

"He knows this forest well," said Beeche.

"I just hope he retains the knowledge of vault training." The Earthlet's voice was high and clear. "Let's trust it's not a short-term memory."

He bent his thoughts upon her. "You patiently worked with him, Salt. I see no reason why he wouldn't fulfil the modus operandi. I have every faith in you – both."

"If the time proves right, and he succeeds, a current will be felt through the whole five elements," said Beeche. "It will be such a joyous occasion. A consequence so monumental, I dared not think it to be possible at first, but with your help, both, I do believe the silenced Ark of the Okarpi could indeed be made voluble again."

"How long do you gage the root system can hold back intruders?" asked Rhuand impatiently.

"Our root system will not give up. Even if intruders escape their first entrapment, the underground network will continue to recapture them. Their progress will be severely jeopardised."

"But not conclusive?" said Rhuand lengthening his stride.

"Not if they are armed. No!"

"And they will be." The Earthlet was adamant. They continued moving together, wide awake and silent, progressively in single file.

It was Beeche who broke the tension. "Once we reach the monitor-hide a clearer picture will be known, such as the point of entry and which entrapments have been triggered – helping us plot out an estimated path of movement to help you both escape from here without chancing upon the enemy."

"You're saying the root systems of the forest show a record of disturbances, and pinpoint each location–" said Rhuand tentatively.

"Precisely!" answered Beeche. "Every vibration felt by the root system is transmitted via many seismic-wave reading machines – the results can then be analysed from the sheet map–"

"And did I hear correct from Arkade that your system will indicate who the intruders are?" interjected the Earthlet.

"Without doubt."

Salt threw a glance over her shoulder, and he caught sight of her brilliant amber eyes which shone and sparkled until they were beautiful. "How much do you know about Tervanous, Rhu? Have you ever fought alongside him – if so it may help us plan a way to defeat him?"

"I helped to design him." There was a fractured pause, and

even though he couldn't now directly see into her eyes, only her proud profile – he felt completely exposed to her.

"Designed him?" She sounded anxious and he knew she'd request a further explanation from him.

"I was co-operative in ascertaining the design from the previous prototype, DMS5, and creating Tervanous DMS6."

"So, he's not – you mean to say – a living – breathing – being?"

"Exactly."

"But how is that even possible?" Her voice raised in pitch, and her lovely eyes were wide but unavailing, and refused to meet his, yet, followed his hand movements as he outlined shapes and symmetrical parts.

"DMS are the initials for the Defence Mark Series. Female Munrah wanted to create a machine that would be reliably programmed and wouldn't have the characteristics of an element being."

"She wanted a collective force of automaton. Machines," clarified Beeche. The movements of Salt's eyebrows alone indicated she was afraid, but unable to explain exactly…

Seeing her unable to define her fear, Rhuand spoke decisively, "Yes. And in time these programmed machines would supervise by creating a subtle magnetic pull on every individual's freewill. Hence, in theory at least, Female Munrah would have a submissive race of subjects beneath her. She was aware an uprising against her could occur at any given time and Tervanous DMS was designed to counteract this crisis."

"So Tervanous is a weapon to be used against the threat of subversive action in order to maintain her supremacy?" paraphrased Salt. She stared at him long and hard, then lowered her gaze once more.

"Not only within her own element structure, but all existing elements."

"And has Tervanous been put into action?" Salt whispered with reverence.

"When I first became a Kielter, this was still very much in the early stages of development."

"And towards the end of your life as a Kielter?" persisted Salt.

"We were on the brink of carrying out tests on a much bigger scale to those preliminary trials within the controlled setting exclusively at Metal Fort's Hub Base." The war hero clenched his jaw, furious with himself for this sworn disclosure of a closely bound oath. He had never divulged such details surrounding the defence of Female Munrah before. It was top secret. But now that Female Munrah had sent for her newest and deadliest weapon to destroy Salt and his chances, any loyally to his old Metalgant way of life, died.

Yet somehow, now resurfaced, his only concern was how Salt would react to this information – as the extent of his involvement really began to resonant through his spirit.

"It's frightening to think what levels of technology are being invented, with the aim to uphold Female Munrah's reign at the expense of taking away element freewill." Beeche looked warily round and about them.

"And you, Rhuand, played a heavy part in all of this." The Earthlet seemed afraid to lift her eyes to his face.

He had to agree, her words spoke the truth.

"Didn't it ever cross your mind – what you were partaking in was morally wrong?" challenged the Earthlet.

"Female Munrah doesn't give options, she gives orders. Once an order is given it is a Metalgant's duty to carry it forward – the complete picture is never revealed. Each DMS precisian is issued with a singular role in pure solitude. Specific instructions are given not to share their work experiences with others – each precisian undertakes a different section. Therefore, no-one is aware of the broader picture to be achieved. If a precisian breaks protocol and shares their role details with anyone other than their assigned supervisor – that individual, and those who received the information would be punished at the Irongate prison along with any remaining family members, regardless of whether or not you are estranged from them."

"Female Munrah rules through fear," said Beeche. "That's power and control!"

"Without doubt!" he stipulated. "No-one was going to get one over her."

"So how do you know the full story of Tervanous?" To his perceptible eyes, Salt looked to be mind-tracing every root word in order to grasp the very essence of Female Munrah's strength of command.

Tight-lipped, the sound of his voice was like a savage salute, "Because the quartz crystals that were introduced into my body, carried a flicker of memory. They had been part of the first Tervanous prototype."

"Did anyone else know about this?" The Earthlet's voice carried concern.

"No. It was an accident by Metal Fort's medical staff. They destroyed the wrong batch of quartz crystals. I've never shared this information with anyone – those who monitored my progress, were clearly unaware. Had I mentioned my personal experience, I would not have been thanked, but instead would've placed myself in dire risk."

"You could always have told me..." she beseeched him.

An expansive wave of love washed through his body-of-spirit from the breadth of Salt's open mindedness and willingness to understand his point of place. It had crossed his mind she may become repelled by his involvement with the Defence Mark Series Six – instead her sound-of-mind capabilities shone through like a beam of sunlight in an overcast sky. She was hearing him out. She was a remarkable Earthlet, and a female who would be willing to change horses midstream on his behalf if the occasion arose, and needs must.

"No," he said, deep in reflection. "I couldn't run the chance of placing you in added danger. When assigned to solve a singular glitch within Tervanous, I began to piece together the echoes I was receiving through quartz crystal memories, and the greater picture became clear. Pieces started to fit into place, and I realised the possible magnitude to the task I was partaking in. But by this time I had met you, Salt, and had decided I wanted to plan a life with you and leave the establishment."

"Plans went awry." Tears came to her eyes to gradually run down her cheeks.

"And I've since found there is no option to voluntary resign from Female Munrah's establishment... that free choice simply does not exist. You are signed for life, until you are either cast out by punishment – or death."

"And even death gives no safeguard." Salt silently offered her hand to him.

Beeche, who had remained quiet, reflected, "Death is intimately dangerous. It guards a power no-one is meant to calculate."

"There is a world of difference between the two." He took Salt's extended hand. "No. The relentless pursuit will never be over until we reach the final causeway colour of red – or – destabilise Female Munrah's monopoly by releasing the silent Ark of the Okarpi."

:

#Jingo! – The grassed over pathway Beeche urgently led them onto was familiar to the Woodlian custom to bear only naked feet – the Earthlet knew there was no time to inure local custom as they walked with fast and purposeful strides through dense shadow, lit here and there by sparks of sunlight as the evergreen trees thinned out, and the sun's rays on Salt's skin felt like hot ice.

Beeche stopped abruptly at the front of their single file. "We're here!" she said triumphantly. "We've made it."

"Here?" Salt drew in breaths of air so sharp and strong it refreshed her as though she had drank from a mountain stream. "You mean to say we've reached the monitor-hide..." She looked around expansively in the luminous shining green hue. "But I see nothing but trees... and... more trees."

Beeche turned to give her a liberal smile. "Nothing is as it seems, Salt – here, let me show you both..." Bending down low to the forest ground the Woodlian began to push aside plant debris and expose a wooden dome cover with two large handles projecting outwards.

Without hesitation, Rhuand, Salt and Beeche reached for a handhold each, and pulled in unison to move the weighted dome aside, revealing a deep narrow passageway of vertical steps which led into an enclosed area beneath the forest ground.

"Gracious me!" The Earthlet was equally impressed as she was apprehensive to entering the confined darkened area. A flashback of the prison cell loomed, threatening her self-preservation. She swallowed a scream and struggled to keep her voice friendly. "Is there only one route out of here, Beeche?"

"The monitor-hide has many resources. Come." Beeche was the first to enter, taking a beaming lantern from an alcove at the top of the stairway. "Careful where you place your footing." Her eyes narrowed in the flickering sodium light that cast imperfect shadows round them. "Access is extremely steep and without a handrail, just a little extra provision." She laughed softly.

Salt bit her lip and her imagination went into over-drive. Her eye-vision turned inwards to find her inner strength of self, dazzled by the sodium light as another tremor was felt through the forest ground and across the land surface. Feeling dizzy, she fought to stabilise herself as she placed her footing onto the worn wooden steps, perceiving the earth floor below seemed as small as the head of a pin. "Jingo!" Was the only expletive that crossed her lips as she slowly placed one foot in front of the other and descended the stairway behind the female Woodlian. Then it was Rafe's turn to follow.

Rhuand was the last to enter, and full heartedly dragged the detachable dome cover back over its purposely designed raid-incursion, above his head, shutting out the brilliant green hue. They were now sealed in – cocooned below forest ground.

Yet she couldn't help but notice, as Rhuand followed them he showed no fear as he scaled down the steps to catch up.

Does nothing ever intimate him?

Because of this, she was full of admiration, nearly worship.

"The intruders certainly aren't relenting to the root system." There was an edge of bitterness in his voice.

"Movements have been constant and disruptive, we'll undoubtedly gain clearer knowledge once we've analysed the readings." There was an air of optimism in Beeche's voice which Salt found reassuring and it spurred her forward with some sense of relief. She called out to Rafe, and immediately the raven flew down from a wooden perch attached to the inside of the large dome and settled on her outstretched arm. His shining black eyes surveyed the depths along the narrow passageway with creature intelligence.

By now, the shifting ground movement had ceased, running her hand over the walls of carved wooden panelling, Salt explored its richly dark coloured contours in the confined passageway as they continued to descend further underground. From the near distance she could just make out a scratching noise at varying intervals of activity. The noise became more acute the further they progressed. "Beeche, what's that scraping?" Her voice sounded small to her own ears.

"You remember I explained every vibration is felt by the root system and transmitted via seismic-wave reading machines – well, the noise is due to the machines recording the results onto a mapping sheet."

Nearing the bottom of the stairway, a brighter light of sodium glimmered, causing their moving shadows to become elongated and distorted against the stairway walls. She could now see bins of grains, dried fruits and unshelled nuts stood in the shadows and the smell of spices filled the atmosphere, purifying the air. By the time her feet touched down onto the earthen flooring, they felt like lead and her lips were salty with sweat.

The room underground was larger than Salt had visualised in her mind's eye – more than twice the size of her Irongate prison cell, she swallowed her pain, trying to eradicate the past memory of incarceration. Before her eyes had time to fully adjust to the bright movement of light, she was startled to sight behind the equipment of record – a dexterous Arkade sat in a wicker chair, studying reams and reams of sheet paper.

Salt, vigilantly noticed the paper displayed jagged, uneven dark lines, reminding her of an irregular and erratic pulsating heart rate on a screen monitor.

Swiftly the raven flew from Salt and landed on the Woodlian leader's shoulder, jerking its head to peer down and view the mapping sheets.

"How did you make it here before us?" enquired the warrior of steel looking about them as if searching for a place of watch.

Arkade glanced up at the closely knitted group with an open expression, "I'm so relieved you made it in time… I travelled through the underground tunnel… the others should be following shortly…" He then resumed his study of the maps. "The findings are truly spectacular… and take some fathoming."

"There are two tunnels that lead off from this monitor-hide," explained Beeche. "The first can be accessed from the forest clearing to here, the one which Arkade took. The other runs directly from here to the extreme edge of forest–"

"And which is the direction you plan for us to take?" asked the Earthlet quickly. She needed to know. Rhuand held his counsel.

"The forest edge," said Beeche. "But the final outcome will depend on the indications from the mapping sheets."

"Come, take a look," said the Woodlian leader. They stepped

forward, and their eyes followed the direction of his Ranhatty cane as he moved it across the jagged lines on the mapping sheets.

"What have you discovered?" Salt leaned forward in sudden urgency to learn more.

"The recordings suggest considerable and frequent movements. Three individuals. One dramatically stronger than the other two–"

"Tervanous," said Rhuand warily.

The Earthlet felt sick in her stomach. Nerve-white. "And the two prison guards?" Tervanous had occupied their thoughts long enough, and now his threat of presence filled the compact room to capacity. Inwardly she cried out, *help! Help?* In a voice buried so deep in the darkness of her inner self.

"Yes!" said Arkade. Still studying the lines of warning. "I believe your suspicion is correct, Salt. It can't be Female Munrah and Skada as their strength would be recorded considerably higher than these two individual patterns."

"Which direction do you advise we take?" Rhuand's voice remained controlled and calm. Outwardly he looked steady, but she knew his inner turmoil must be raging – self-same.

"In my interpretation of the maps, the intruders appear to be following a direct line which shall overlap the second tunnel – therefore I would strongly advise against this route." Again he pointed at the chronicling records.

"In that case, we'll take the scenic way above ground." Beeche's face remained pale and serious.

"Advisable. While this shall take considerably longer, the route is safer, and–" But before the Woodlian leader could finish his recommendations, an almighty vibration shook the monitor-hide causing the seismic-wave reading machines to go haywire.

In the violent tremors Salt was thrown to the rustic floor. The raven began to squawk in alarm and take flight round and about them. Rhuand helped her back onto her shaky feet and placed his hands round her upper arms. She wavered... then swooned against him, in no hurry to recover.

"Salt, are you alright?" Concern ran through his words like a string of accompaniments.

"Hmm, just a tad woozy. I'm fine though..." She tried to blink away seeing Rhuand in treble vision.

Focus, now is not the time to paint out of the bigger picture...

Failing this she decided to concentrate on the middle vision of him and it was like looking back at herself on another planet.

"This is like nothing the machines have recorded before—" shouted Arkade above the raucous sound of rumbling. "It would suggest the root system of the first tunnel is going into some sort of indirect spasm – inhibiting its defence of trapping the intruders."

Salt felt Rhuand pull her closer to him as he leaned over and flipped through the heap of maps. "What's this marking? It's not present in the earlier readings."

Arkade hesitated. "It looks like an electro-wave."

"An electro-wave?" parrot-phrased Salt in a voice she barely recognised as her own.

"Tervanous could be transmitting electro-waves into the root system and causing this upheaval..." She felt Rhuand take an uncertain step back; she followed suit, not wanting to be left behind.

"I can't rule that out," shouted Arkade. "And neither should you!"

"If this is so, the dangers could be, unknown and—" Rhuand

didn't complete his thoughts into words as the reading needles suddenly flat-lined. In contrast, the growing noise of destruction travelling through the tunnel Arkade had earlier passed through, entered the monitor-hide.

"Whatever that sound represents, it's coming straight for us!" Salt wrenched from Rhuand's hold, feeling caught in a backwash of fright and more.

Mind over matter! She willed her unsteady body to react in time to this danger. *Now isn't the time to be fragile, burdensome…*

"The readings are no longer reliable–" Arkade's eyes were ablaze with a new-born fear for them all, he grasped the flat-lining results in both hands, soundless evidence.

"We're not safe here, we must move!" yelled Beeche.

The mesmerist blinked himself out and away from the readings. "Yes, yes…" he answered, releasing his hold on the mapping sheets. "We must abandon, with immediate effect. Rhuand!"

The two male warriors began negotiating the unstable stairway as the relentless violent tremors continued in their assault, carrying their voices away with them.

It took joint strength to shift the detachable cover above. Salt knew before Tervanous had entered this causeway of colours, Rhuand would have needed no assistance in removing the heavy wooden dome, but circumstances had changed significantly since that time. And the Tervanous effect was unchallenged and unbroken for now. All they could do was keep on the move, and avoid the weapon of destruction for as long as possible.

With great persistence, Rhuand and the Woodlian leader pushed the dome upwards and across to reveal the familiar mystical glow of green hue which seemed to glaze over them as it began to filter down and into the sheer passageway.

Spanning, then beating its wings, the black raven soared upwards and out of the monitor-hide and into the forest, letting out a haunting call that sent a shiver through Salt's being.

She breathed in a jagged, almost painful breath of trepidation. Places of confined space brought back too many long, hard-baked memories of sufferance in her cell of imprisonment.

Forcing the grievous memories aside, *the past is the past*, she told herself, *so leave it right there where it belongs, firmly in the past.* Such recollections would only dull her perspective − slowing down her reactions. She must not be distracted.

"Salt, hasten!" shouted the steel warrior from above ground level. He reached down, and she extended her arm and hand to touch his...

"Look out!" yelled Arkade, forcefully pushing Rhuand clear from the escape hole.

As she opened her mouth to call back up to them, the escape hole into the green hue above her and Beeche became overcast, and they were plummeted into darkness from a great crashing sound, and a sudden whoosh of dry air hurled them back down the stairway... reeling, tumbling, until they re-entered the sacred monitor-hide room, stunned almost into senselessness.

Trapped!

:

"Salt! Salt, are you o-kay?" The voice sounded far-off to the Earthlet's ears amidst the unyielding vibrations travelling up from the compacted earthen floor as she lay face down breathing − still breathing.

Wearily she pushed her body upwards by pressing the palms of her trembling hands onto the hard floor; dragging her knees forward to rest underneath her in a kneeling position. Slowly she raised her head and let out a loud piercing scream, her scream followed her mind and led her nowhere else.

The Earthlet then lowered her head, and closed her eyes while trying to control herself, taking long, deep, even breaths to help gain composure… "That was unintentional, Beeche…" she uttered in a sibilant voice, shaking from head to foot. Her head throbbed with the exertion. "Are we now trapped down here? Tell me, we're not–"

"Yes," said the Woodlian. "It would appear the spasms from the root system have destabilised the Ranhatty trees above us, causing them to keel over and block our way out of here via the stairway."

"No! Nooooo…" she shouted. "Rhuaaand…" Her amber eyes brimmed with tears. She thought she was all cried out from her time at the Irongate prison. But here, now, when there was more to life than just her own existence, she couldn't stop the outpour of frustration and rage. A heated rage born out of the harsh truth – other forces outside their control had come between them.

Again!

"There's no choice. We'll take the second tunnel. It's now our only route out of here." Beeche offered the Earthlet a reserved backpack. "Here! Wear this – it could be the difference between your live or your death!"

The Woodlian remained matter-of-fact, she didn't rebuke the Earthlet's behaviour, neither did she comment on it. She simply remained practical.

Through Salt's despair, she couldn't help but wonder if this was because destruction wasn't unfamiliar to the Woodlian, and she was left with the distinct feeling the other's practicality had been learnt from the practiced routine of frequent disappointment.

"A lifeline?" she mumbled, feeling the weight of the heavy bag. Her hands felt limp, not ready to pick things up.

"Exactly! A lifeline – containing essential reserves – if there are any further tunnel disturbances we may need the contents of these backpacks as a measure to dig our way out."

Salt wiped the palm of her hand across her wet eyes. She couldn't afford the luxury of moods.

Crying won't make it clean! She told herself fiercely. *Must get a grip of myself, stop this self-indulgence of emotions... I'm an Earthlet and a show of weakness is to be frowned upon.*

"What about Rhuand and Arkade?" she said in a voice strained tightly with suppressed dread.

"It stands to reason we have only one option," said Beeche. "They'll know where we're heading."

"But didn't we all agree that the second tunnel was out of bounds because we'd cross paths with Tervanous and company?"

"Well, we can't stay put!" she rebuked sharply. "The first tunnel's certainly not viable, possibly twisted from all recognition and full of pit-falls. I just hope the other Woodlians evacuated in time."

"Oh, of course... I'm sorry..." The Earthlet visualised the other Woodlians she'd briefly known, crushed to death in the tunnel. She shuddered and feared for their existence.

"You make it sound like they've stone died!" reprimanded Beeche, as she reached for two sodium lit lanterns that hung from hooks jutting off the walls. She passed one to Salt. "Remember, we Woodlians are in limbo, already dead in the traditional sense – protected from death – one cannot die twice."

"Couldn't we just wait here?" Suddenly, Salt was afraid to leave. "Rhuand and Arkade may be trying to dislodge the barricade above us."

"Highly unlikely. Arkade will have moved onwards into the forest where they will be safer in the short-term."

The Earthlet struggled to her feet, if only Rhuand had his true strength of Iquique, he'd have been able to remove the barricade before she'd finished this thought. "This has been one hell of a day... if I had a diary, I'm sure I'd write something in it, even if impressions came first, then afterwards I'm sure I'd relate them to the facts."

"Well it isn't over yet," said Beeche impatiently, pulling on her own backpack and bringing her plaited hair to one side. She stood ringed with the scent of her own hair, heavy with the burden of her sanity, or sorrow? Salt couldn't tell and couldn't guess.

With dread mounting, the two females hastily entered the second tunnel, and the violent vibrations they experienced in the monitor-hide appeared to die-down into a ripple of echoes the further they strived into the dimness.

"How old are these routes underground?" Her words, like seeds, scattered, too light to fall onto the grey clay-like soil held in place by interlaced tree roots.

But Beeche seemed to hear the resonant words, "Work began shortly after we arrived here."

Detached and curious, she is a natural traveller, thought Salt. "So all this technology is your own design?"

"Arkade's primarily. He sparked up the idea of the root systems transmitting vibrations to a monitor-hide. Collectively, we took that idea and ran with it, improving the stages as we went along." Her voice then changed from a fact tone to a more hankering one. "I must say, Salt. The lengths you have gone to in order to help Rhuand find his salvation. I mean, you willing entered his dwelling of limbo while you are still life-form, bound into a different dimension – your gift is beyond word."

The Earthlet thought a moment before answering. "It just felt the right thing to do. The hardest part was accepting Rhuand was still out there, instinctually I felt I should have known within myself that our bond wasn't broken, only fractured through time and distance. But I was completely unaware, and instead had to learn this secret through another, Lapis-Lazuli."

She paused at the recall of memory.

"As an Earthlet growing up, I heard stories of the dead coming back to visit their loved ones, bringing a unique message. After a time of nothingness, a bleakness followed, and I realised the barrier between life and death was out of reach to me. For if the dead could get in touch with the living, the living would live a life of death, and what would be the point in that?" She hurried her words, so that she could answer the question herself. "One may as well be dead in that case, but then, everything was turned on its head when Lapis-Lazuli made contact, and once I could let myself believe Rhuand was indeed out there – somewhere – even wild horses couldn't have held me back. And while it crossed my mind, it could be a cruel lie bestowed on me just for the hell of it by Female Munrah, I had nothing to lose and reacted the best way I knew how..." She felt a spasm of ironic pain as the words left her lips.

"Lapis-Lazuli found you because you emitted a signal of loss. You wouldn't have been found if those questions had faded from your mind–"

"How do you know this?"

"Because Arkade received a similar message from me via, Lapis-Lazuli."

"You mean to say you have been in the same position as Rhuand and myself?" A shiver of fearful surprise quivered through her being, her voice cracked against the new knowledge as it unfolded before her.

"Yes. Arkade found me here in limbo – we were bonded together because I took the place of his scheduled death issued by Female Munrah, and so the order of death became unstable and circumstances against her escalated into volatile times."

"So, Arkade was in life-form when he arrived?" Salt felt she was coming, at last, nearer to an understanding.

"Just like you are now! Female Munrah and subordinates pursued us with relentless cunning and killer instinct, until she succeeded and unmercifully murdered Arkade and–"

"And now he's in limbo too." The echo of their lives-to-limbo resonated like giant nocturnal insects frantically beating their wings against the flaming lanterns.

"That's why Arkade harnessed the root system – to transmit ground movements back to a monitor-hide – so that when Female Munrah returned, we'd be warned. Ready for her."

:

#DeafSentence – Rhuand Mezarron opened his leaden eyelids to see a canopy of Ranhatty trees above him flashing passed at dizzying speed – yet, not sufficiently to screen his sensory.

Beneath him he could feel uneven spasmodic movements as he fought against fatigue and the mental cloud of disorientation. He made an attempt to sit upright. To his alarm he found he could not move!

Captured!

The word flashed into his mind like swords.

He strained his neck forward and looked down at his body-in-spirit – shocked to see he had been expertly tided with Ranhatty wooden straps round his wrists and ankles onto a device consisting of two wooden posts with a cross bar between.

Sometimes the speed at which he was being dragged through the forest slackened; sometimes the pathway reared upwards to unexpectedly fall sharply into a small ravine, causing the transversal vehicle to slither and backslide in guttered substances – this friction to his being was like red-hot rods of steel.

Clenching his steel hands into fists, he strained against the wooden straps – would they eventually yield or break under his pressure of resistance?

In the distance the distinctive haunting cry of Rafe ended in a warning screech of discord. And within moments the raven began circling above him in the transparent green mist.

"No! No!" uttered Rhuand under his breath. He didn't want any forthcoming attention before he could wrestle himself free and off the wooden sledge, but before the Metalgant of limbo could struggle any further the continuous dragging and heaving came to an abrupt stop.

Rhuand closed his eyes tight, better to be thought to remain in a comatose state while at such a disadvantage. Acutely he listened for any signs that would give insight as to who had captured him…

Hearing the sound of a reign creaking from the burden of towing tension… then released, hitting the ground with a dull thud. Rhuand detected an individual by the sound of even paced footsteps crushing plant life. Yes, only one being moved from the location behind his head, and now halted over him, casting a shadow across his closed eyelids.

It couldn't be Female Munrah – her steps were smaller paced... he would have heard her stiletto heels sinking into the dry forest ground...

"Rafe! Are you praying, or are you cursing?"

Immediately Rhuand's eyelids flew open. "Arkade!" he croaked, finding the strength to be suddenly savage. "The duty of an advocate."

"Rhuand Mezarron!" There was a burst of relief in his voice. "I was beginning to think your light was out indefinitely."

"The anxiety has almost unhinged me. I was afraid I might find myself in someone else's mind, or at least, in someone else's memory. Untie me. Immediately!"

"Hey, no need to sound angry. It's for your own good – how else was I meant to contain you from falling off the sledge – when there's no other means of transporting you through the forest?"

"What happened?"

"You don't remember?" The Woodlian lent over him and began the task of untying his warrior friend.

"No." His voice went tight as he strived to remember... *the forest... and the monitor-hide...* "The last significant memory I retain was reaching out for Salt, then... I was wrong-footed and everything turned black."

"Black. That sounds about right from the disturbance that occurred–"

"Disturbance?" Rhuand's eyes fastened upon him, he felt both dark and intense with a secret power of endurance developing deep from within.

Lithely, Arkade moved to the other side of the wooden sledge and started the same procedure of releasing Rhuand. "Yes, the uprooted Ranhatty tree. Before it crashed to the ground, I managed to push you out of its way – only narrowly missing myself – though I feared the branches crashed upon you. I couldn't be certain to what extent the impact had – tell me, how do you feel within yourself?"

At the back of his mind, Rhuand rested the inclination. Was he his own creation, made, lost, and recovered? He still existed, and that was enough for the Metalgant of limbo for now, and at this point in the friendly talk there was one predominant question that overrode all others – "Where's Salt, and Beeche?" Rhuand looked deep into his eyes, appealing for information as he threw all four loosened wooden straps away.

The Woodlian avoided his appellant eyes. Rhuand detected something pass across the face of his warrior friend... the expression gave little away but hinted at trouble within the silence. And the underground seemed to close in on him, giving the impression that Salt was numb with the repercussions – he wanted to bring her closer, to warm her, even though he felt cold himself. "Arkade," he persisted. "Don't give me a deaf sentence. Speak up!"

Straightening from his bending position, the Woodlian leader flexed his entity in the process to stand erect, then he took a measured step backwards – as if preparing himself – steadying himself before committing to the answer. He cleared his throat. "The uprooted tree... landed badly... completely obstructing the way out from the stairway in the monitor-hide."

He wanted to pour a flood of generosity over Salt and Beeche. Salt had had too much death, he must promise her life.

"As far as I know, the females are still down there!"

Rhuand, now on his feet swayed with stiffness. "So, why aren't we digging them out?"

"Because I couldn't shift that great tree on my own without Tervanous and his aides reaching us. It was far too risky. Don't forget you were knocked out, unconscious for some time. I took the decision to move you for all our sakes."

"But the females!" He eased himself forward through a mighty sufferance as the Tervanous effect intensified throughout his Metalgant spirit. Unsteadily, he re-seated himself on the sledge, his mind reeled at the implications, something not yet fully understood – for now – not ready to be put into words or action.

Arkade broke into his way of thinking. "Beeche will assist Salt through the second exit tunnel. Not all options are lost." He concentrated his gaze on Rhuand, and the steel warrior felt uncovered to his dilemma. "I'll ask you again, how are you feeling?"

Rhuand didn't trust himself to answer, he remained detached, not impersonal – not ready to extend his personality. What really mattered to the Metalgant of limbo was seeking the whereabouts of his former lover. He needed to gain a clearer understanding of the catastrophe. "How long have I been unconscious?"

"How far has yesterday gone?" replied Arkade, his eyes still riveted upon the other.

"As long as that?" Rhuand heaved at the thought of being a passenger for all that length of time, it went against his whole system of self. He hated and begrudged the thought of relying on another, he did not wish to be anyone's burden even though his training had included comradeship.

Furthermore, who knew what sufferance the two females may

be going through with the perilous Tervanous in mechanical pursuit? The Earthlet and Woodlian could even have been separated…

Rhuand felt a terrible recognition of betrayal from letting her down, from letting her go. He should be there – with her – but he wasn't. Extending his steel legs in a bid to regain stance from the vehicle of transport, he moved with instability, staggered uncontrollably, nearly falling.

"Hey, steady there Rhuand." His companion held out a helping hand. "You must take things easy, now!"

"Easy?" He smiled wolfishly, somehow managing to keep composure. Nothing in this state of limbo had ever been *easy*… the word simply didn't translate to his mind-set.

Their eyes met and held, he recognised something in the Woodlian leader, a knowing shared between them, both in silent agreement: find the females, then continue their part to aide discovering the Ark of the Okarpi and attain freedom – he was drawn to Arkade and happy in the reflection of him.

While supporting the Metalgant, Arkade reached into the long pocket of his jocund green robe. "Here, try this – it should sustain you to a better level of endurance."

"Spirited limbo means I don't need to eat."

"Don't be so insular, Rhuand. Just because you don't need to, doesn't mean you mustn't." With a practiced movement, Arkade cracked the curious looking root vegetable against his knee, and the spiky oval shaped food opened into three segments, revealing an internal flesh of exotic orange. "Believe me, this will set you up – eat well, we have much terrain to cover when heading for the second tunnel exit."

With a degree of improved spirit strength and perception, Rhuand helped Arkade haul the wooden sledge for some distance through the forest-land, leaving drag marks behind them in an effort to lead Tervanous and company into a misleading direction from their planned route.

Adroitly, they had tied a standing-stone onto the sledge to emulate the weight of Rhuand's spirit-body and ensure the drag marks that cut into the forest ground looked unchanged in appearance to the earlier ones.

Rhuand knew the misdirection wouldn't fool Tervanous DMS6 for long. The magnetico-electrico warrior's programming would detect a metal attraction to the Metalgant of limbo elsewhere, but any amount of gained time, no matter how slight could mean the difference between success and failure.

Meanwhile, the ground tremors had ominously ceased for some time, making it all the more troubling for the two warriors of limbo, it surely indicated a calm before a rage.

Rhuand glanced up to the raven of prey as it left its perch on a Ranhatty tree bough to swiftly glide high and wing-span through the beautiful glow of green hue. He felt his spirit rise up to touch Rafe's shining black feathers, but the precious moment was lost as the bird flew out of sight, leaving him with a feeling of heightened wonder into the skies beyond. "Birds have such liberty," he said with a slip of a smile. "It would seem they are not restricted by boarders or barriers like us."

"There is a freedom to the skies, yes…" agreed Arkade. "And creatures of flight are unique as they have the innate ability to enter and exit any bow system."

Rhuand turned to look at his warrior friend as they trekked unrelenting, side by side, through light and shadow across the forest-land. "Any bow system." He mused to weigh in his mind. "Whether that be Rainbow, Moonbow, Icebow or–"

"Yes, they are the closest life-form to the spirit–"

"So," Rhuand interjected, inspired to clarify his reasoning. "Rafe may have entered this limbo accidentally in life-form. He may have just flown into it without, instinctively knowing?"

"And he has the freedom to leave at any time, through any bow..." Arkade continued to swing his Ranhatty cane in his left hand and with the motion and timing of his right leg, use it as a third leg for extra vigour.

A kind of white noise infiltrated Rhuand's mind. "It had been rumoured within Metalgant circles that air is part of the evolutionary process, and will advance one sola day to become the sixth element."

"And what do you believe?" asked Arkade. "For as I see it, air crosses all five elements to abridge them, holding them together."

Rhuand thought for a moment before voicing the depth of his mind. "I would extend that thought further and say, not only does it abridge the five elements in life and limbo, but also the continuation that connects us in limbo to the infinite beyond."

"I've always believed that the answers are locked within us already, we just forgot how to access them–"

"Yes." Then his voice changed, it sounded distant. "Salt once told me, part of the Earthlet practiced faith leads them to believe, they don't hold grudges in the place of the infinite beyond. They simply won't let you in if you hold them. And part of living is learning to let go, so when you leave the home planet, you leave resentment behind.”

“That may be easier said than done!” replied the Woodlian leader, coming to a stand-still while at the same time making an impatient conciliatory gesture. “For those of us trapped in limbo, we have been cast out here with the sole purpose that eventually the home planet will forget about us. We are unreachable to most.”

Rhuand nodded, showing his agreement. “With no ties to pull on, we are unable to retreat back to the home planet, and without marked assistance, we can never enter the infinite beyond.” His mind brought Salt instantly to the forefront. She was the anchor to his past and the route to his future. Her face filled his mind’s eye, her voice his inner ear.

“Some things are not devoid of light or blazonry. They can also be obscure.”

“Obscure...” Rhuand held onto the word. A word that came to mind after the overwhelming feelings of happiness at sighting Salt at Lake Gardenia, his place of restrained limbo... visualising her intangible aura that gifted her a spiritual diffidence, and there in that moment of her arrival, the raw truth had hit him just as hard as a fisted blow, and he knew, their enemy, Female Munrah would never know the true strength of Salt Delray until she attempted to break her spirit...

His thoughts found speech. “I fear I have become obscure to Salt in my state of limbo. Sometimes I want so badly to embrace her, but the realisation she doesn’t know me as known before — holds me at arm’s length.” He had a moment’s inclination to keep sacred personal thoughts.

Arkade gave him the time and space to reflect by not breaking into his deep-seated isolation.

"And then there was... and still remains... an emotional barrier to overcome." His voice strained at the hurt burnt into him. "While I knew the Regard brooch would ground her from my condition of Iquique, ensuring she wouldn't receive a harmful shock from my spirit... I was aware I would nevertheless alter the jewellery structure, twisting, disfiguring it if no other foreign metal came between us to buffer the electric charge... and surely if I had allowed this to happen, it would have gone against everything we stood for... especially when the brooch has been the only thing that's remained a constant symbol of our unity – our love – while everything else round us has changed, including ourselves, the Regard brooch is untarnished – a sacred personal symbol for us, and as we've since learnt, a key to unlocking the gateways into salvation."

Arkade broke his silence. "No-one can reside in limbo and be unchanged from who they once were..."

Rhuand pulled open the top part of his enforced steel overcoat to reveal and point to his chest. "Here, in Metalgant life I had a scar from a medical procedure where quartz crystals had been introduced into my bloodstream."

The Woodlian leader narrowed his eyes to condense his sight. He shook his head. "And now there's no trace?"

"Limbo takes some things away, and their absence shouts louder than if they still existed."

"You have to learn from this, whatever will help move you forward," encouraged Arkade. "See it as a new beginning, while you are a different version of yourself, you are in the promise to become transcendent."

"Aren't promises made to be broken?" Rhuand said bitterly, "Or merely to be forgotten?"

"Not necessarily. What matters is who makes the promise in the first place – we're all here because our best laid plans were deranged and resorted to dust."

Rhuand knew with certainty nothing in life had been pulled out from beneath his feet as quickly as a Metalgant pitch-white carpet.

:

#ShadowsMakeACrowd – The stale air down below in the secret forest territory smelt damp, chilling Salt's soiled skin to a bluish transparency. She strove further into the depths of the escape route, crouching, shivering with cold. Her dread mounted and her dismay grew to terror, hearing in the far distance the subsiding rumbles of the earthquake.

With eyes wide open but unavailing she glanced down at herself, seeing vaguely the vibrant turquoise all-in-one was now completely caked in soil, and the Regard brooch only hinted at its once superlative shimmer.

Smoothing back with great effort her dishevelled hair from the coolness of her face, she felt the roughness of her matted hair trail heavily through her fingers.

She blinked away her dullness, reduced to an edge of gladness she was still within the perimeters of a fighting chance to live and breathe. For everything they had collectively worked towards could be shattered at any place and at any given time. Even the moth-like insects she noted, no longer fluttered about and burnt their delicate wings against the lantern's hot glass shield.

Quickening her pace, afraid of losing sight and sound of Beeche; she could not reconcile herself to the deep dread of going without her, she needed her to get out of this land sliding underground. Raising the lantern, its yellow tongues of flames and vapour with no wind to blow them away, rose up straight and mingled with every other smell.

Head down, feet slithering over slimy rounded stones that hurt her insteps and rolled over her plimsolls, she grasped cold wet tree roots which mercifully acted as banisters. The further they progressed, the wetter their location became, indicating to Salt they were nearing the forest borderline.

In front of her, she could hear the sound of Beeche's footwear scrapping over stones, hearing the other's voice stifled from the closeness of the space between the tunnel and her spirited-body and the words were lost...

Within the escape route were a series of alcoves, allowing an individual enough room to stand up straight. From first experience of stepping into one, Salt couldn't help but think it was like standing in an upright, lidless coffin. But she had quickly learnt to block her mind away from this fearsome comparison. And force herself to rearrange her morose thoughts, for the alcoves proved to be a brief respite from the claustrophobic conditions – aiding a wing of sanity to their struggling survival.

"The intermittent alcoves have been designed against a hostile incursion, so that if intruders ambush the channel, those of us down here would be concealed from their sight," explained Beeche. "Their design ensures they are a black-spot, whereby light cannot readily enter them."

"A safe hide!"

"Yes, they are placed at certain turnings within the tunnel. Some, like the ones we will shortly come to, have to be rolled into from a lying position on the tunnel ground, while others can be stepped into, as you've already experienced–"

"After my time served at the Irongate prison, I never thought I could deal with an enclosed space again without losing my sanity…" confessed the Earthlet as her heart rate immediately raised like a thinly veiled secret. The sheer exertion of crawling through the tunnel left her with a resounding rage calling for revenge.

"Everyone has a different way with them to survive painful experiences, while I can't pretend to know your mind-map, if it's any help, you're not facing this alone, Salt. I hope that goes somewhere to offering you, at least, small comfort…" She could hear empathy from Beeche, indicating she knew something, and more than just a little, of what she was striving to express.

"Yes, and no," she answered truthfully. "I'm just trying to concentrate on moving forward by placing my mind elsewhere… a skill I learnt in solitary confinement." She turned her face away to visualise the end result of seeing the brilliant green hue again. If she let her mind wander, the Earthlet could almost feel and taste the misty greenness of light air – the cool refreshing breeze as it caressed and enveloped her being.

Intervening between her longings flashed Rhuand, and she didn't challenge them – *Where is he this moment – already at the tunnel exit, waiting for us – or battling on into the unknown with Arkade?*

She took in a deep breath to steady her impatience to get out of the Woodlian escape tunnel. *At least the tremors have stopped, for now – should this irksome silence be taken as a blessing?*

She wanted the silence to speak, giving an indication that something may have gone wrong in the face of their scheming enemies – *or could this all be part of the treacherous game-plan programmed into Tervanous DMS6?*

"It's possible Tervanous has taken a different route to the one Arkade predicted–" Beeche broke into her mediation.

"Possible. But not certain." Salt was quick to pick up on her female friend's cautionary tone. "Tell me, how accurate are Arkade's predictions, generally?"

"Spot on!" she said without hesitation. "In fact, the more I think, well, I just can't name a time when Arkade has faltered on any of his previous predictions."

"Where there is hope, not all is dead, right?" To her own ears she didn't know who she was trying to convince more, herself or Beeche?

"We mustn't out rule an alternative–" Beeche was an arresting movement; round her the insects had returned and fluttered, the pale yellow lamp flames flickered upon her in misty infatuation, and with their shadows they made a crowd.

"That being?" Salt felt her morale lift, while a shiver of fearful surprise ran through her body.

"I'll let you know if or when it occurs to me. But I can't believe it's cut and dried one way or the other."

She paused too long during breath for Salt to ignore the break. And suddenly Salt's optimism plummet again and she hardened her heart against Beeche in secret. "Our chances look lean and close to the bone when spoken out loud."

"Well, we mustn't give into this kind of morose talk, Salt Delray!" the Woodlian said brusquely. "I come from the school of thought of diamonds, not daisies – whereby one can only be found if you're prepared to dig deep enough below the soil, while the other is just below surface level."

In reflective consciousness the Earthlet glanced down at the Regard brooch again, and rubbed a dirty palm over the cut gemstones. One, the sixth precious stone, being a diamond. And while its brilliance failed to glisten in the sodium light, its importance was no way lessened. "Diamonds," Salt said positively. "I also choose the hard work of diamonds, they last forever unlike the short payoff of daisies."

"Wise thinking," said Beeche. "Anything worth having is worth fighting for."

:

Fretful, the Earthlet stopped short. "Beeche, Beeche! Wait up–" she yelled, longing for the hemmed in feeling to cease as it might be too much to bear.

"Why, what's the matter?"

"Just stop a moment from chopping and clearing. I thought I heard something."

The only immediate noise to Salt's heightened senses was her own laboured breathing and rapid heart rate pounding mercilessly in her own ears.

"I hear – nothing," replied the Woodlian. "Nothing other than the underground atmosphere."

The unnerving feeling persisted and began to press heavily on Salt Delray's being. Warily she remained statue-like, open-minded to the relative stillness. Only now she had drawn Beeche's attention to her concern, the mysterious sound seemed to elude her altogether. Until – *There!*

And there again!

She reminded herself how she had become self-reliant. Reliant on her instincts to alert the natural impulse within her being. "Do you hear it now, Beeche?" she cried out urgently. "I certainly can!" she felt herself shrinking back instead of moving forward away from the faint low tone which appeared to be way behind them in the far distance.

"Barely, but whatever it is, I don't believe we should wait round here until it makes itself known to us."

"Maybe its Rhuand and Arkade–" she said hopefully, feeling hope was only a wish. A whistle against the wind.

"Well, the noise is unrecognisable to any sound I've come to know. And it's certainly not Rafe's distinguishing call."

Alarmed the two females resumed their desperate pursuit through the narrow tunnel, only now with extra edge to their inhibited movements. Quickly the noise increased in volume, but curiously not in pitch.

"Can we dig upwards and out of the tunnel?" shouted Salt in sudden panic, feeling their escape route was rapidly turning into a tunnel of devastation and about to take them with it.

"No! We're too far below ground to make it out in time, and with nowhere to place the excess soil from above, you'd end up suffocating from lack of ventilation, furthermore, the probability is high that we'd hit rock anyway because of the terrain in this location."

The low continuous buzzing noise began to dominate the compact space, so much so that Salt could hardly hear herself think. But one thought presided over all others, and that was the unknown disturbance was heading straight in their direction. "What are we going to do?" she yelled, her voice cracking under the pressure of the unknown.

"Strive on!" commanded Beeche. "We're incredibly close to the next set of alcoves. You take the first one, there isn't space for the both of us. I'll take the one adjacent to it." They crawled, slithered and relentlessly pursued forward with all their might of will. Salt, now only a handbreadth away from Beeche.

Suddenly, a sensation of prickles spiked along Salt's skin. And she sensed something foreboding had pinpointed her with a skill of marked precision.

Swallowing the fear close within her, she turned her neck to peer over her cramped shoulder into the dimness behind – focused, the Earthlet sighted a piercing dot of white light. "Beeecche!" Her voice rose louder in pure fear. "I don't think we're going to make it–"

"The turn in the tunnel's coming up, Salt." Her voice carried through the twisted and fallen debris laid strewed across the subterranean passageway. "We're almost there. Keep up with me. Don't fall behind."

As the intense dot of piercing white quickly enlarged in size, Salt rapidly blinked and turned from its mesmeric influence. Even though she was no longer looking directly into it, the echo of the light remained in her vision as though she had stared at the sola sun.

She knew she could quite easily become entranced by its unfathomable attraction – feeling susceptible to its placement of magnetic pull on her. But this magnetic pull was nothing like the magnetic attraction she had to Rhuand. That was passionate and heated, whereas this magnetic pull of white light gave her the distinct feeling she was being coldly and chillingly targeted.

Fighting against the mind-trap of lethal energy, she heard an echo of a memory replay over and over in her fearful thoughts: the enigmatic words of Rhuand Mezarron when describing their differences of life and limbo to salvation, *'They don't pull on the same handrails of the past'.*

His words had the resounding ability to motivate her onwards, she mustn't give up, mustn't give in, she must fight to stay alive. He wouldn't want her to willingly join him in limbo form. With renewed resourcefulness and commitment on her part to keep up with the Woodlian in front of her, she fought on –

"Now! Salt!" shouted Beeche, still crawling over fallen debris. "Roll into the alcove on your left."

Just as the Woodlian had stated, there was her respite out and away from the path of rapidly travelling light. She uncurled herself from the intense crawling position, to lie flat on her stomach, then roll her aching body into the alcove and onto her back. She turned her face towards the tunnel, shouting out to Beeche. "Have you reached your safe-hide?"

"Almost. Turn out your lantern." Salt did as Beeche stated, only to find they were not sheltered into direct blackness, but instead a dull dimness.

Salt's utter relief at finding the shelter of alcoves in time was short lived and quickly replaced by an increased terror. For as the Earthlet stared across at the tunnel wall from her place in the alcove, the wall became completely exposed to the intensity of white light.

Salt could see for the first time the true structure of the tunnel wall. The soil was expertly held back in place by dark brown roots of the trees growing in the forest ground – the root system – she could clearly identify the intricacies of the interlaced and interwoven roots against the greyness of soil. It was beautifully designed, but in that split moment of added knowledge came trepidation as the intensity of bright light began to burn and sting her eyes – she felt her breath had stopped, even though her body shook from the loud hammering of her heart beats.

Tightly, she closed quivering eyelids against the fearsomeness of lightening pain and edged further into the depths of the alcove, rolling over onto her side with her face pressed against the alcove back wall, while with one hand she clasped over and round the Regard brooch pinned to her garment.

Salt began to utter a loop of recital that had entered her mind when she had slept recently in the forest enclosure – it felt the most natural thing to do to level herself into a measured calm and seek out an inner strength, *'He is a Metalgant who was there when white horses left for the shore, but I failed to recognise him as once before, in the days leading up to Capricorn...'*

She hugged her shoulders up to her ears, lowered her face into her chest, as a most peculiar and unsettling experience occurred – even with her eyelids still tightly closed, she could – see – the bones inside her own body – her skeleton hand across the Regard brooch – even her own rib cage.

X-ray vision.

With great preservation she held onto her mind, body and spirit.

What is this source of bright white light?

The Earthlet had been brought up to believe light was pure, holy and good. Now she understood it could also be used as a deadly trick, misleading its subject into a falsehood of honesty.

She felt the want to call out Rhuand's name against the low hypnotic buzzing sound as it rapaciously passed her safe-alcove – and in those few moments of terrorising distress, the intensity of the noise along with the bolt of harsh white light hurtled passed their alcoves and travelled like a storm-wind further into the tunnel – leaving Salt too weak to lift her head.

She put one hand up to her head as though to staunch a wound, and tears of fears lay inside her closed eyelids – un-spilt.

:

#BehindTheLogganStone – The warriors' foot-tread sank into the moist spongy ground, leaving deep impressions like punctuation marks interrupting long sentences.

Arkade used his Ranhatty cane as a pointer. "At the bottom of this ridge, we're now approaching, are two large standing rocks partially submerged into the hillside..."

Rhuand nodded, his vivid green eyes following the line from his ally's cane into the depths far below them.

"There, we will find a sentry Loggan stone positioned in front, concealing the second tunnel exit."

"Ab intra – from within," said the former Head Kielter. And he was reminded of the Metalgant motto: *'Failure is your own creation'.* He hoped he'd not sabotaged their possible success.

The scenery was hard to distinguish through the denser layers of misty green hue that had come to settle in the valley below. Rhuand found this veiled environment could so effortlessly draw a comparison to the magnetico-electrico warrior named Tervanous DMS6 – for while their antagonist had fallen silent for the time being, he was still very much present in Rhuand Mezarron's thoughts – not knowing when the next disturbance would be unleashed on them proved to be more unsettling than feeling the tremors travel through and over the ground.

Yes, Tervanous DMS6 had become hidden from them, and

while they had no inclination as to where he may be, this indicated only one thing to Rhuand – the worst was yet to come.

Watchful, while zigzagging their way down the rocky ridge and into the dense green fog, to Rhuand's surprise they soon reached the bottom. In the distinguishing stillness he heard Rafe's familiar call, followed by a rush of air across his face as the raven swooped down with natural grace before soaring high above the dense fog. Spontaneously, Rhuand cupped his steel hands round his mouth – "Karh, karh, karh!" he called into the green cloak of mist.

"Water vapour can be rather disorientating when it's too near the ground," said the Woodlian leader. "Beings are known to lose their way. I'm told, they wander round in endless circles believing they're walking straight, and with no-one there to teach them what they have to know about the curve of the bow, they are their own experience." His words had a sinister sound. Words which drew Rhuand closer to him. In the full light of opposition he felt this would make him dangerous as memories burnt into him, remembering every last thing about his own past life. Like many Metalgant warriors with secret lives, he touched others often, and bravely. Yet hating it.

Rhuand forced himself forward and together they approached the two large standing rocks partially embedded into the hillside with a Loggan stone camouflaging the open exit, just as Arkade had described.

The two grey rocks were twice the height of the warriors in limbo. Each one stood boldly, not entirely covered by moss. Rhuand studied the droplets of moisture which ran down the rocks' exposed sections. Tracing the nearest one to him, his thoughts leapt to Salt and Beeche, leaving him with the distinct feeling they hadn't exited the tunnel as there was no imprints in the spongy, mossy grass. His eyes travelled up the Loggan stone placed between the standing rocks, the moss on the edges of the rocks had not been disturbed in anyway, in fact there was no indication anyone had been in this vicinity for some time – his heart sank beyond belief – he'd felt positive Salt and Beeche would either be here already – waiting, or have left an indication as to where they had gone…

In sheer desperation Rhuand heaved the Loggan stone aside and shouted into the darkness of the tunnel. "SALT! SALLLT…" He then waited, his eyes cast down to the ground in deep concentration to hear any forthcoming sound in reply to his call… but nothing came his way… only the echo of his voice, and the drips of moisture hitting the irregular pattern of stones jutting out from the ground soil.

"I would have thought the females had already exited…" Arkade said warily, sharing Rhuand's frame of mind.

Rhuand tried to control the rising dread in his being. He knew he mustn't give into anxiety, little would be accomplished if he failed to think straight. "There's nothing for it. We must enter the tunnel and find them." His mind was made up, resolute in his own decision.

Arkade signalled agreement with a single nod of the head. "The more I think about the lack of Tervanous's show of movement lately, the more I find it troubling." The Woodlian leader handed Rhuand the Ranhatty cane, then squeezed himself through the slim gap of entry. "One must think small when entering through here–" His voice went tighter as he drew in his body-of-spirit, making himself transferable.

"I've never thought small in all my life!" said the steely warrior, ignoring his real feelings. Arkade's hand appeared through the gap in order for the cane to be placed in his outstretched hand. Rhuand obliged.

"Well, this is limbo, not life remember. And we all must adapt–" replied the other with terrible pleasure and resolute humour.

"Adapt to survive is like seeking asylum, isn't that the saying?" He kept his guard up, fearful for all their well-beings.

"Right, I'm through to the other side." There was no denying the triumph in his voice. "Now it's your turn, old friend."

Nothing could have held Rhuand Mezarron back from entering the downward slope in an effort to search and find Salt and Beeche. He had never been a Metalgant to stand and stare. He had always been a Metalgant of action, and he refused to alter that impulse just because he was trapped in a state of indefinite limbo.

"Halt! Halt!" shouted Arkade. The loudness disturbed the other's combat thoughts. "Something's not right."

He had squeezed his body-of-limbo halfway through the gap, but stopped immediately to the Woodlian's words of alarm, yet seeing very little.

"I've never seen anything like this before..." Arkade's voice rose beyond recognition.

Rhuand peered down into a length of dimness within the tunnel not clearly seeing the formation of the other, only an image, or a shadow, or a likeness of the mind, bent over with hands resting on his knees and the Ranhatty cane tucked under his arm.

The dugout was narrow, while its height could accommodate them standing, so long as they stooped unmeasured.

"What do you mean you've never seen anything like this before?" he demanded, with an edge of impatience in his voice.

Rhuand was used to giving direct orders, with clear and succinct descriptions, not taking evasive ones for an answer. His eyes searched for something to fasten onto within the imperfect shadows. Then he became conscious of a sudden low tone of noise beginning to travel towards them from the tunnel depths.

"Do you hear that, Rhuand? Can you hear that oncoming sound?"

The Metalgant's mind latched onto the sound, deciphering what it could be… "Yes!" he countered slowly. "I hear…"

"I'm not picking up a good vibration from this. In all honesty I believe we should back up and move out."

"Out?" That went against all his principles of searching for the females. He had made his mind up, he wouldn't settle for wasting any more time.

Arkade swiftly turned his being towards the phenomena of personal existence, Rhuand, still wedged between the rocks.

And in that split moment of movement from the Woodlian, the steel warrior caught a glimpse of bright white light. "Look, I've not come this far to turn back. I'm going in there, and I will bring Salt and Beeche out if it's the last thing I do!"

"No you're not! And that's an order. Until we know what that travelling noise and light is – we're not advancing."

The low tone quickly began to increase in volume and for the first time didn't sound like a wall of noise, but instead, a tremendous buzzing. Its subtle measure of vibration was almost hypnotic. Rhuand stared back into the Woodlian's eyes, half in light, half in shadow, smoky-orange, golden-black, neither revealing nor altogether concealing.

"I know you're resolute to finding Salt and Beeche, and while I admire you for that quality, I have to insist, we must retract. Immediately!" He made a palms-up gesture.

Rhuand searched the shaded face of the Woodlian, and he knew Arkade was right. No-one in their right mind would tattle something unknown to them before assessing its strength and weakness. A blind battle was often a lost battle. While they had the option to retreat, it would surely be wise to do so. "I'm not averse to changing my mind. I just don't like to." Rhuand said in pure stubbornness. His mind flickered back – *What was it Salt had said not so long ago, 'Any Earthlet who never changed their mind, never changed anything'.*

Well, he could apply that way of thinking to himself. Now.

But before he could act on these thoughts the intensive light began to surround Arkade's body-in-limbo, and immediately Rhuand was burdened by a weird prickling sensation travelling over and through his spirit. "Can you feel that, Arkade? Can you feel something deriding through your senses?"

"Without doubt! I think I've attracted some kind of atmospheric discharge. I'm trying to keep calm, but I think we're in serious trouble."

Left with the solemn feeling they had placed themselves in imminent danger – Rhuand wrestled into action and freed himself from the rock gap and out again into the dense green fog, while at the same time reaching out a steely hand to help Arkade out after him. Together they fell to the ground and onto the cold porous moss.

Looking up above them, a raging bolt of pure white light sped from the tunnel's exit and streaked into the density of green mist, turning the atmosphere momentarily into a deadly cloud of milky whiteness, before gradually returning to its threatening look of appearance.

"What was that monstrosity?" Arkade looked half asphyxiated by the cloud, and half deaf by the volume of sound.

The steel warrior rapidly blinked away the impression of light that remained in his vision. "I would hazard a guess that was a magnitude of electricity." His voice turned colder, darker. "And that could only be sourced from one entity, Tervanous DMS6."

The two warriors in limbo witnessed three further bolts of intensive white light shooting into the atmosphere round them within a relatively short space of time.

They moved to stand either side of the rock gap, mirroring each other with a tense and frustrated expression fixed to their faces.

"It's impossible," the Woodlian leader said passionately. "We're going to have to come up with a secondary plan if we are to reach the females inside–" But before Rhuand could respond in agreement they heard a distant call located deep from within the heavy green mist in the valley.

"Yallo, yallay!" the caller repeated over and over again. Arkade appeared to shake all over with tides of recuperation. Then, unexpectedly Rafe appeared to the two warriors from the opposite direction, like an uninvited guest who had come to stay and had forgotten to leave.

"That sounds like Beeche!" said Arkade. "She's calling from the vale."

Rhuand's harboured rage of the impossible, quickly lifted and changed into expectant hope. He held back from speech, but held the Woodlian's meaningful stare. Then the convivial moment was over.

"Yallo, yallay!" mimicked Arkade as he stepped further into the mist of green, eager to encourage a response.

Rhuand remained silent, though his spirit was far from quiet – his inner self was rapidly questioning – *if that really is Beeche, the odds would imply Salt must be with her, surely – unless…*

His mind couldn't reach into the depths of despair and what came with that contemplation. In turmoil he closed his eyes tight to block his mind from travelling on and – he felt a light touch placed on his steel arm. His eyelids flashed open, and to his amazement there stood – Salt.

"The mist gave you back to me," he said awkwardly. Her smeared skin and cinnamon-black hair was smattered with underground soil, but in her dishevelment of appearance her beautiful amber eyes seemed to penetrate brilliantly into his very soul, recognising a shared sufferance from their separation. He swallowed his pain. "I thought you were still trapped below ground or…"

She traced a soiled hand down his arm and paused at his steel hand, then laced with some difficulty her blistered fingers round his. Instinctively he moved his other hand to find hers, and gently squeezed her hands, not too tight to cause further discomfort, but enough to show he didn't want to let her go again.

And when she did speak, it was like the sun had come out shining. "We had no alternative but to dig our way up and out, well before reaching the exit – otherwise the destructive bolts of white light would have…" She was lost for words, and it showed.

"You thankfully made the right choice," he said supportively. "I've seen the magnetic light war-heads and the power they contain is unsurpassed." He looked at her closely. She smiled generously, and he felt her squeeze his hands before releasing, and instantly he felt her radiant warmth leave him.

"Once we heard Rafe's call, we knew it must be safe to approach the standing rocks – and you and Arkade must be close by."

Both Arkade and Beeche joined the couple with exuberant smiles. Their arms placed round each other. And within their small group of mutual happiness to be finally reunited again, a heavy darkness came over Rhuand. For he still hadn't realised a dependable and harmless way of deprogramming the magnetico-electrico warrior from carrying out specific instructions of destroying their causeway plans. And without an alternative safe plan, Rhuand knew their only chance to halt Tervanous DMS6 would be to bring about an Icebow, but the horror of this calculative action would mean placing Salt directly in death's doorway. Framed. The details of which she was still firmly in the dark about.

As he stood here now, opposite her, looking into her captivating deep amber eyes – to actively seek harm towards her went against everything he stood for. He would not potentially destroy this beautiful Earthlet female – together they had shared a life, no matter how fleeting, and he was damned if he would be disloyal to her by seeking their limbo together.

The steel warrior in limbo felt internally obliged to voice his opinion. "Salt!" he said slowly but firmly. "I think it would be for the best if you returned to the home planet. We should seek a Rainbow with immediate effort and–"

"What?" she demanded. "Did you just say – the unthinkable? The unspoken…?"

Arkade stepped closer to Rhuand. "What are you suggesting?

We have a plan to take you both to the next sandsomme stone building – remember?"

Rhuand turned to face the Woodlian leader squarely on. "The risks are far too dangerous and hostile to allow Salt to come any further, and we all are aware Tervanous could appear at any given moment…" Rhuand then turned his gaze back to the Earthlet. "You could go into hiding on the home planet. Assume a new identity while Female Munrah is searching for you here."

Salt's open face showed super-induced disbelief with mixed hurt and disappointment. "I can't turn back now and just leave you here – in limbo – where's the sense in that?"

He blocked out his recognition to her feelings. "I'm not asking you to, Salt. I'm ordering you to. It isn't safe for you to be here!" he said harshly. He upheld his choice to be cold and detached, for if he allowed himself to become sentimental he would become weak and selfish and demand she remain with him.

Yes, this was the correct action of approach, by letting her go he would be saving her from an almost certain existence of limbo, and he wouldn't let Tervanous DMS6 hold such power over the Earthlet.

"You cannot order me to go against something I'm adamant about. I'm here at my own freewill!"

He could see she was standing her ground and she wouldn't be budged from her own sensibility.

He would have to tell her the vicious, chilling truth about how an Icebow would need to be created in order for the termination of Tervanous, and how this could only occur by rupturing the ice crystals within the Regard brooch – and from this wave of catastrophe unleashed by the ice crystal trauma, any living-being would almost certainly die, only those in limbo would be unaffected. Whereas the magnetico-electrico warrior, Tervanous DMS6, being neither of life or limbo would suffer severe consequences followed by eminent system shutdown.

Yes, Rhuand Mezarron knew in his spirit he would need to be merciless and brutal with the facts to ensure she changed her mind, and left this menace of jeopardy.

:

(6) PINK RAZ REZ

:

#GameOfUnsulliedDarkness – Entering the fourth sandsomme stone building, quite by chance the Earthlet caught a glimpse of a wound deep within Rhuand, and at once she pulled back from asking further questions.

Instead she secured the Regard brooch back onto her garment. Then, noticing the particles of damp soil from the tunnel had dried on her bodysuit she began brushing them off, and as she did, the tears in her eyes belonged to the draft of wind channelled from the closing door.

Painfully reflecting on the stark news Rhuand had disclosed to her – adamant against her carrying on through the causeway colours, explaining the dangerous repercussions to her life-form from rupturing the ice crystals in the sacred Regard brooch, and yet, knowing herself, acknowledging her own needs, needs that flew in the face of his advice, she wouldn't be untrue to her mind-set, not just for her own sanity, but also for his – without reaching his salvation surely meant to be without sanity.

In the past she'd thought nothing of changing horses mid-stream if the feeling took her imagination, but on this personal matter she would not be moved.

Arkade and Beeche had loyally brought them to the edge of luminous green hue, and their final words still echoed in the Earthlet's ears – the pledge to remain in the forest and deliberately obstruct and slow down Tervanous DMS6 and company from entering this building where she and Rhuand now stood.

Together they took up the eerie call from the bird of prey, and began to tread warily through the building as the curious raven flew from one end to the other of the majestically long fourfold interior.

Salt's glittering eyes began to study the abundance of differences within this fourth building compared to all the others before it. The large windows now held intricate designs of coloured glass within them, and as the light shone through the glass from the outside, clear, well-defined lines cast onto the sandsomme stone floor. While above their heads they sighted a superb ornamental roof, sheltering them from an unknown climate outside.

Despite the opulence of the building, Salt and the Metalgant in limbo did not share a word of dialogue within their awakened surroundings, instead they each held a personal silence while in fierce disagreement with each other – he'd wished her to go, but she would not!

His choice of words and the way he had said them in such coldness had rooted her to the spot. But since learning his overriding incentive was from a concern for her safety, she had listened attentively to his words of warning, yet feeling she had nothing to go back to the home planet for – Rhuand was to her mind worth the prevailing risk.

As they continued to stride testily across the full length of the stone floor and approach the door opposite their route of entry, side by side, they automatically raised the palms of their hands to rest against the door, and in that moment before pushing into the unknown, Salt felt the strong compulsion to break their agreed silence.

Turning to study his face, he seemed to instinctively pick up her need to halt. "I know that by disagreeing with your advice I have in some way wounded you, but I'd like you to respect my choice to carry on. It's just *not* part of my Earthlet makeup to bail out at the last moment."

"I respect your choice, completely," he said in levelled, and almost too reasonable tone to her ears. "But I would rather you didn't deliberately place yourself into an almost inevitable darkness of trapped limbo."

She swallowed hard. Her thoughts circled a desert of space at the thought of experiencing her own limbo. Then, taking in a steady controlled breath she spoke – "You mustn't forget, not all is lost, for if I was to enter limbo, so long as Rafe flies into the Icebow, there would still be a chance of salvation for all limbo sufferers once the Ark of the Okarpi is reinstated to the elements." She hesitated. "Hold on, when you said all life-form would succumb to the devastation of the ice crystals – does that also include, Rafe?"

"As a creature of flight, provided he takes high to the sky and in a position close to the Icebow, he should be alright to glide straight through and back to the home planet – though one must remember, there are no securities. No guarantees."

Salt looked at him closely and tried to probe the hidden calendar times ahead, and to know if she'd made the right decision. "In that case, shouldn't the *'no guarantees'* also be extended to myself – and say that I may not be predestined to suffer a state of limbo from the effects unleashed?"

"The chances are extremely remote that you could survive in life-form."

"Well, I'm prepared to take the risk!" she said stubbornly, knowing she would either be proved damned or brave from her decision. Either way she had to go with what felt right to her at this time. She would not be disloyal to her own nature.

"Well! That's, that!" By the abrupt tone of his voice, the matter was closed. And a small comfort washed over her as together they pushed the door open to enter into their new environment.

And one with the other, boldly stepped into their new causeway colour and found themselves embraced by a delicate hue of pink, with blankets of pink effervescent carnations covering the infinite acres of space ahead of them. While in the distance, their eyes travelled and settled on the outline of a golden spine of mountains.

"Looks like where in the pink..." She smiled, intoxicated from the scent of rapturous floral fragrances filling the air. Pink carnations always sparked her mind to floral bouquets intimately held in the hands of hopeful brides. No Earthlet bride had a wedding without pink carnations. It was a strongly upheld tradition within the element, the flowers signified the unity of carnal desires – the body – the flesh – a celebration. A public display of vows and settlement.

Attention seeking, the raven flew from its chosen position: the roof of the sandsomme stone building, and into the elevated warm pink-salmon coloured skies, calling out his awareness. In her mind she acquiesced. Her mind was in ecstasy. "The horizon appears much lower than normal," she said, while looking happily into the vastness above their heads, momentary dazzled, it seemed to reach downwards, to touch her like a spearhead of brilliance.

"Pink," said Rhuand, in a tone that removed him from the beauty and serenity she was experiencing, "is related to insanity!"

"Insanity?" she blinked, not knowing where his thoughts were leading.

"Yes. The colour pink evokes bloody memories from the demanding training practices endured before learning if I had successfully gained admittance to the Actimm programme." He paused for one vivifying moment, and Salt glimpsed the anguished joy at the relief pain brought forth as he repeated in remembrance – "The pink room!"

"I've never heard of that term before," she said cautiously, knowing skill lies in objective interpretation. They began to walk amongst the pink carnations, her fingertips catching and trailing lightly over the luxuriant petals only to lose them to the soft breeze.

"No! Well let me inform you, Salt. That's due to the fact it is used as a test for prospective candidates. A technique to measure individual mental stability. There was some talk the test would be introduced to prisoners at the Irongate prison for auxiliary punishment–"

"A proposal of auxiliary punishment? I heard nothing of the pink room while I was imprisoned there."

"Good!" he replied through a series of imposing facial expressions she found hard to translate. "The timely results found that by placing an individual into epoch isolation: an empty square room, void of any distractions, with the walls, floor and roof painted a block bright pink – they would eventually go stark crazy and lose their grip on rationality altogether."

"Eventually," she said warily. "Are you saying it is inevitable under such controlled conditions?"

"It is," he said in a flat, unhurried voice. "That's the whole purpose. A pragmatic exercise. It's an ancient practise. A cruel perverse game."

"Game? You make it sound like it's fun, when really it sounds mortally harmful." She continued to look at him, but he didn't move his gaze to meet hers, instead he continued to look straight ahead, seemingly unaware of crushing the florescence flush of blooms beneath his footsteps. *He walks like a king*, she thought, breathing in the diffusible essence of oils.

"You're correct, in both ways," blatantly he continued. "Those who are trained to withstand their own limits and surpass them when needed in combat, would refer to it as a game of unsullied darkness. While it is true, others who succumb to their own weakness of mind, rarely can, or do, recover from its detrimental consequences, and this is where the idea of a secondary punishment arose. If one delves deeper into the pink room's history it was at first designed as a tool to test the limits of selected individuals – Female Munrah requested only the strongest minds reach the top."

Salt hesitated. "Did you also go... the same way as *'those'*, or of the *'others'*?"

"My resistance was much higher than other candidates, but I reached my personal limit and felt close to borderline fracture when the psychosomatic professor stopped the test."

"So what does that indicate to us here in the now, in a hue of pink?" She turned her face upwards, seeing the pink clouds moving, reforming, shifting, and dissolving. And she realised as a consequence of their different element backgrounds, certain things triggered a completely different response in them. For her the colour pink instigated thoughts of unity and love. Whereas for Rhuand, it represented mental torture.

They were both still learning so much about each other's past. Their romance had been such a whirlwind of attraction, an action on impulse. They had been led by a feeling that was right for them, and together they had been denied the opportunity of time to learn about each other's roots.

But here in the causeway of colours, Salt understood, they had sighted why the depths of themselves made them who they were, and now are. And she thought, the past makes the present... and the present makes way for tomorrow... but tomorrow never arrives... it can never be caught up to. It remained as elusive as catching sparks in the fire.

His voice penetrated into her reminiscence, "I'm over-cautious to the power of a colour – how it has the potential, under certain circumstances to be used for good, and bad – to sooth, to break a mind – to elevate or to break a spirit."

There were no words she felt she could add to his. His experience remained part of him. She could only listen. They had each suffered different experiences for different reasons, but nevertheless they had been tested and almost broken by the sadistic enjoyment and calculative minds of others.

Could it be? They had unconsciously recognised something of themselves in each other at the very beginning of their romance – and while opposites do attract, Salt realised here and now, they were more alike than she'd at first sight known, and their individual likeness had been unconsciously sort and found.

The Earthlet certainly knew from experience she could never be with a weaker soul than she herself. While she didn't lack empathy towards others, she had felt on more than one occasion, if she came across a male who she perceived to be weaker than herself, she had the curious temptation to want to weaken him further. While she didn't like her persistent inclination, she recognised as an Earthlet whose element had been devalued in status – she couldn't always fight the urge.

To her rationality, who wouldn't enjoy doing the same thing as she – and in her position? Enabling her repressed feelings to rise to the surface.

Female Munrah had allowed powerful high-ranking Metalgants to socialise with Earthlet dancers for coarse fun and entertainment as reward for their loyalty to her and the regime, but love was staunchly forbidden. The tradition was introduced after Salt had joined the elite dance company Amharik, proposed as a courtesy and a privilege for the dancers to mix with the Metalgant dominant. But to her way of thinking, it was more like dining with hunting, hungry wolves.

Salt always drew a firm line of not crossing that boundary and entering into causal or paid intimacy. No. She refused to be drawn into meaningless couplings, or one night encounters where Earthlet dancers were merely prey to the self-elevated element of metal.

Though she had been caught in some tight situations with Metalgants of great distinction who had taken her generosity of company, and assumed it led to one conclusion – intimate favours, with no emotional attachment – but that impersonal approach had never appealed to Salt.

While her Earthlet dancer friends had remarked about their often disappointing, sometimes brutal sexual encounters, she had always yearned for a relationship of depth – of meaning – of a meeting between both mind and body. And so she couldn't encourage a weaker soul to herself, or a clinical, cold-hearted experience, not after the struggle she had ensued to find and earn a place in the Earthlet elite of the dance world.

From meeting Rhuand Mezarron, she had never once felt that familiar surge of distain against him, instead she had always been left with a mind imprint that together they would add to each other's strength – with the potential to be a strong unit that no-one could infiltrate or lastingly divide. They could be a force for good, smoothing out each other's edges.

In their separate lives before meeting, they had been absorbed and self-aware in order to progress and accelerate in their careers, but priorities can and do change, depending on who one comes into contact with along the way of life – and limbo.

"We should head for the mountains, Salt." His deep, rich voice reached her from the depth of preoccupied thoughts.

"Yes," she answered, more in response to her internal acceptance of known facts than to his advice. This stage of their causeway colours, seemed to her, to be one arrangement after another, flying straight towards her out of the heart of the sun.

"We will stand a greater chance of being reunited with Lapis at that height." He pointed into the near distance. "Where the mountains scrape the rain clouds."

Salt gave one sharp nod, as though she had closed her eyes barely for a moment, thinking he hardly asked questions, he made statements, which one either contradicted or agreed with. And she knew she'd paused too long for breath for him to ignore the break to consider whether or not it was time to go. "Yes," she spoke with more clarity. "I noticed even when we walked through the damp green fog earlier, it wasn't strong enough to bring Lapis-Lazuli to us."

"It would appear to me, Lapis only becomes known to us when he feels so inclined. But there's no doubt, the more water round us – the stronger his appearance of limbo becomes."

The Earthlet could sense a line of tension in Rhuand's voice, and the way he held himself told her this colour of pink, would be the most testing of all colours they had conquered so far. And for this reason, she knew they needed to reach Lapis-Lazuli before the magnetico-electrico warrior caught up to them.

Lapis was a reliable and knowledgeable source in limbo, perhaps he could offer up scope of an alternative to the predicted threatening shadow that cloaked her life-form.

She had to prove Rhuand's prophesy wrong, show him she had chosen the right decision to stand with him – side by side – soul by soul.

Salt Delray was a female Earthlet who believed in the alternative. Nothing was set in stone to her way of thought… it could always be removed or adapted. Just because it wasn't sight visible, did in no way mean it didn't exist.

No, she was not of the standard: seeing is believing. She was of the strong and dedicated opinion: all possibilities and infinite sequences in patterns already exist out there in the airwaves. Nothing could be thought or invented that wasn't already possible – it was just a matter of harnessing the possibilities and bringing them to mind, tapping into that hidden knowledge.

She fervently believed in the power of the mind, for as every Earthlet knew, one's mind was the other side of one's soul.

:

#MaskOfBeauty – The cold space of emptiness Rhuand had carried inside himself for an age blazed up with an answering warmth as he watched Salt.

Salt was a movement, zigzagging her way, insects hopping and settling round her hair as she bent beneath hanging tree branches laden with florescent blossom, scented like rose coloured promises – but when he came face to face with her, he was perfectly controlled as they ventured onto the foothill below the mountainous incline.

The Metalgant in limbo had to admire her resolve to loyally remain with him. He couldn't imagine anyone else with such strength of character and yet gentle nature going to the lengths she was prepared to take – and all for him! He had been quite conquered by her impenetrable resilience.

While he had taken every care to demonstrate to her his prophesy of Earthlet limbo, he had to acknowledge if this was indeed her destiny, at least she was in some way prepared – whereas he entered his own personal limbo without concept as to what the spirit of entrapment held for him. There had been no-one to teach him what he had to know to be conscripted into the unconsciousness. He was his own experience. He had to learn the onerous way, fathoming out for himself as best, and worst, he could.

Yes, looking back, only when Lapis-Lazuli came into his milieu of limbo at Gardenia Lake was he then able to bridge the gaps and gain a magnitude of accuracy through hidden truths.

The immediate truth at this moment was Salt Delray's contagious enthusiasm for an alternative had begun to rub off onto him. Perhaps she was right, Lapis may know of an alternative. After all he was an expert on all things limbo which indicated to the Metalgant in spirit, Lapis must have been in this tainted intermediate place for some time. He always had the habit of remaining steps ahead of those who were comparatively new to this capacious space between.

He let out a toneless laugh and with a surge of spirited energy, the wayfaring Metalgant of limbo moved forward with the Earthlet to increase their pace up the golden mountain side.

Rhuand glanced warily below to the pink acres of flower heads basking beneath the clear pink-salmon skies. They looked even more threatening from his new sight of elevation. The floral scent carried forth on light whispering waves seemed to seep into his soul and poison it for being.

From the east, fast moving rain clouds began to cast dark shadows onto the golden mountain, blocking out the salmon-pink skies directly overhead shimmering, as though the whole wide territory was on the move and might at any moment take off into the above wilderness – a place of the lost.

Which brought his troubled mind to Rafe. He knew the raven had flown ahead of them into the mountainous expanse, then, as though the bird of prey had picked up on his turbulent thoughts travelling through the airwaves and converted the waves into a message to its antenna brain, he reappeared, to swoop down close to their heads, before again surging into the future skies. Eagerly calling to them, encouraging them in their ascent to reach his code of locations.

And Rhuand was reminded of some other time, some other place, very remote, yet bearing a resemblance to this moment. The memory escaped but continued to plague –

The Earthlet interrupted his flight of thought, "How do you feel?" He could hear a tentative quality to her voice.

Rhuand hesitated for a moment. Now was not the time to help protect her from his knowledge. He had opened up to her about his fearful concerns of reproach from the magnetico-electrico warrior, and vowed to himself he would remain as open and honest as time was long, for she had chosen to see this battle of wills through to its dire conclusion – almost as if the experience somehow gave her a borrowed freedom – and the more he thought about it, the more it bothered him. "Tervanous is never far from my mind. He shadows all my thoughts. So much so, at times I could swear he is becoming part of me." Sharing his deepest, darkest suspicions of the magnetico-electrico warrior, the true devastation of the situation magnified to him...

Salt seemed taken aback by his answer and didn't hold his stare. Instead, when she answered, the words that came out of her mouth sounded to him to be well rehearsed, "Spiritual gestation should not be suppressed, nor should it be overshadowed. It should be honoured. You are a Metalgant warrior of super intelligence, Tervanous is a machine."

He confronted her, almost angrily, "My thoughts are not all my own. He is, and shall remain strictly controlled to home in on me and our location." Rhuand willed her to stare back at him, to show apart of herself, her thoughts, but her face was set, a mask of beauty.

Is she numb with the repercussions?

"Does that also work in reverse?" Her words collided into his thoughts and fell into the darkening shadows. "I mean to say... if Tervanous can read your thoughts – can you read, his?"

He could not help but notice, even in the dimming light, her beautiful eyes shone brilliantly with an untraceable purpose, and a sudden doubt crossed his mind until it became whole...

What if Salt had made a deal with Female Munrah, and that deal was programmed into the magnetico-electrico warrior. A deal that ensured her survival for his capture – for if he could read Tervanous DMS6's programmed thoughts, he would learn of such a secret – a betrayal – a plot against him – and she would be found out! That could explain the Earthlet's eagerness to carry on and into this next causeway colour, which may well send him insane, and why she refused to heed his advice of finding a Rainbow to return back to the home planet.

Is she sincere, or just pretending?

He hardened his heart against her in secret. She had stung him, and at that very moment Rhuand felt an immensely strong current of electricity discharge down his spine. It wasn't the kind of current that gave an instant spurt of energy and vitality, it was quite the opposite – a sharp burning pain that left behind a long dull ache in its place.

But what if his suspicions were a distortion of the facts channelled to him through his connection to Tervanous – he would never forgive himself for getting her wrong. To him, love must be founded on a solid rock of trust, and if he accused her and was found in the wrong, he would grind their rock foundation into dust – any trace of love could be lost – and that action would be a betrayal in itself on his part.

But in holding back and remaining quiet, he was denying himself.

:

The heavily burdened rain clouds blanketed their perceptive view, and the temperature had now dramatically dropped.

"The air pressure feels different up here?" she shouted through her strands of hair as they whipped across her face. She quickened her pace.

He pulled the long coat about him and fasten it securely. "Yes. The air is highly charged…" He'd already observed white dust rising above the steep, deeply-rutted path while sighting the intelligent bird of prey angling itself adeptly into and away from awkward positions in flight. He wheeled closer, and squawked in boisterous protest against the refracting airwaves.

Quite unexpectedly, a distinct and familiar voice spoke into the charged air, "Isn't the world of limbo a small place, though I have to admit, I wouldn't much like to paint it!"

Both Rhuand and Salt turned round in equal surprise, which turned into pleasure.

"Lapis! Dear friend," Rhuand said in outward relief, and the water vis-viva gave the couple a generous smile and a raised eyebrow of acknowledgement. His fringed grass skirt fluttered flirtatiously in a current of air.

"I received message via the verdant mist – your plans to reinstate the Ark of the Okarpi. I trust you were well guided by the fellowship of Woodlians."

"Agreeably so!" Rhuand exclaimed in a jovial manner. "We've come in search of you and you're fervent knowledge."

"Well, don't be backwards in coming forward. Fire away, sir!"

"We are seeking an alternative," she said.

"An alternative, to overcome an encumbrance?"

"Indeed!" Nodded Rhuand.

Lapis-Lazuli combed his fingers thoughtfully through his long wavy hair. "What is the name and nature of the particular encumbrance?"

"The possibly of rupturing the ice crystals from within the Regard brooch," beseeched Salt. "Is it more than likely I shall suffer as a life-form, and enter an Earthlet limbo?"

Lapis-Lazuli's forehead furrowed. "A trauma will occur from the effects, yes..." He gathered his windlestraw skirt back round his legs. "Bound to be a sort of blitz."

"Could there be an alternative to this outcome or is it a written certainty?" Salt cupped her mouth with her hands against the harsh winds.

"I see – well, as you're an Earthlet with a prevailing sense of an alternative to any situation – there are two options that can be put into place to prevent the catastrophe from running out of total control–"

"And they are?" interrupted Rhuand, straddling himself against the wind force.

"Well, the first is the simplest, but has major drawbacks like most things–"

"You have my full attention, Lapis–" enunciated the Metalgant. He peered needle-eyed at him.

"Discard the Regard brooch and find a supplement to it."

"Discard?" cried the Earthlet. "But the brooch is key to unlocking the sandsomme stone doors into each and every causeway colour... how could we possibly proceed onwards?" Her beautiful eyes grew larger and her full mouth smaller.

"By discarding the brooch, you would then need to steal one of the skeletonised keys which Female Munrah and her subordinates are using for access."

"And so another set of risks and dangers would arise from this territory of action," offered Rhuand. They circled one another with an amorous enmity that called for constant wariness. "This solution requires proving, not once, but over and over again and we just don't have time."

The water vis-viva inclined his head.

"And the second option?" she enquired with anticipation.

"Well, this is the most touch and go of the two options, involving heightened risk–"

"We wouldn't expect anything less," voiced Rhuand in a sarcastic tone followed by a toneless laugh.

Lapis paused for a moment, almost daring himself to carry on the dialogue. "It would require direct intervention from the steel Metalgant of limbo himself." Lapis smiled into Rhuand's eyes, and then raised a wicked enticement of the eyebrow. "All depends how far you are both prepared to go, really."

"Our limits are constantly being tested!" acknowledged Salt. Her concentration appeared almost fanatical. These limbo-beings clearly puzzled her deeply and moved her with excitement which didn't escape Rhuand's shrewd observation.

"Well, dear Earthlet, you will have to reach the very edge of life before you can be pulled back, it is a dependence of trust. And do you both trust each other implicitly that is the question of questions?"

"Yes!" she said without hesitation.

Rhuand looked deeply into her lovely sparkling eyes, her open and youthful face and again a wave of suspicious fractures entered his mind, but before he could place them together in order, a curious wave of calm came over his spirit of limbo. Instantly he knew what this meant.

"Rhuand?" whooped Lapis-Lazuli. "What is it?"

The Earthlet turned her attention from one to the other, her lovely face creased with concern.

Rhuand regained his crystal stare. "A sudden weight has been lifted from my spirit. It feels like Tervanous has switched off his magnetic impulse in the search of me…"

"My goodness!" shouted the Earthlet into the winds. "That's the best news I've heard in a long time–"

"So you've completely regained clarity, strength and purpose?" Lapis-Lazuli spoke guardedly.

"Completely!" said Rhuand. "And that indicates one thing only."

"We've gained time?" offered Salt hopefully.

"No!" corrected the Metalgant of limbo. "It means Tervanous is so close to us that we are now in his immediate radius, causing his signal to cancel itself out."

"You mean it's a trick?" she uttered in disbelief. Her eyes brimmed with tears.

"It's *so* much more than a trick. This is not meant to mislead. This is for real." Rhuand saw a dullness of movement over Lapis-Lazuli's shoulder, and in swiftness of instinct the Metalgant in limbo lunged to forcibly grasp Salt's arm and pull her close into him.

But before he could say another word, the magnetico-electrico warrior pressed an insignia on its chest of solid armour. Distinctly a loud charge resonated and Rhuand felt the effect as the magnet pull dragged on his spirit, dulling his senses, yet allowing him to see and know exactly what was going on round him, while unable to spring into action and protect Salt any further.

With nature's velocity, Rafe appeared as if from nowhere and began to fiercely swoop down into the danger zone – its talents spread wide apart to take its prey with practised balance. But Tervanous DMS6 was pre-programmed to detect any brand of force opposing him, and advancing his purpose to win by escalating his level of dangerousness. He was strong by design. Solid. This, Rhuand Mezarron knew darkly well as he'd skilfully helped to place these characteristics in the Metalgant hard-head machine.

There was no expression or attitude on the face of Tervanous, simply because he didn't feel – emotions had not been introduced into his design, only the drive to forcibly carry out instructions by his planners.

His machine body was encased within crimson metal plates containing black haematite. His appearance was stocky, with a thick neck and heavy shoulders and had an easy gait of movement, but he was rigid in mind – focused – through a programme of intent.

The two Metalgant prison guards edged into Rhuand's view and moved to stand either side of the machine warrior. The corners of their mouths turned up in a united show of contempt at the sight of Salt, causing Rhuand to feel an instant burning desire to attack them, but how could he fight them all – and win – without any harm coming to Salt? His mind was moving every which way.

The relentless black raven's attempts to bomb dive and take prey proved no distraction whatsoever to Tervanous, and while the Metalgant guards ducked and cursed violently at the ferocious bird of prey, he, the programmed machine, would not be separated in mind-set from his programmed mission of action.

Then, all at once, Salt let out a loud scream of terror and thrust her hands up to cover the Regard brooch pinned to her bodysuit.

Rhuand knew the powerful magnetic pull from Tervanous had now diversified to the brooch.

"Lapis!" called Rhuand through a magnitude of sufferance and strained willpower against the machine's pull. "Tell me, what do I do? What's the second alternative you began to speak of?"

"You do the only thing you can, Rhuand Mezarron," shouted the water vis-viva while searching both his and Salt's tortured facial expressions. "Wait! Prepare! Shock!"

:

#WordsOnIce – With all her willpower born out of adversity the Earthlet continued to clasp her fingers onto and round the mud-caked Regard brooch still pinned to her. But as the pull of emitting magnetism began to intensify from the magnetico-electrico warrior, who had intentionally locked mnemonics onto Rhuand's metal virtues – and now, scanning everything containing metal traces, including the sacred brooch, she knew her hands wouldn't be able to hold onto the jewellery for much longer. Her physical strength was meagre in comparison to his. She had no self-preventative defences against Tervanous DMS6.

"And so we meet again, Salt Delray," enunciated prison guard one with perverse pleasure. "I always knew we'd find you either up a mountain or down a well – it stands to reason your element sort like to take the long, arduous route, instead of the more effective Metalgant way."

"What are you trying to say?" She panted in laboured frustration and fear, unable to think straight.

"What I am saying, is this." He narrowed his eyes against the tumultuous winds and white dust pounding against his face. "You can run all you like, but can never outrun the final Metalgant punishment demanding your charter of death. All you're doing is prolonging the process. Don't you think it would have been better, cleaner even, to have taken the administered metal pellet..." He narrowly looked round in a contemptible manner, "instead of dragging us out here on your claptrap excursion?"

Before she could answer, or even think of an answer, the second prison guard jutted in with insolent disregard, "You do know Rhuand Mezarron is only using you. I mean, what other explanation could there be? You're a pathetic sham!"

She stepped away from Rhuand's hold, and glancing up at him she couldn't be wholly sure his bond to her was purely driven by a death deifying love...

"Now that's more than enough!" Rhuand carried arbitrary tones in a seemingly controlled and dark voice. Though Salt knew he must be severely impaired by Tervanous's effect now the machine stood only five strides away from them. "You have no authority to judge or condemn something or some-being you know absolutely nothing about! You are both a replication, employed by the Metalgant compartment that executed the original – you're just an answer–"

"Oh, we've been informed," interrupted prison guard one. "The escaped prisoner here." He jabbed a hand signal at Salt, "carries some vain notion she has the power to release you into salvation. Well, I'm here to tell you both that simply isn't going to happen. You're coming back with us, prisoner Delray to honour your death decree, and Tervanous is going to make it possible by using his power to anchor this Metalgant of treachery! You think you're the first to attempt a feat like this? Well, you're not!"

Salt felt her spirit trail, as a Lapwing trails her wings.

Rhuand clenched his hands. "Don't mistake me for a Metalgant who's worried about the likes of you two, but if you are as well informed as you would so like us to believe, you will of course know that shortly after Tervanous DMS6 attains his goal of maximum magnetism, you shall succumb to the dire circumstances."

"Is that a threat, Rhuand Mezarron?" scorned the other guard, while spreading his legs wide.

"No, not a threat. Fact!"

"Seems you two chappies have been well and truly hoodwinked… and old Tervanous here – well, he's not big on words, or original thoughts now is he?" intervened Lapis-Lazuli.

And a mixed expression of insolence and doubt passed over the prison guards' faces as they turned to look at each other, as if to say, *how long do you wish to stay?*

Then, glancing at Rhuand, Salt caught a glimpse, so disturbing that while the image only lasted the length of a few brief moments, its effect would be with her for as long as she would exist – riveted, in her mind's eye, Salt had caught sight of Rhuand's aura pulling away from his body of spirit. And she realised the true extent of the magnetism placed on his being.

She was afraid!

Afraid for him. Afraid of the unknown, oncoming circumstances.

While having no idea how they would make it clean away from here, Salt continued to make every effort to hold onto the precious brooch. Looking down at herself she noticed her knuckles had turned white, then filled with dread, she looked across and focused into the magnetico-electrico warrior's eyes – *Will he show any relent to our struggle?*

To her utter dismay she saw nothing reflected back at her –

only an opaque obscurity – his large black pupils showed no display of emotion – and she realised, Tervanous, the hard-head was as cold and computerised as Rhuand had described earlier – he was a machine devoid of many element-life qualities. He didn't even speak, he simply acted on order which made the happenings even more chilling to the Earthlet.

"We've wasted enough time," stated prison guard one, indicating with a knowing nod of the head to the other. "Let's get this over with. Once and for all." And as if answering an Earthlet's prayer, the turbulent rain clouds above them began to release loud thunderous rumblings in the highly charged atmosphere, causing the prison guards to reassess their surroundings.

She glanced back at Rhuand, and then Lapis-Lazuli in an attempted to gain support from this frightful situation, but Rhuand closed his eyes on her – and she suddenly felt isolated from him.

Has he closed his mind to me, as well as his eyes?

And as the thought washed over her, she witnessed Rhuand's steel reinforced overcoat begin to deplete – all the entwined threads of metal from the source of the Braska sword speedily unwound from his coat fabric in wild, spiralling movements, and hurtled dangerously towards Tervanous. Darting like needles through the turbulent air, the silver threads collided with one another and formed a thousand and one sharp daggers, only halting once they had speared Tervanous's metal body plates. But the machine remained utterly obdurate, unlike the two Metalgant prison guards who were shocked into a loud silence of time.

Rhuand's original coat now hung in tatters round and about his body-of-spirit in the blustering winds, and the Earthlet knew the change of consistency from metal threads to metal daggers was

Rhuand's own doing. And immediately, the mass of burdened clouds above them began to release their moisture.

He always did think ahead of his time, she thought with gratitude as great lashings of rain droplets hit directly, soaking them clean. A flash of lightening projected from the magnetico-electrico warrior and zigzagged high into the angry clouds above him, followed by a crash of thunder that vibrated down the mountain side and further flash lightening.

Is Tervanous controlling the weather?

If not, he was definitely effecting it in some way – inhibiting them every which way possible.

Uncalled, Rafe navigated close by her. "Stay away!" Her voice broke under the strain of not wanting the raven to be struck by any electrifying pulse. And in that precious moment of concern for someone else, she felt the Regard brooch surge forward, ripping away from her bodysuit, parting her entwined fingers.

The surprise was all too great to take in at first, and her mouth gaped open in shock as her mind strove to keep up with the rapidity of unfolding events. It felt to her as if she was watching the show of aggression in slow motion, almost suspending herself from events, but all the while knowing she was part of all this.

With a resounding clatter she heard the Regard brooch collide with the magnetico-electrico warrior's plated chest. Salt recoiled at the sudden impact, but against expectation the brooch didn't smash into pieces. No. It remained intact, at least from her perspective. Tervanous DMS6's magnetic force had locked the brooch into his now dented armament.

But what of the ice crystals inside?
Are they still intact?

Before the Earthlet could judge or contemplate any further, the Regard brooch began to glow fiercely, and all at once a flood of light began to escape from the brooch and wash over them, dampening the thunder in the darkened clouds above like a metal plate across a smoke-duct furnace. The humming energy emitted by Tervanous ceased in abruption.

He, had shut down!

Instinctively she knew, Rhuand had been released from Tervanous's pull as fast as a switch flicked off. The crazy memory was branded on her brain, but the nightmare, she knew, had only just begun as she heard Lapis-Lazuli's voice lament into the crazed pink atmosphere, "The ice crystals – they've breached." His face went white, less damning white than a blush, but his mouth fell open and that was an unfamiliar sign to her.

This is it, she thought, petrified.

This is the moment of my life-end and my travel into limbo…

Even though both Rhuand and Lapis-Lazuli stood close by her, and she knew she was not facing this alone – for they had both faced something very similar before entering their own personal state of limbo – nevertheless, the knowledge did in no way lessen the intensity of terror pumping through her veins, leaving her Involuntarily shaking from fear of her own life-demise.

And while she had listened to Rhuand's experience of being separated from life and discovering his placement in limbo, she realised in true clarity, hearing his worded descriptions from her distance of life-form, was now very different to actually encountering it for herself.

Rhuand's voice resonated into her throbbing ears, "Salt! Hold on… all is not lost… it's only beginning… Salt!"

Bracing herself against her unknown future, she felt a dreamy tide cleanse over her as the ice crystals and their charged energy continued to barrage them all, even traverse across, to shift, travelling high into the clouded skies. And from the hailing down of rain droplets, suddenly the weather changed, to falling snowflakes – the wet ground beneath their feet began to ice over with severity, cracking and straining, until it had become completely covered in joining sheets of ice.

The Earthlet began to shake more violently against the razor-sharp chilling air, but unexpectedly, she felt a strange lull of warmth radiate from within her, and a heaviness of sleep began to dark blanket round her body.

"Must stay awake." She told herself. "Must not give into this comforting feeling." Her eyelids felt increasing heavily as exquisite ice crystals formed on her long eyelashes like diamonds. Her body called out to her to shut down, but her mind fought the feeling away with all her resolve.

Looking up at the two Metalgant prison guards who held their positions at either side of Tervanous she saw a reflection of what was happening to her, happening to them – as they too were life-form. They had become completely encased within a frozen shell, unable to move – and suddenly the horror hit her, she too couldn't move. She had become iced. Fixed ridged to the mountain.

I am dying…

These three words reverberated through her head as the uninvited guest called claustrophobia, took hold.

She began to panic, feel nauseous, her mind jolted back to her days and nights locked into the cell at the Irongate prison at the request of tyrannical Female Munrah – the similarities were all too alike, only now it was worse – Salt was locked within herself.

Through sheer force of will she managed to part her lips – only slightly, not enough to let out a churning scream. She could just move her eyes, but for how much longer? Every other part of her body had become immobile – she was mentally reeling on the cusp of going mind crazy, or was she going pink crazy?

Dully, her thoughts broke to Rafe, his survival – *How is he?* Unable to turn her neck, she moved her eyes to the left, detecting through a curtain of swirling snowflakes, the brilliance of a pale pink arch in the sky. A profound sense of relief overcame her – an Icebow – and the Icebow by its very nature in this unnatural environment represented hope. Not immediately obvious to her senses, Salt faintly heard a sweep of air pass her shoulder. *Rafe,* she thought, *Rafe is still alive and in flight…*

She recognised Rhuand's voice from a mind-distance, "How much longer do I hold back, before–"

"As soon as Rafe touches the edge of the Icebow – that's when!" Lapis-Lazuli's words trespassed upon her mind in a cavalier manner.

"I can't wait any longer! Salt's at the brink. I won't lose her, Lapis. I'm telling you, I just won't."

"Don't jeopardise Rafe's chances," the water vis-viva responded in a more levelled and controlled tone. "Think about the Ark of the Okarpi. We must wait until everything comes into alignment. Don't waste this one and only chance…"

Deep within herself, the Earthlet felt the closeness between herself and Rhuand magnify. It was tangible and went a long way without speech. While still unclear as to what the second alternative involved, she was aware some shared knowledge had passed between Lapis-Lazuli and Rhuand. But whatever the procedure involved, she knew it should happen sooner rather than later, as she didn't know how much longer she could remain aware in this increasingly dulling state of mind and freezing body.

Rhuand moved into her now fading line of vision. She was responsive to nothing and no-one else, but him. His vivid green eyes shone expressively into her now half-closed lids. He held out his steely hands to place round her upper arms, pausing tentatively only a hair breadth away. She could feel a faint current, or was the sensation simply in her mind of imaginary?

Salt longed for him to pull her closely into his strength of spirit which shone and glimmered between the gaps of his tattered coat, as snowflakes melted on his being in silent promiscuity. And for the first time ever, she noticed the puncture wound on his chest had diminished from where the quartz crystals had been introduced into his bloodstream during life-form.

Slowly, opening her gaze to reach his, Salt uttered in a forced, shallow breath, through her slightly parted, yet not moving lips, "I'm fading, Rhu... I think... I know... I'm about to–"

"No! Salt, stay with me," he spoke through a clenched jaw. "I don't want you to become like me! This is no life, this is and can only be a bearable existence. And only bearable because you're here with me..." Then turning his head so she could see his beautifully balanced features against the darkened skies, he shouted, "Lapiiiiis!" His beseeching call echoed down the side of the mountain like an avalanche of rolling rocks that had broken free from the summit.

Aware of the snowflakes continuing to settle round and on them, she had time to know Rhuand's words as her own thoughts, and expected other thoughts to follow…

"Now!" shouted Lapis-Lazuli. "It's now or never!"

And then everything in her vision went black – with only Rhuand's last words echoing round her… "Salt Delray, stay with me! That's an order!" Until the sound wound down and stopped.

:

#TasteOfTorments – Upon instant contact with the Earthlet, Rhuand felt the dulling thud of an electrical jolt occur deep within her body. He let go of her arms, fearing more than one surge from his condition of Iquique could tip the balance of bringing her back into life – but as he looked searchingly into her frozen face for any trace of recovery, he saw – none! She remained lifeless. Like an ice statue. Even her eyelids were sealed together by the ice. Concealing her from him.

Rhuand repeated the procedure once more. Again, as soon as he broke spirit-to-body contact with her, the dulling thud faded to nothing and she showed no change from his transmitted electrical shock.

"Lapis!" he shouted in desperation. "The shock to her system isn't bringing her back to me. She's leaving us–"

"Most things go in groups of three… or five… even seven. It's called the balance of display. Much like the group of frozen three I'm looking at right now…"

Rhuand glanced in his direction and caught sight of both prison guards and Tervanous stood dormant in their frozen ice shells. "I don't care about them!" He didn't endure any delay. "All the spoken and unspoken care and love I have is for *this* female, Salt Delray. And nothing will make any sense to me without her–"

"Maybe you should increase your electrical shock." The

intensity of his spoken words carried clear but not sharp across the now heavy mantle of snow, covering the region on the mountain side and way beyond.

Alerted, Rhuand looked up to the cloud dominated skies above as though to gain mental strength and inspiration. And as he did, he noticed for the first time in the far distance the pale coloured Icebow in the expansive sky, and he witnessed Rafe, soaring high on the wing in the heart of the illuminating bow. In the blink of an eyelid, the black raven disappeared as the last of the snowflakes sparsely fluttered down round them like a last reply from the Regard brooch.

"Salt!" he pronounced slowly on the verge of desperation. "If you can hear me – help me to help you – you can't go on like this." For the third time he placed a grip round her frozen arms, tighter than normal, aware now, if he was too careful and reticent it was almost as bad at being too forceful – he could lose her either way. He must give her a full burst of his whole-heart of Iquique, no half-measure.

With this thought clearly set at the front of his fraught mind, Rhuand lent forward, closing his eyelids while taking a respiration breath as deep as a draw-well, then slowly, deliberately, pressing his lips over her frozen mouth he tasted his own torments and doubts apart even from what he called love...

As if suspended in a sensation of calm, he felt moisture gradually begin to trickle from her ice-sealed lips and gently, so gently, he parted her cold lips and breathed into her his Iquique spirit-force.

In the stunning short space of time, as though by accident, he felt her intake a gasp of air. At once, he pulled his lips away from hers, his eyelids flew wide-open alert to her changing condition.

She had a way of catching him out which made him, at times, rather afraid of her.

Asserting himself to her, he detected through his metal fingertips an intermittent current flowing through her frozen body, accompanied by sharp cracking sounds as the frozen ice on her body began to sharply splinter and fracture – regardful, he released his hold on her, and stood back. To his keen ears the acute sounds didn't stop, they continued –

Eagerly he turned to Lapis-Lazuli who honoured them by standing a little distance away with his back politely turned, arms folded, gazing onto the mountain side.

Sensitive to change, he came to stand by Rhuand's side. "Signs of life!" the water vis-viva said triumphantly in the stilling overcast atmosphere. Though Rhuand dared not feel too happy. A relapse could easily take hold.

Checking for vital signs, Rhuand saw a thin wisp of air leave her mouth, which quickly vaporised in the chilling climate. No, she was not safe yet – but she was – breathing.

"By golly… the process, it's working!" said his limbo companion in a heightened tone to his usual sophisticated voice, while rubbing his hands together sublimely.

With a sensory jolt the spirited Metalgant rapidly blinked himself away from Salt and into mid-air. "You make it sound like… you're surprised."

"Well, it was a suggestion of an alternative brought about by mere deduction," he said shyly, allowing his glance to fall as if by accident.

"Deduction?" shouted Rhuand, his eyes scolding him. He stayed where he was, his metal hands now clenched into fists as if ready to fight.

"Hey, steady on now, Rhuand Mezarron." He pulled away from the former Head Kielter. Any tendencies to this being a social outing quickly appeared to evaporate from him.

"You mean to say, this was guess work, blind faith? Yet you advised it as truth?" Rhuand's eyes were ablaze with anger as he pin-pointed Lapis-Lazuli with an accuser's charge.

"Risk always comes before a reward, sir," he offered in a reasonable tone that infuriated Rhuand even further. "And nothing can ever be certain, except death, or so I was led to believe..." He gave the other a conciliatory smile, "until I discovered the layers within limbo... and so it turns out not all of us can and do find the sanctuary of death... it's all about trial and error, and trial again in these obscure times. But next time–"

"Next time?"

"If indeed there is a next time." He paused, as though reassessing Rhuand's response. "I'll state when my suggestions are not fact."

"Indeed you shall." Rhuand's eyes widened.

"Hey, you were searching for alternatives, and that's what I presented to you. I can't simply know all the answers to all the questions. Though I admit, I am not far from the knowing of total limboisum..." The water vis-viva sounded more than a trifle indulgent.

"You're both in the right," whispered Salt in a waif-like voice.

"Salt!" He was alarmed, and immediately cleared the heated dialogue from his mind, she took centre stage in his outlook.

They watched with bated spirit as she slowly opened her frosted eyelids. To Rhuand it was like seeing her anew all over again. He looked attentively into her dilating pupils, then her amber eyes, studied the minute flecks of green and yellow within them, and then seeing her hair dripping round her white face like dark tears.

"Rhu, am I going to be alright?" Her voice was still faint, wavering full of uncertainty.

"Yes!" he said. "You look, like you–"

"I feel so warm," she said weakly, as sheets of frozen ice on her body began to rapidly slide from her and fall like pointed weapons to the snow covered ground.

"That's due to the electrical shock you received from my spirit."

"You used Iquique on me?" she whispered, fear mingled with reverence in her voice. "That's why I'm feeling pleasant astringent, feelings of a beginning–"

"It was the only way to reach you through the biting encasement of ice and restart your heart."

She paused for a moment, looking down at her released body as the encasement of ice now lay in shattered particles round and about her ankles.

Attentively, Rhuand watched, as with as much muster as her body could bear she stepped out of the cutting ice shards, looking thankful, she took the water vis-viva's eager hand. And he thought, the lengths Salt had gone to by placing herself in limbo's doorway, confirmed to him, there could be no premeditated conspiracy against him through her. She was here, for him, due to the bond they shared in life. Salt Delray wasn't leading Female Munrah to him in order to trap him further and benefit herself. No, Salt was here for all the right reasons gone wrong!

She spoke slowly, "I remember a sudden blackness taking hold of me, then a lulling feeling, and I stopped feeling frightened… and I struggled to hold on–"

Lapis-Lazuli interjected, "Your body was closing down, accepting the bitter chill, so you would be free from all pain."

Wearing a hunted look, Salt allowed herself time to think. "My inability to recall that particular moment more precisely is disappointing, although I do recall a strong feeling of jagged impulses pulling me into – the now." She let go of Lapis-Lazuli's hand and stared straight into Rhuand's eyes, and he felt a far-reaching energy locate his very essence, so strong that it mirrored their past life together. She smiled into the respite of his soul – and the relief he knew, would only be temporary, for their hardship was not over yet – knowing they still had two more colours to endure. She let out her breath. "So I've not stepped into an Earthlet limbo?"

"By no means, Salt." He felt the need to reassure her again and again, and a compelling rush to hold out his steel arms and draw her close towards him and enclose her safely into him took over, then remembering – he had no buffer of foreign metal between them, he spirited away and across to Tervanous, who stood dormant with the prison guards, frozen in time – or at least for the time being.

With such relentless force Rhuand heaved out the daggers of steel from Tervanous's body plates. Each drag of the steel; a razor sharp metallic sound pierced the chilled air.

Quickly he transformed the daggers back into steel threads, until once more they became entwined into the fabric of his tattered overcoat, restoring it to a recognisable shape – and by this time he became aware, Salt and Lapis-Lazuli had come to stand either side of him, deliberately studying the bodies of their frozen opponents.

"You're not planning on transforming Tervanous with your Iquique skills, are you?" She closed her eyes and appeared to give herself over to intense thoughts.

"No!" he said in force. "He is a machine with moving parts. The complexities are numerous. The only chance we have is to immobilise him by removing the chief programme of signature from his machine body – the Metalgant CPU."

"Central Processing Unit," confirmed Lapis-Lazuli, in his foretelling tone of voice.

Rhuand nodded. "It's located where a beating heart would be in a life-form." He narrowed his eyes while further inspecting Tervanous, feeling both Salt and Lapis-Lazuli leaning forward with him, following his line of eye sight. He indicated with a strong steel hand to the location. "There, directly behind the embedded Regard brooch in the chest plate." Then skilfully running the palm of his hand over the iced jewellery, he shook his head in thought – this magnetico-electrico warrior had shadowed his every move, from one location to another, relentlessly inhibiting the swiftness of his spirit – his thoughts – his actions – but now the weight had been lifted, Rhuand could sustain his true potential while entrapped in limbo – he couldn't allow Tervanous to regain momentum over him again. This machine had to be destroyed!

The Earthlet reached forward to trace her fingertips over the iced brooch, making contact with Rhuand's hand. He felt a bond of unity draw them closer together.

"I feel almost sure I wouldn't even recognise the Regard brooch in this state…" she said in a lingering soft voice, as though there was more behind the meaning to her statement.

Does she intend to say more? If so, she isn't filling the space with words or mannerism.

"Everything changes in the space of time..." brooded Rhuand. Drawing a link to his own state of being.

Yes, everything changed it would seem, apart from the character of beautiful and resourceful Salt Delray. His thoughts went ahead of him... but then, the changes she had endured by staying with him was beyond most individual's capabilities – and yet, she had fought through with such fortified admirableness, and without her, where would he be now?

He felt a sudden rush of love radiate through his spirit, and he realised all this love he had been carrying round with him since being an adolescent Metalgant had been a burden – a burden in the sense, he had never be able to give it away – while he had so willingly tried, he always knew the brief encounters of intimacy were not emotionally sustaining to be fully embraced by an all-consuming love. And so, Rhuand had been left with this overwhelming feeling of great passion and devotion, but with no-one to give it to – until Salt Delray arrived in his life, and in his limbo. And now he was forced to listen to his inner-self without escape.

Looking into the intensity of her spectacular eyes, he felt sure something of an acknowledgement moved between them – or was he simply imagining it, seeing something that wasn't there, but what he chose to see?

She parted her mouth and moved her lips, as if silently communicating to him, then she found words – questions – "For what reason is the CPU placed there, surely it should be within the machine's head, to replicate a brain?"

It wasn't what he had expected to hear, but she always did have a way with her, to constantly surprise him on nearly every level. Keeping his interest. Filling his innate needs by being just her. Just Salt. "Female Munrah isn't an advocate of the heart, while she sees it as a source to pump blood round the living body, she also holds onto the firm notion that the heart symbolises sentimentality, and this causes a distraction from the puritanical Metalgant way of prolonging dominance–"

"Therefore she sort to place a CPU within the heart space to eradicate any heart tendencies," interrupted Lapis-Lazuli, shaking his head, making his curls dance round his shoulders.

"In short, yes! It's a representation of Female Munrah's theory. The CPU is a symbol of strength. By displacing the heart and mind, which together make an individual automatous by instigating emotions and thoughts–"

"I can't for the life of me imagine an existence without primary emotions. What would be the point?" said Salt. "She must be mad!"

"She may well be mad! Female Munrah has prolonged her own life through ways we have yet to learn," said Lapis-Lazuli. "She intends to hold onto her Metalgant domination of reign and the servitude from other elements at all cost."

Rhuand turned to meet Lapis-Lazuli's eyes recognising he knew so much more than what he let onto. "We must remove the CPU to guarantee when Tervanous thaws out, he will not reset to his programmed state." He moved, ready to put his words into action. "But first the brooch–"

"Remove the brooch?" cried Salt, avid for information.

"No matter what condition it's in the brooch is key to unlocking the sandsomme stone doors and therefore must come with us."

"In all honesty…" The water vis-viva wiped his lips with the back of his hand as though to spread out these softly uttered words as long as possible. "I'd be surprised if Tervanous could regain any form of power, considering he was a vessel for the ice crystals to escape from the Regard brooch... did you see... I mean, not only did the crystals project outwards into the atmosphere from the brooch, but they also entered Tervanous and were emitted out through every aperture – ears, eyes, nose and mouth. He lit up like a beacon!"

"My foremost attention was placed on Salt." Rhuand turned to re-examined the magnetico-electrico warrior's metal plated body. There was distinctive traces round the machine's face from where the ice crystals had scorched him badly with ice burns. Tervanous looked the discharged shell of a machine, no spark, no flicker of comeback. Rhuand carefully inspected his black deadened eyes. "It would be detrimental to our welfare to walk away from him without tying all loose ends. We can't afford to be reckless at this late stage!" Forcefully, he wrenched the Regard brooch clean away from the machine with one solid steel grasp of foreclosure.

"It looks a shadow of itself," the Earthlet said with profound disappointment as she reached out and received from Rhuand the item of jewellery, carefully bringing it closer into her awakened gaze.

"At least it's still within reasonable shape considering the force of rupture endured. And be assured, Salt there are ways it can regain its sparkling allure." Lapis-Lazuli smiled softly. "Once you reach the next colour – band of gold."

"Band of gold?" repeated the Earthlet, beginning to sound like her old self.

Lapis-Lazuli shrugged with a friendly laugh.

Rhuand watched her, noting she had made a full recovery

remarkably well.

With a concentration of mind, Rhuand placed a hand into Tervanous's body of steel and disengaged the CPU from the main circuit route. Then swiftly turning to face Salt he reached for her hand, she responded by intertwining her fingers round his. An immediate surge of happiness took hold of his spirit. Gently he pulled her away from Lapis-Lazuli who continued to closely regard the three frozen statues.

"This," he said, showing her the CPU, "has been a rod in my consciousness–"

"Mine also," she said tenderly, her eyes appeared larger, more beautiful than ever to him.

"But I want you to know, this shall never hold us back, or come between us again..." He lent forward, not knowing if she would pull away from him. She didn't. Instead she reached up onto her dancer's toes and placed a tender warm kiss on his moving lips, silencing his words.

He closed his eyes, savouring her, remembering her, and then... she released him... and feeling the breath of her life on his spirit, he knew he wouldn't want to be released from her if he had his way. Ever.

Then, placing a hand on his chest, not to push him away, but to support her balance, she drew forth and brought with her a cloak of seduction – enveloping him. He closed his eyes tighter. Willing this moment to exist beyond the all so briefness of splitting time. "I want you to know, Salt... I..." How could he say his thoughts out loud – *I want you, I need you, I simply can't be without you?*

Tenderly she lingered, moving her mouth closer then further away from his, like a tease – even with his eyelids still closed, he could feel the proximity of her by her breath, she soothed him, he was eager to feel her once more – but he continued to hold his hands down by his sides – it had to be on her terms, and at her pace in these dire times of uncertainty, he didn't want to get this wrong by inciting something then risk the pain of her backing away from him emotionally and physically. She was far too important to him to mess this up by rushing her with his wants, his needs – after all, Rhuand knew well what he was missing, as he recalled the tenderness and passion of intimate unity they experienced together in life... He opened his eyes slowly, taking her in, her enigmatic beauty. "I remember so clearly when I first presented you with the Regard brooch."

"Yes..." she answered breathlessly, a recognition of secretive happiness spread across her face as she held his unflinching stare. "You came to visit me backstage in my dressing room. It was only our second meeting and you masterfully removed a Metalgant of rank who was attempting to get fresh with me–"

"He had no right to think he could take advantage of you." Just the very recollection of the Metalgant male trying to cajole, then force himself on Salt made Rhuand's past anger resurface. He knew the individual male, Breon Leviathan through reputation in the elite establishment.

He was an acclaimed defence warrior, who had risen to the position of Head Architect – designing Metal Fort's Hub Base at Female Munrah's request. But his lurid and depraved ways with Earthlet women highlighted his character for what he really was – a prime specimen for Female Munrah's new order – whereby she would remain the only important female in his Metalgant life.

"I could handle myself," Salt offered with gracious gestures.

"Self-defence was incorporated within our dance company contract."

"I never doubted you could, but giving into help shouldn't be seen as weakness. No-one can accomplish everything on their own. Even I'm reluctantly beginning to acknowledge that fact after years of denying myself the right."

"And I'm still learning," she confessed. "Anyway that predatory male didn't stand a chance once you placed him in your perceptible sight. He was well and truly put in his place! Whatever happened to him?" Her eyes shone like crystalline glass. "I never saw him again after that night."

Rhuand's mind flickered back – he'd never told Salt the reason her home, the narrow-boat was destroyed by fire was because of that lecherous Metalgant male – Breon Leviathan. Yes, he was the architect of that fire. The arsonist. After much persuasion, unwillingly he'd confessed to Rhuand, a combination of being repeatedly turned down by Salt and humiliated by the Head Kielter had drove him to such an extreme – Rhuand personally took the Metalgant in hand. Then shot him in the head with one fatal metal bullet. Life annulled.

In his mercenary thoughts, the then Head Kielter would not risk another attempt by Breon on Salt's life. He had to be stopped. At all cost. The murder file had gone missing before it had chance to gather dust – Rhuand had seen to that!

"Last I heard, Breon Leviathan was found with a fatal head injury, face down in the north beach sands," he said honestly, her eyes looked long and hard into his vivid green eyes from receiving the stark news. Yes, Rhuand Mezarron would do anything for this Earthlet then, and now.

"So, *The Hound* was eventually hunted, and put down?"

She didn't seem all that disturbed by his answer. *Did she already know? No, she couldn't.* No-one but Rhuand knew the true details. The mysterious killing had been hushed up, covered up, and Female Munrah didn't want Breon's demise broadcast beyond her inner circle – it would reflect badly, making her look weak – threatened.

He watched Salt push aside the strands of cinnamon-black hair from her face, the pink hue of breeze began to envelop them high on the mountain edge, and then, she kissed him again. Her sensual mouth began to turn up at the corners, and he felt her smile generously on him and the heartfelt words he had intended to express earlier came to the forefront of his mind again – but before Rhuand could express the words, they heard Lapis-Lazuli shout out in alarming bad grace.

"Time to shape up and shift out comrades! We have an imminent problem developing here..."

Reluctantly he broke away from her and the intensity was channelled to a new feeling of danger as he stared into her locked gaze. He could sense her swaying on her feet with emotion, almost like an echo of shadows.

Lapis-Lazuli's voice cut through the dreamlike pink hue like a cleanly sharpened knife, "The frozen encasements of body ice surrounding the Metalgant prison guards are indicating – a change!"

"Change?" Rhuand forced himself to move forward. His eyes now riveted upon the ice-bound figures. "What sort of a change?"

"A formidable one. Irreversible..." He gathered up foreboding tension. "I fear the prison guards have crossed over the threshold between life and limbo. Shortly to see their own reprisal!"

#Syzygy – "They'll keep our feet to the fire, now they've crossed over to limbo," Rhuand said darkly.

"I'm with you all the way," she replied in honesty. Catching a flicker of something in his flashing green eyes. Something she couldn't quite grasp, but knew it wasn't anything to be afraid of. His look held a wealth of knowledge, not like hope – that often led a scenic path to an empty promise.

"Energy doesn't end, Salt. Remember that. It just moves to a different state of being." And an overwhelming feeling of trust came over her.

Yes, she trusted him beyond any male she'd ever met before in her life. Though she knew trust could be broken in a single word or action, but for now she believed in him. Believed if anyone could fight the hostility from outside influences that took delight in disguising and hiding themselves from open sight, to lurk in the lengthening shadows, surely he could, along with herself and their respective aides in limbo – succeed.

For when the next strike against them would occur she couldn't be sure, only that it would. And its result would force them to regroup, rethink, react...

"Come!" shouted Lapis-Lazuli urgently. "I'll take you both to the next sandsomme stone building." He glided passed them with a light step, she felt the breeze of pink hue displace round them. "It's positioned at the highest point along the spine of these mountains. I'm sure we can reach it before cloud cover lifts, giving us a measure of concealment, while allowing me the time necessary to re-enter the moisture of the skies and locate Rafe on the home planet." And with a fluidity of movement, the water vis-viva excelled further on while offering an encouraging hand wave into the beyond…

And they followed.

Relief beyond belief.

Salt was glad to ascend further up the mountain track. To leave behind the bad experience of entrapment within the ice.

She shuddered, reminding herself earlier she'd jumped to ludicrous thoughts and suspicions – momentarily suspecting Rhuand's involvement in Breon Leviathan's death.

So that was the Metalgant's full name!

She'd heard him being referred to by other Earthlet dancers as, *The Hound* and from experience, Salt could testify he certainty *did* hound. Many dancers had mentioned the only way of ending his relentless sexual attention was to give him what he wanted – to succumb to his advances. It was common knowledge after the hunt was secured he would lose interest in his target and rapidly move onto his next sighted prey.

But Salt Delray just couldn't bring herself to surrender to him. It went against her whole being, and she hated being cornered. It brought out the worst in her.

But that was what *The Hound* had found exciting about her – and had stated this on more than one occasion. Her fury and resistance was a game to him; to her, his behaviour was brutal.

Thinking back, she had been sinisterly pursued by him for some time before she'd met Rhuand. But after the Head Kielter had come into her life, *The Hound* just disappeared from sight, and she'd thought no more about him. Rhuand had taken up most of her thinking time as their courtship had begun to blossom.

The warrior gave her hand a squeeze, as if to signal his

presence – had she given something of herself away through her facial expressions while considering the past. Or had he just felt the tension within her?

Either way, she actively lifted her face and took in a deep, slow, long breath, and let his hand go. He looked searchingly into her eyes as if seeking an answer. She gave none. She wasn't ready to talk.

Her mind flooded back to her Irongate experiences, there no-one had held her hand, or given reassurance that everything was going to be alright. No, quite the opposite.

Until her introduction to Lapis-Lazuli she hadn't heard one kind word, let alone the kindness of touch – but she could sense Rhuand wasn't rushing her to open up to him. He was patient, and held a quiet internal strength, allowing her to go at her own sweet pace. He was not demanding, and right now that was exactly how she needed him to be – yes, she needed him, and that realisation reverberated through her soul.

Whatever he was trying to tell her earlier, while it appeared to mean so much to him, she would rather he didn't say it, in case – her mind lingered – in case, the words indicated a demonstration, a declaration of perpetual togetherness, for she couldn't allow herself to hold onto a false promise.

How much stronger, she pondered, are events than one's futile efforts in shaping them? For they were far from in the clear and nothing was certain.

All Salt knew was they were both here for each other now – that would have to be enough – until later: in the final colour call of red.

In a moment of distraction, her thoughts fractured, as curiously hundreds of pink carnation petals began to whirl and dance round them in the air, like wedding confetti. She held out a hand, but they didn't settle on her for long as the breeze lifted them in the arts of coquette, into the pink hue.

. "They've travelled on the wind from the carnation fields below." Rhuand sounded as surprised as her to sight such a random display. She gave out a burst of unexpected laughter, any unhinged craziness from the pink hue seemed to dissipate without delay, and instantly Salt felt calmer in knowing, if the opportunity arose, she would kiss Rhuand again, in fact she'd kiss him and then some more. She only hoped their kiss here on the mountain edge earlier wasn't a kiss goodbye, but instead a kiss hello. A reintroduction.

Walking side by side, instinctively, together, their pace fell in sync further behind Lapis-Lazuli's steps. And as the pink petals settled onto the mountain side, her immediate thoughts found speech, "I remember, like yesterday, the first time we ever... we..." Her emotions nearly choked her as they suddenly rose in her throat from active suppression of her mind.

"The first time... we ever made love." His tone was hushed, discreet, carried away from the water vis-viva's ears by the breeze. Through her own sufferance she nodded, noticing his eyes began to take on a polished look and glimmered in the light. "And we found a meeting of two minds; two bodies; two souls. Yes..." His voice lingered over the words in remembrance. "Something I have never been able to forget, nor would I want to."

She smiled openly into his face, his memory imprint hadn't paled from existing in limbo. "Does our connection mean as much to you now as it did in life?" She daren't take a breath until he answered.

"Salt..." His eyes misted over. "We have and always will be strong, independent individuals, but together we make the bad better. I endeavour to be your rock when you are weak. For I have never wavered from the intensity of pure heights we found together in each other's arms. We shared ourselves, and in return, something truly spectacular happened, something I've never experienced before." He held her gaze with an intensity that meant she couldn't look away from him – neither did she want to. She felt he meant every word he said, his words mirrored her own feelings.

"Our past connection has held me together in spirit, I couldn't let our memory die, so waited for you in the place of our forced separation, at the edge of Lake Gardenia, hoping beyond hope to see your beautiful self again. You give me reason when I'm in doubt – that bond of love we ignited together in life must be carried forward with care into the future – never to be dulled by sinister adversaries."

It was more than Salt could wish to hear – her heart fluttered uncontrollably and her throat muscles contracted as she swallowed down her tears of joy… "I shall never forget how generous you were in offering me a place to stay after my home on the river was destroyed by flames." She lowered her voice, "And from the devastation of losing all my Earthlet possessions, with only the clothes and jewellery I stood up in…" Her fingers trailed over and across the Regard brooch.

He smiled right into her heart, again now, just as he did then. "Salt, as I recall, you took some persuading–"

"You were very persistent. Looking back that's what I needed but couldn't acknowledge to myself…" Her voice faltered. "It had been ingrained within me, better to go without than accept or ask for a helping hand. I just didn't want to be anyone's burden or slave."

"Salt, you have never been either to me." His voice became firm but friendly, "Until you came along, my life was empty. Loneliness was like an absence following me. I filled it with blind loyalty to the establishment, thinking this would fill the darkening void, but it never did, and how could it, it only formed as a sufferable distraction." He paused in reflection. "You brought an addictive warmth with you and placed my life into perspective. Slowly I realised from a role of destroying and enforcing control, I wanted to change, to breathe a life and feel freedom to love and be loved."

She nodded in silence, as her mind flickered back to when Rhuand insisted she move into his recently acquired apartment within the manor house, situated on the boundary line between Earthlet and Metalgant districts.

Visualising the large rooms with high ceilings, sash windows and substantial mahogany furniture. Decorated in sumptuous purple, red and gold, overlooking the East River. He had insisted she stay there until she'd gained her strength from the smoke inhalation rather than bunking down in the dancers' communal dressing room.

Rhuand had surprised her one evening at the manor apartment, by filling an entire wardrobe full of new couture dresses designed by Madam Miriam, a specialist in Earthlet dancing gowns who'd kept detailed records of Salt's body measurements and previous dress designs.

Following that moment of disclosure, she'd thought, *could this Metalgant male be anymore wonderful or beautiful to me?* Her heart had turned over with pure joy and happiness as she couldn't imagine a world without him. He had become everything, by encouraging her to be everything she could be. To reach out and meet her true potential, and fight to recover from the smoke inhalation by having a visible aim – a wardrobe full of dresses designed to be danced in, not just left on the hangers in remembrance.

Salt had thrown her arms tightly round his strong muscular neck, and kissed him with a glowing passion, but her enthusiasm had been short lived as breathlessness took a grasping hold, from the scars on her lungs caused by the fire's smoke. But Rhuand was a gentleman, lifting her off her feet, carrying her to her bedroom, lying her down... telling her, she needed rest to repair from the internal injuries, something only time could take care of. He'd held her, made her feel safe, secure, until she'd fallen asleep...

Time together seemed so short, not long enough. Once her health had significantly improved, Rhuand celebrated by taking her out to her favourite venue, the Imperia, to see the latest stage production...

Salt had chosen to wear a shimmering gold dress with the Regard brooch pinned at the centre point of the V-neckline, while he'd worn a tailored-cut suit for the black tie event. He made the best companion, funny, attentive, while remaining effortlessly handsome and available.

Back at the manor apartment, he handed her a glass of sparkling champagne in the parlour room, they naturally clinked glasses, and she knew there and then, she couldn't resist him or her own yearning desires any longer.

In the pink hue, Rhuand broke into her recollection as they continued along the mountain edge – "Everything seemed so perfect, so possible, but looking back that's when everything accelerated against us – Female Munrah refused to accept my resignation after much strained and bitter dialogue, and I came to warn you at Lake Gardenia – but she struck out, and now here we are." His voice hardened, "in a darkened place away from the home planet."

"Yes," Salt agreed soulfully. "In the sunshine of our love, an ever growing cast of shade was moving in, counting down the time, before she would deal a hand of intended death, with the sole intention of uprooting our bond."

Salt fell silent, thinking – could she reconcile herself to the alternative of doing without Rhuand?

Her answer was clear and firm –

No!

Nunquam!

Never!

With only two more colour of causeways remaining, she could sense the result they had so strived for in this dimension was almost touchable, almost within sight.

A growing strength of energy continued to circulate in her body from Rhuand's shock-start impulse that saved her from limbo. She was blessed with a renewed focus. Left with the distinct feeling he had given her some part of his metal strength, to prevail and get the better of their adversaries bad.

:

(7) GOLDERIZE

:

#Rejuvenation – Except for themselves with noisy drawing in and out of breaths and their footsteps striking the grassed over pathway there were no other sounds. No voices of any sort. No cry, only oppressive silence.

Impatiently, Rhuand cast out the silence, "Don't be precious with your thoughts, Lapis. What do you plan to do once you reach Rafe on the home planet?"

"Limitations mean, our Rafe cannot fly the Ark from the base… so my initial thought is to create a flood within the Hub Base, allowing the Ark of the Okarpi to float right out and off Metalgant premises and into the heart of the capital city, whereby all five elements will rediscover its written knowledge–"

"That would be a triumphant feat!" exclaimed Salt. His words seemed to deeply move her with burning excitement, and her large brilliant eyes sparkled until they were like polished amber.

But Rhuand was wary of the repercussions for the Earthlet. He concealed his concern as best he could – "You have given this some thought, Lapis. And I dare say, your idea is possible as there are many chambers and water tunnels beneath the base which lead directly to the capital."

"I believe in you and I'm glad of that!" She voiced with optimism. And together they followed the path up and along the mountain side, edging ever closer to the fast moving clouds over head.

Below, Rhuand noticed the fields of pink carnations had reduced to a memory, lost in a blur of vision from the increased space and height over which they had trekked, reminding him how Salt had at one time become a memory to him, until she'd found the bridge of gateway that linked the home planet to where he'd waited in limbo for her.

He couldn't go back to that existence of separation. He would find a way to ensure they could be together, no matter what. If there was one thing she had taught him, it was an alternative could always be found. It was just a matter of finding it…

Every so often, he threw a perceptible gaze over his steel shoulder to the foot track they had keenly walked along. "Still no sight of the prison guards," he said cautiously. "Though I suspect they'll need time to adjust to their new form in spirit…" His voice trailed off as he reflected on his own personal understanding of limbo and the startling realisation, traditional death doesn't always follow life.

"Once their shock dissipates, we can only hope to be far enough away from them. And don't forget," added the water vis-viva in urgency. "If indeed you do sight the prison guards, they shall not look as they once did in life-form. They will be completely changed, unrecognisable."

"Just as Rhuand was…" the words burst out of the Earthlet's mouth and her eyes went larger and her mouth went smaller, so the rest of her words were lost.

"Absolutely!" said Lapis-Lazuli, filling the gap. "My advice would be to suspect anyone new you come into contact with from now on. As any significant features the prison guards had in life will be lost to their state of limbo."

"Noted!" said Rhuand firmly. "Leading from this, what can we expect to find at the other side of the next sandsomme stone building?" His voice lacked emotion to his own senses, he was purely interested in detail and fact.

But how can you prepare for the unknown?

He answered his own question: *by being alert at all times to any changes.*

Lapis-Lazuli continued in the same breath, "At the place called band of gold, you shall be met by Erasmus."

Salt found her voice. "And will Erasmus be our guide?"

"Erasmus will wish to tell you her own story in her own words. Be sure, she is a great source who will aide you both to see things much more clearly. She is the balance between endings and new beginnings, and will indicate the way ahead. Preparing you for the final colour."

Providing we reach it – thought the steel warrior in limbo, who, to his way of thinking, was certain everything was uncertain.

"How will we know her?" accentuated Salt.

"She is born from the ashes of fire–"

"Erasmus is of the earth element?" Rhuand turned towards her instinctively.

"Like me–" Salt gravely raised an eyebrow, her features more mobile.

"Yes. But take heed, she will appear to you in a form you shall be familiar with. Do not be scared of this." Lapis-Lazuli's voice sounded conversational, steady, but practical. "It is just her way of insuring the message stays with you, leaving a resounding impression."

"You make the experience sound so cryptic, Lapis." She caught his eyes and stared at him, her eyes were like antenna, reaching, sensitive, searching into the future.

He looked back at her benevolently. "That's because Erasmus is exactly that. She is a source who can tap into your psyche without you even being aware she was there. She will only become known to you when she is ready and has something of worth to offer."

"Erasmus is a force for good, yes?" Rhuand needed confirmation. A smile outlined his face and he felt in a moment both cruel and jubilant.

"In surety and without a shadow of doubt. She is a light," he answered with an implication of secret busyness as he moved his gaze to the grassy path.

"Lapis?" The Earthlet paused as if suspending her thoughts in time. Was she debating whether or not to ask something, or was she about to demand something? Rhuand couldn't tell, but held his breath as he felt a tension rise up.

"Lapis," she repeated in emphasis. "I have to insist on an honest answer as to why you didn't save the Metalgant prison guards from limbo, while Rhu saved me from such a fate?"

In swiftness, the water vis-viva turned his head to momentarily sight Salt and Rhuand eight steps behind him, before turning back to face the future winds. "You sound somewhat accusing, dear Salt."

"I am merely airing my thoughts out loud as I cannot find a solution to quieten my own mind."

Rhuand felt great admiration for the Earthlet who kept a friendly face, yet firm voice. It took mettle and attitude to ask a hard question that could potentially imply their friend, Lapis-Lazuli could have undeniably caused them serious harm by not acting in their favour. And by asking an arbitrating question, she also risked tarnishing their solid friendship.

"You do right to ask me." He continued at a steady, even footing across the mountain terrain, and they followed. Then, he cleared this throat before choosing his words carefully. "In response to your question, dear Salt, neither I nor Rhuand Mezarron would stand a risible chance of saving their Metalgant derrieres–"

"Why not?" He was as eager to learn the answer just as much as Salt.

"Hey now, you do trust me after everything we've been through together, don't you?" The water vis-viva sounded cold, ice-flavoured.

"We've never doubted you," she said, answering for them both... too much was a stake to blindly disregard a nagging feeling of uncertainty, this Rhuand knew, and surely Lapis-Lazuli would understand too?

"Just answer the question, Lapis!" Rhuand said sternly, more on Salt's behalf than his own.

"Fine," he said bluntly. Stopping, to turn round and face them both squarely on. "I'll quench your curiosity. Due to the fact neither one of us shared a unity of bond with either of the Metalgant prison guards, there was, and never could be a connection of tie to help pull them back from limbo. Surely you both now recognise, only love can break down barriers and transcend through into the infinite, below all levels of skies to reach an intended."

There was a marked silence as the couple took in the magnitude of Lapis-Lazuli's words.

"What did you expect me to do?" The water vis-viva broke into the silence. "Use a reversed version of my Iquique water skills on their encasement of ice to free them? Surely not, for I'm much more inclined to cause excessive fluid to enter porous body cells and drown an individual from the inside out."

From these words, Rhuand felt a shudder reverberate through his system of spirit. He felt his face fall, and immediately, Salt seemed to pick up a tension from where he had let go – he was reminded of his own demise, drowning in Lake Gardenia after saving her life.

She reached out a hand to him, but he had become unreachable to her for the time being as he fought to focus through his glazing eyes and sight into the future distance ahead. Blindly walking passed Lapis-Lazuli, as if seeing nothing and no-one, only his own pertaining thoughts until he steely regained an outward control of silent despair.

He heard Salt run closely behind him, to catch him up. Then, sensing her eyes wash over him, Rhuand felt a sudden peaceful feeling settle upon him, as though their hearts and minds had connected, soothing him, almost as if she was part of him somehow, becoming one – and he felt his internal electrical current of jagged flow calm to a ripple of circulating energy, allowing him to gain a silence deep within.

In recovery, while still walking at speed, Rhuand looked straight into her eyes. "What was that? What did you just insight, without even placing a hand on my spirit?"

"I'm unsure," she said wide eyed. "I just reached out to you with my thoughts, ever since you kissed me from the edge of limbo I've felt different – stronger – as if some of the transferred energy you gave me continues to echo round my body. Sensing your pain as if it were mine also."

"Well, however you did just what you did – it worked, in fact it worked more than a lot, Salt Delray." He felt the corners of his mouth turn up into a smile. And he watched as she swallowed down emotions on the surface, to bury them deep within, and bravely graced him with a generous smile.

"We're here," shouted Lapis-Lazuli, breaking into the tender moment. The couple moved the intensity of their gaze to his direction. He pointed at the lower part of a monumental sandsomme stone building, the upper regions were concealed by cloud cover. "Once you've entered, I'll spirit away through the clouds and back to the home planet to discover Rafe's whereabouts."

"You are the only limbo-bearer who can see this through, Lapis." He reached out to shake the water vis-viva's already outstretched hand.

"It's a collective task, one which has involved many of us, but it will mean nothing without an end success. I hope to grant the wishes of every limbo sufferer – but fear not, you shall feel the results should I succeed."

"What about Salt, for if limbo is lifted, how will she, as a life-form be effected?"

"Erasmus..." He nodded thoughtfully. "She'll be able to help answer that question. Whereas I'm a message giver, rather than a prophet."

"I hope you wasn't offended by my question earlier, Lapis?" Salt looked oppressed with guilt. "It wasn't meant to sound impertinent, or cause you displeasure. I've always valued your friendship and careful advice."

"You asked a straight question, and I hope I offered a straight answer. There is nothing worse than assuming and then reaching a wrong conclusion, it can and will lead to all sorts of misgivings and misguidance." He paused momentarily, as if to take a mental picture of them both and hold it in his mind. "Wish me luck, I hope to see you both again, under better circumstances."

The Earthlet unpinned the distorted Regard brooch from her skin-tight bodysuit, her eyes dilated with obstinacy as she carefully adjusted the item with both hands into the stone door, Rhuand held his breath tentatively. He reckoned they had little light-time left in this pink hue before darkness fell. "This is going to work, right? I mean, it has to work as the brooch isn't completely ruined from the ice crystals erupting out of it earlier." Salt looked sad. She must still ache from her repercussive recovery, he thought.

"It has to work!" He heard a strain of emotion in his own voice. "This is our only key to entry. Tervanous sealed his great fate by being a machine and irrevocably dying."

They waited for a moment, then another. Nothing happened. The door remained locked as they stood tense in the moving pink hue – Salt stiffly repositioned the item of jewellery.

"Take your time." Rhuand could see she was exhausting herself with rising fear.

"Belief holds great strength," said Lapis-Lazuli. "One should never be too keen to give up on a belief and the power of visualisation, it can transcend the mind beyond limits."

Not one to give in easily, Salt wriggled the brooch slightly this way, then that way, while taking in a deep concentrated breath, as if visualising the words of Lapis-Lazuli. And, with overwhelming relief, the door began to slowly grind open.

"Don't look back," shouted the water vis-viva, saluting both Rhuand and Salt with a firm and quick gesture of the hand. "Remember to keep moving forward." Together they did just that. Leaving Lapis-Lazuli on the other side of the immense stone door to go their separate ways, but with one shared goal in sight – to release the chains of limbo.

:

Internally the great sandsomme stone building appeared completely finished in all detail. The tremendous spherical rose window they looked upon when entering illuminated beyond all imagination, with strikingly vibrant clear colours reflecting down onto the stone flooring as though meditating.

"I guess we must be fleeting with our appreciation of this magnificent building." Salt replaced the Regard brooch onto her garment. "Time is everything right now." She tapped the brooch pinned close to her heart to mark the spot.

"The precious moment isn't lost. It's just placed into a memory, to be revisited in our minds' eye…" He reached out a steel hand to her, and together they hurriedly walked across the light shafts and headed for the exit door. And he felt a ripple of gentle electricity from her, as her individual current fell into sync with his own spirit flow through the palm of her hand. Together, for the fifth time, they walked purposely out of a sandsomme stone building and into the next prismatic colour of the Rainbow.

The large ornate door closed behind them and they found themselves walking into a band of gold hue. Its particles rose in the air glittering and shimmering in the striking golden light of sunbeams.

Then, by rule of practice, looking down to the ground beneath their feet, Rhuand released her hand and bent down, carefully surveying the blackened ground. As he picked up the small rocks in his hands, quickly he discovered their texture was unstable, crumbling into dust. He studied the land, it looked to him as though it was like a mass of convoluted rock that had lain maturing forever without number, and had now reached its strength and was terrible: the ground he stared at was pitted with craters.

Leaving his side, Salt walked further on and up a gradual

incline, only to stop abruptly. "Rhuand! Come look at this."

Swiftly, he shook away the particles of dust from himself and moved close to where she stood, his eyes were greeted with a most unexpected sight. They were now standing on the every edge of a massive void beneath. The opening to a mighty volcano. Instinctively, he placed an arm round her tiny waist.

"Do you think it's dormant?" she said warily, her arms hanging limply by her sides.

He stared down into the blackness. Seeing its edge was as high as the tip of an ancient seabed, such abysmal depth. "Let's walk further round for a better view." His mind used up its energy in the thought of reaching the other side, thankfully there was no glowing colours, or plumes of smoke signalling alarm. Everything appeared calm.

He pressed his hand against his brow, lulled to an appreciation of the very large skyline. In the immediate moment, there was no middle distance to his way of thinking.

As they made their way further round the volcano opening, they began to hear dull thudding noises from a great distance away.

"From the depths a rejuvenation is taking place isn't it? Like a circle of rebirth..." Her perceptible words suddenly jogged his memory to the chief programme of signature he'd taken from Tervanous's machine body, the CPU.

Carefully, Rhuand placed his hand into the pocket of the slate-grey overcoat then pulled out the CPU in his palm. Clenching a fist round the device and without saying a word, he took a step back, and with all his metal strength he swung his weight forward and launched the metal device into the shimmering golden air. In continued silence, he watched vigilantly as the CPU descended down into the great depths of the volcanic crater below.

Once it had left his sight he turned to face Salt, seeing she looked as relieved as he felt. "No-one will ever fall under its potential programme of influence again," he uttered bitterly.

"It belongs to the volcano, now. As an Earthlet, I was brought up to acknowledge from the ashes, a new earth is formed–" All at once she stopped in mid-sentence. He followed her sight-line into the distance – to see a dark cloaked figure moving towards them.

"We're not alone." Inwardly he was not so sure. He placed a hand on her shoulder as though to ground her. "But remember, Salt, Lapis told us to be suspicious of everyone new – this may not even be Erasmus." He narrowed his eyes as the distance between them lessened. "The flesh is insubstantial, but the memory is a more formidable preserver."

The mysterious figure came closer into their view. He heard Salt take in a jagged breath… "Mur… Mother!"

Rhuand recalled her mentioning both her parents had died, under what circumstances he did not know, only that the memory of them she held dear. They had taught her how to acquire an inner strength in times of need.

"Mother, it's me, Salt!" she hollowed across the open space of gold hue. With immediate concern, feeling something wasn't quite as it appeared, he reached out to pull her back. But she slipped from his grasp and was gone like a thin Zephyr wind.

:

#Erasmus – The figure, shrouded in a shimmering petrol-blue cloak, with golden threads weaved through long strawberry blonde wavy hair, contrasted beautifully against the blackness of the volcanic landscape.

"No, Salt Delray," she smiled warmly. "I am Erasmus. I am the source who will help bring a clarity to your endings and new beginnings with mind to the final colour of outcome here in limbo."

The Earthlet was immediately stunned. "Erasmus? But you look so much like... her... I... don't understand..." Not knowing how else to say it. Her Earthlet mother had always been her fireside, and the unexpected emotion of sighting the female caused a strike to Salt's heart which reverberated through her body. She fought to catch her breath as the spoken words from the female echoed round her distraught mind to be followed by a sudden let-down – this was not her mother, and yet – as Salt studied the approaching female, it was almost unfathomable to her mind... when she looked so compellingly like the mama Salt had known and loved.

How can she be anyone else?

She moved with such grace, sure of foot, and just like Mama, her large amber eyes were her best attribute, handsome, deep and liquid, expressing a gentle sensitivity that could seldom be put into words.

In a significant manner, Salt felt the steel warrior close by, his hand brushed against hers, signalling he was there, but allowing her space to breath in the unsettling situation. "Rhuand, this is..." She paused, her body shook from the loud strokes of her heart. She couldn't form the name on her lips. It was almost too much. Such an out-of-the-way experience like a blot from the blue.

"Erasmus." He finished her sentence while turning to hold her gaze, but she lowered hers, not wanting him to see the true extent of her stark disappointment. "Salt," he said tenderly, "it is never the love you haven't yet met, but always the love you can never forget."

And she realised she hadn't hid her emotions from him as well as she'd hoped.

He had seen through her.

He knew her too well.

But then, if she allowed herself, the Earthlet could take comfort in that knowledge – and this led her to think, while she was with Rhuand, he was her home, anywhere else would just be a place she lived. But all Salt could do in response to the warrior's words was nod her despair away...

I'll be alright in time... while I have him, I will surely come through the darkness and find a heart of strength.

The female source interjected. "There is always one face imprinted on the memory that can be taken into the dark. I fear, I may have shook your system, Salt, but the reason is in no way malicious – it is for your own and Rhuand's benefit. As I appear here, in the echo of your mother's appearance, any guidance I am able to give will remain clearly at the forefront of your mind, and this guidance may mean the difference between success and failure. In times of great need, everyone remembers a mother's word." Erasmus came to a sweeping stop in front of them while inclining her head in a handsome motion.

"I was born an only child." Salt heard her own voice crack under the stress of buried emotion, bravely she carried on. "Both Mother and Father were older parents. They sort for me to find a substitute family of my own through the dancing profession, for when they sadly could no longer be there for me. And dance led me to meet Rhuand." She smiled sadly at the warrior in limbo. "They had already died of old age by the time we met, so never had the chance to meet you. And I would so dearly have wished you to have met them."

"But they are part of you, Salt. They have helped make you into the resilient, independent female that stands beside me now."

She saw his eyes soften to hers.

"People remain alive through our memories," he said, "and while we talk about them, they are never forgotten."

Erasmus moved closer towards them. "Together, you have successfully come this far against premeditated odds, therefore it is critical in the final colour you find the opportunity to reach eternal salvation–"

"You will help us reach the end purpose?" Rhuand turned a shrewd gaze to the source of enlightenment.

"While I cannot completely prepare you for what is to come, I am here as a guide and will indicate any obstacles I can foresee, but the overall ability and action can only be taken by the two of you, together." Erasmus brought forward a small bag from an inside pocket within her stunning cloak. Its shimmering golden fabric caught the late-summer sun as she pulled back the two draw strings. "I invite you both to pick out two volcanic rocks from the bag to represent endings and new beginnings." She extended her arms towards them with her offering. "The volcanic rock absorbs the energy round us and can transmit fractions of images to me. And with your help – bridge the gaps."

Cautiously, Salt went first, feeling the luxurious fabric against her skin until she became conscious of the contents. Tracing her fingertips over the cool rocks concealed within the bag. She selected two, going by nothing but the feel of the rocks for preference, then pulled her hand back out into the evening sunshine.

Warlike, Rhuand placed his hand into the bag as though

experiencing a sensory moment. Salt couldn't help but think anyone would have thought he was placing his hand into a bag of reptiles.

"Good!" said Erasmus. "Now, once you've selected two rocks, Rhuand, I want you both to not think too hard about the past, present or future. Instead, just be with the magma rocks, allow your own energies to spontaneously flow through you and into them."

Salt emptied her mind of all frightful thoughts, breathing deeply and evenly she held her hands out, palms to the sky, displaying the volcanic rocks.

"The rock held in your left hand signifies the past, the right hand, the future." Her voice was low but penetrated into Salt's mind.

"How did you come to be here, Erasmus?" the Earthlet acquiesced.

"Like you, I am part of the earth element. I found myself cast out here due to the actions of Female Munrah."

"What did you do to insight her anger?" Rhuand removed his hand from the bag. He had made his selection.

"I predicted her downfall." She paused. "And from this, Female Munrah sort to remove everyone who would pose a subsequent threat to her reign in order to disprove my prophesy, this in turn came full circle in my direction, as she gravitated to the blind belief the prophesy could only be destroyed if I, and those close to me were murdered." And further words fell from her unguarded lips, drawing Salt closer to her. "Female Munrah and I are second cousins. In her youth she was never with others, they were in her presence. A natural born leader. From the moment she leaned forward, fate saw her, and Female Munrah took control with both hands. Because of her want. A woman warrior, she could do it. And did."

Salt watched as Erasmus pulled the draw strings together on the bag, then replaced it into the inside pocket of her stunning petrol-blue cloak. "Female Munrah has destroyed many lives and loves without any form of trial and retribution, as I have experienced first-hand with Rhuand–"

"Trial?" interrupted the source as she looked into Salt's eyes. "Female Munrah is well aware of the destruction she has prevailed over others to gain superiority. She does not deserve a prolonged trial, this would only serve benefit by allowing her the opportunity to devise an escape plan. No! The less time permitted, the better. However, retribution on the other hand is quite a different punishment."

Erasmus narrowed her eyes, seemingly to pull herself away from her own personal thoughts and centre herself to find a deep telling concentration. Salt focused on her own choice of rocks, to her mind she saw nothing distinguishing about either one of them.

After a short while, the source broke into the golden silence – "Both ending rocks signify a clash of swords, a clash of will. Before the two of you arrived here separately, there was an incident that had the potential to put an end to your courtship... but instead it forced you closer together... action taken outside your control..." She paused in mid-thought. "Yes... a deliberate attempt to destroy the seed of your attraction... a warning sparked into raging flames–"

"The narrow-boat fire." Salt cut into the other's words with swiftness. "Could that be what you're describing?"

"Yes!"

"The fire-starter was never discovered, though." Salt hesitated, noticing Erasmus looking doubtful to hearing her choice of words.

"No, Salt," she continued. "The fire-starter may not have been openly discovered, but his actions came to the knowledge of the few."

"The few?" said Rhuand harshly, Salt sensed unrest prickle through his spirit by the way he stood stiffly next to her.

The foreteller, having the power to pervade made plain her affirmation. "The culprit was architectural in his intention to do harm to your blossoming relationship..."

Salt held onto the one word – *architectural*, sensing something familiar, something at the back of her mind that rang true, if only she could grasp onto it... a link to the past. Then, a name jutted into her thoughts and she said it out loud into the band of golden hue, "*The Hound* – of course – Breon Leviathan, he was an architect!" She looked straight at Rhuand for confirmation. "And he mysteriously went missing about the time of the fire, didn't he..." Her voice trailed off at the painful memory.

Erasmus's concentrated gaze did not waver as she studied both rocks held in each of their left palms. "This calculated devastation speeded up the process of your strengthening bond, but that in turn also speeded up the process to further devastation... your enforced life separation at the hands of Female Munrah on Lake Gardenia." Erasmus took a deep breath. "You. It was you, Rhuand Mezarron who sort revenge on the architect!"

"Rhuand?" Salt was alarmed. Her eyes searched his face for answers.

"Yes!" he said bluntly. "I suspected Breon was responsible for the heinous act on your home as soon as I heard about the arson attack. Luckily you were not on the narrow-boat when he set light to it – but I could only imagine what he would be further capable of. And I knew, Breon wouldn't stop after one warning. He would progress. He had to be stopped."

"Why didn't you tell me?" She sounded agitated to her own ears.

He held her eyes. "Because you had enough trying to regain your health, recovering from smoke inhalation when you discovered the fire – I confronted Breon, heard his laboured confession and acted out my justice on him." He then deliberated, "Erasmus, you said it was known amongst the few – but no-one had seen him carry out the attack on Salt's home – and following his death, I've remained silent to this every sola day."

Erasmus's eyes focused closely on Rhuand's ending volcanic rock. "After you killed the architect, you left him."

"Yes," the steel warrior agreed.

The prophet raised an eyebrow. "Breon Leviathan was revived. He was brought back to life!"

"What! How could he be? The shot was fatal – I made sure of it." He showed a flood of double forced anger not only through his words but in his facial expressions.

"I see snap-shots of images, the architect in a coma, medics standing over him, orders for regular reports of his progress... Yes. He survived to tell his story."

"To whom, did he repeat his story too?" asked Salt as a dread came to settle heavy on her shoulders.

"Female Munrah!" the source said in slow confirmation. "Your courtship has been constantly tarnished by a powerful force of energy against your connection, and this aggressive willpower to break you both has relentlessly followed you through from the home planet and into the now–"

"But do we stand a chance to end all this conflict?" Salt felt her eyes brim with tears.

Rhuand had selflessly sort to keep her safe by removing a dangerous predator from her life, this she now knew, and yet, their short life together seemed fatally destined to follow one act against them with another, even crossing over to this alternative dimension. Salt fought not to let the tears flow down her cheeks, and looked up into the band of shimmering gold above... all roads clearly led back to one individual, Female Munrah.

Erasmus turned her attention to the second set of volcanic rocks that represented new beginnings. "I see more crossed swords." She sounded heavy hearted. "So many clashes of force... more than anyone should have to endure in their whole existence." She hesitated. "I don't often ask this, but as this is an exceptional circumstance, would you both turn over your beginning rocks to show what lies beneath?"

They complied as she requested. Salt heard the source exhale a sigh of relief – the lovers looked and held each other's strengthening gaze.

"Yes, I can see a symbol of a great sola sun."

"And the sola sun represents good?" Rhuand sounded optimistic.

"The very greatest of good The sola sun represents a new dawning. A new beginning. But beware, while the sola sun offers a brilliant warmth of sanctuary, it can also burn." Erasmus took a measured step back from them, and surveyed them with delightful curiosity.

"What is it, Erasmus? What have you seen?" Salt was eager to learn anything more that might benefit them, even if the female prophet thought it could be over-sharing.

"Something which I have never known possible before..." Erasmus glanced back down into the palms of their right hands, still holding out the beginning rocks. "It would appear, Salt Delray that a change has already been felt through you... does that make any sense... have you felt different recently?"

"Well, yes! As you mention it."

"And how would you describe it?" asked the source searchingly.

Salt blinked herself into the moment of detail.

How best to describe an obscure, yet growing sensation?

"I would say... I feel a force in both mind and body, almost to the point where I catch glimpses of fearlessness from an inner self." She lowered her hands down to her sides, while still holding a volcanic rock in each. "I can only describe it as different from myself, yet familiar to me, as if it is an echo to something I had once lost."

Erasmus cupped her hands round Salt's jawline and looked deep into her eyes – just like her mama used to do when she wanted Salt to be reassured. "That is because you and Rhuand are becoming one, I never thought it would be possible for a life-form and a spirit to find union in such a way... this may prove to be your underlining advantage... a shared strength."

Salt felt the tender hands let her go, and the prophetess moved to stare meaningfully at Rhuand. "Caution. Remember as you go forward, with every acquired strength there is always a point of weakness – and your weakness is the love you have for each other. Beware, Female Munrah and her subordinates will prey upon this, for it is their only means to defeat and destroy you as a couple. Be in no doubt, plans have already been meticulously drawn up and a vicious trap has been placed into motion. How you fight through your designed downfall will mean the difference between two possible consequences… damnation or salvation."

:

(8) RED OR DEAD

:

#ThreeShouts – With reverence, Earthlet and Metalgant handed back the volcanic rocks to Erasmus.

"Before you both leave this band of gold and enter the last sandsomme stone building, Salt would you be generous enough to attempt something for me."

Rhuand could hear a sensitivity in Erasmus's voice that indicated a mark of importance. He looked towards Salt, she was smiling back at him. Then he looked at Erasmus, and looked away. She reminded him too much of Salt.

He moved aside impatiently, hearing Salt say graciously, "Thank you, Erasmus. I would be glad to take advantage of your offer."

And in the beat of silence, there was nothing predatory about her manner that he could sense. Then Erasmus spoke. "I'm asking you to harness your energy, and in doing so, not only shall it prove the change taking place within you as a life-form is real and you can therefore use it to your own benefit, but it will also recreate an image of symbolism which shall act as a constant reminder, dear to your heart and mind and so carry you both forward."

"Symbolism?" repeated Salt genuinely enough, appearing to leave behind no impression of ill-will.

Rhuand searched the face of his lover and instantly he understood what Erasmus was asking of Salt – she was encouraging her to repair the distorted form of the brooch by using her new power of energy acquired from him. "Restore the Regard brooch to its original condition."

A small spurt of excitement, he sensed, sharpened her glances and her tongue, "But how do I harness the energy?" She appealed to both him and Erasmus, reaching out her arms, her fingers caught and lost the air... "I haven't much to hold onto and what I have seems to fall like rain – hot rain."

"Visualise what you want to take place before you make contact with the brooch. Make sure you hold a clear image in your mind, and whatever you do, don't waver from this image. Self-doubt will only impede the outcome." He willed her on. "I know you have a good sense of self-preservation, Salt. Use it."

"But you've had more time to perfect the quality of Iquique, Rhu... this is all new to me... what if I get it all wrong?" Doubt began to spread across her face.

"And it is for this very reason you must attempt the procedure now, Salt," said Erasmus, "before using the technique against your adversities. It is utterly imperative to experience that something yourself, and by doing so, you will not hesitate to use the energy again, safe in the knowledge it works. There is no room for self-doubt, it will only hold you back."

"But to use it on the Regard brooch, what if I distort the brooch further – render it ineffective as a key to open the final sandsomme stone door." He could hear the desperation in her voice.

"Precisely why, pertaining to visionary, this item of jewellery should be used in such a way, because it is of great importance to you both. Nothing through the causeway colours has been thoughtless. Everything has had its place within the progression of evolutionary colours and has subsequently led you to where you both stand now – right on the edge of an unknown outcome, but nevertheless stronger in your unity of bond together."

"Salt." Rhuand had to support her like a protective cloak through the realisation that while she knew she had a force growing inside her with the potential to equal his own, she must now learn how to use it. And understandably with power came responsibility – a responsibility to help, not harm their circumstances. "Salt," he repeated, lingering over her name, giving himself the time needed to find the right words. "I trust you with my whole spirit being, you came through for me, found me in this vast place of limbo. You believed it was possible to be reunited, and that's just what happened. Belief holds such power. Never let anyone sway you against that knowledge."

Reaching out to her, she met him half-way without hesitation and gave him her hand. He gripped it, to confirm his belief in her. She in turn squeezed back.

"I know how serious this is, but we are in a serious time. And as I trust in you, I ask you to trust in me also."

"I do trust in you, Rhuand. I trust in you an awful lot." She released her hand from his. Then, placing an even weight over her feet to balance herself, she inhaled in a long, steady, slow breath and closed her eyelids. He knew she was visualising, some aesthetic sense, long sleeping inside her that had been capped and now responding to joyfully. And he, visualising along with her – the Regard brooch resuming its designed shape of beauty.

Vigilantly, he watched as she brought up her hands to place over the dulled and deformed item of jewellery. As soon as she made contact with the brooch, it slowly, very slowly, began to change in form and through the gaps between her slender fingers, Rhuand and Erasmus studied its changing shape, until... until it appeared to be restored to its once intended splendour.

Salt flashed open her eyelids, "Did it work? Has it... I'm sure I felt..." She peered down at the brooch. "Oh, my..." She smiled, and smiled some more. "A world of colour opened up before me, exquisitely pleasurable, promising revelation after revelation."

"All the brooch needs now is spit and polish to let those precious stones shine brilliantly in this band of gold hue," confirmed Erasmus.

"Yes!" Laughed Salt good heartedly. "Thank you, thank you both."

"What for?" Erasmus looked intrigued. "It was nothing."

"It was everything! You believed in me, and therefore let me believe in myself."

"You cannot put something where it does not already exist," he said. "The belief was always there within you, Salt. It was just a matter of reminding you. You've been through so much with me from the home planet to this alternative dimension, and yet, you never cease in amazing me." He lent forward and kissed her on the lips, and he felt an instant ripple of energy surge through his spirit. Her face lit up with an effervescing happiness, as if she too had felt the ripple, sharing a joyous moment of being in tune with each other's being.

"Now I can see you are both ready to face the final sandsomme stone building. My thoughts shall remain with you both." And as they turned from each other, they looked about for Erasmus, but she had vanished with an inmost swiftness into the dancing air particles that shimmered and glowed in the spectacular band of gold.

"We're on our own now."

"We may be on our own, but we have each other." She swallowed hard. He fought to remain as normal as possible to her reflecting amber eyes in his limbo state. Now was not the time to go against his own choice of words and self-doubt himself. Together they held the possibility to forge ahead and survive against the perishing odds set into motion by Female Munrah and her obedient dark followers.

And his mind flashed to Lapis-Lazuli and Rafe who would be striving to accomplish their part in saving the limbo element forces. "We must now concentrate on achieving our own personal accomplishment," he vowed in a resounding voice as they moved along and further into the band of gold.

:

Salt moved with intensity to position the renewed Regard brooch into the final sandsomme stone door. It fitted into the indented shape with ease and perfection. She sounded hard with triumph. "No sight or sound of Female Munrah and the others, but I fear there is more renewed commitment to retaining her power."

"Yes," replied Rhuand. "We mustn't drop our guard for one moment and relax. She may already have entered the colour red."

"I just want you to know, regardless how this ends, I wouldn't wish to be anywhere else. I'd follow you to the edge of rationale if it meant we had a little more time together." She smiled into his eyes, but he could feel her anxiety beneath the outward look of keeping face. His heart went out to her in plain sight.

"While we're in the causeway colours my main concern is if Lapis releases the Ark of the Okarpi to the five elements back on the home planet, and limbo is lifted, then what will happen to this alternative dimension – will it just cease to exist, with you in it?"

"The answers will appear when the time is right," she said bravely. "Remember, Rhu. I came here with the sole purpose to aide you through limbo so you could reach the sanctity of salvation. I'm sure whatever is to happen, it will not be the total end. We will find each other again in the future when we are both of spirit. Walking alongside you in your sufferance of limbo has been my gift to you, as you gifted me by saving my life from drowning at Lake Gardenia."

He held onto each and every word she said. Her soft amber eyes showed a tenderness he longed to dwell in, but time was against them. "Yes, Salt, but the gift of life I gave to you on Lake Gardenia was no real life at all, was it?" he spoke in sadness. "Instead you were forcibly incarcerated at the Irongate prison. In truth, when you really think about it, we both merely existed before we met each other, after which we found a glimpse of full life, however short-lived. And we have existed through the strains of punishment ever since."

Salt nodded courageously. "Then we must fight to attain the blessing of the final colour. I strongly believe there is a spring of hope to eternal happiness." The Earthlet removed the Regard brooch from the stone door. Then, hastily repined it onto her turquoise bodysuit. There were tears in her eyes as she tried to smile back at him.

Rhuand was quiet and watchful. "Are you ready?" he spoke against the familiar grating sounds of the magnificent door as it opened.

"We've waited long and hard to reach this borderline, and if I've learnt one thing, it is this, love transcends the life we are born into and is carried forward with each and every one of us."

Their eyes locked together in silent meaning. He knew with each and every step he took, he would fight and strive with all his spirit to ensure their bond of love and unity remained endless. Abruptly their engrossment was broken, as the sandsomme stone door suddenly stopped opening. It had opened as far as it possibly could before it would begin to close.

Concern immediately tightened their faces and looking away from each other to sight the enormous space beyond them, they hurriedly stepped across the threshold. As Rhuand's eyes adjusted to the internal setting, a sinister feeling settled upon him. His concern sharpened his voice, "Something's not quite right." He couldn't identify the feeling for what it was. Rapidly, the uneasy feeling grew, he reached out a hand to her as the door juddered to a close, swiftly he turned round to the direction in which they had entered, only to find she was nowhere in sight – a frantic numbing chill ran down through his spirit.

Where is she?

"Salt!" he shouted. "SALLLT..."

A uniformed pace of stiletto heels struck the sandsomme stone floor. Slowly he turned towards the direction of the sound, under no illusions as to whom he would be faced with...

"I spy with my little eye something beginning with... T," Female Munrah said in sing-song voice before letting out a burst of wild laughter. "Any suggestions?"

As though on cue, from behind one of the many pillars within the elaborate building, a shady figure stepped forward. "Traitor!" the figuration shouted.

"Correct!" she said approvingly. "We have a traitor amongst us! A traitor to the Metalgant regime."

Rhuand narrowed his eyes in deep concentration to sight the figure who stood at some distance from him. Seeing something proverbial in the way the figure moved – instantly he knew it could be no-one other than the architect. "Breon Leviathan!"

Erasmus had spoken the truth earlier.

For, *The Hound* was indeed, *alive.*

"Well now, Rhuand Mezarron. Surprised to see me, I'm sure. Considering you left me for dead on the north beach sands." The architect allowed his distaste to show through the deliberation of his words. Rhuand knew, the architect was not a being of limbo, he was still very much a life-form, looking remarkably similar to how he was when Rhuand last set eyes on him, only now, proportionately less muscular, the result of time spent laid sedentary in a coma, he thought shrewdly, which no amount of training could act as preparation.

And as he moved steadily forwards, Rhuand noted his adversary wore the same type of grey tweed suit he'd always favoured, with plush crumpled animal-skin gloves and his mid-length dark hair swept immaculately off his face, clearly showing the furrows from an oily toothed comb.

The former Head Kielter separated his mind and his senses to where Salt could possibly be. But he felt no trace to her. "You deserved to be left for dead following your calculated action against Salt Delray." He voiced in equal force and frustration, not knowing where she was.

She has to be within these four walls, but where?

"Many deserve certain things to befall them, Rhuand."

Menacingly, Female Munrah began to walk alongside the architect. "But when it comes to one of my high ranking Metalgants taking upon themselves to kill another Metalgant without being given permission from me, well, I can't have such disorder of free-thinking within the establish. Order must be adhered to. And you, Rhuand Mezarron were proving yourself to be an individual, not a game player. And *all* for the sake of an Earthlet." She spat out her contempt. "There is, and never will be a place in my system for such reckless Metalgants who choose to benefit themselves and not me, their leader."

"You are no longer my leader, Female Munrah. I am my own spirit."

"Perhaps, but from where I'm standing, Rhuand Mezarron you are far from being a free-spirit in this dimension of entrapment. You should know by now, I have no need for your unique qualities to be taken back with me to the home planet, I've already acquired two new specimens who will be cheered and adorned by the establishment for advancing Metalgant technology. Yes! I have great plans – you had your chance, and you threw it away. Therefore you are free to languish in this pitiful existence once the condemned girl is dead!"

Rhuand knew he mustn't rise in anger against the provoker just yet, he must keep a level head until he understood more.

Glancing round the interior he searched for a sign, an indication as to where Salt could be, then something arrested his attention, something he'd sensed earlier as they'd stepped into the building, but couldn't put into words at that time, and his unrest formed into a recognition – every subsequent sandsomme stone building he and Salt had walked through was more elaborate, more intricate, more grander than the last. But this final building was different, its interior was not symmetrical – his eyes settled on the tremendous spherical rose window high above the exit door that led into the next colour – only this window was unlike all the others, it was not circular but instead a semicircle shape, as if the other half of the window had been obscured from view…

Of course, the building's interior has been divided into two – by a false wall!

Rhuand's eyes came to settle on the architect, Breon Leviathan. His face looked quietly smug.

He knows something I don't – sensed Rhuand.

Female Munrah must have instructed him to redesign the interior of this building, and Breon cleverly designed a false wall with deadly intentions.

Salt's either hidden within or behind the wall.

A sudden fury began to build upwards from his feet and throughout his entire spirit in limbo. They dared to be so relentless, so predetermined in their pursuit of harming his one and only true love, Salt Delray. Rhuand would stand no longer for words. He would take only action.

And where is Skada?

As he surveyed the grand building, two shadows moved, one to guard the entrance door, the other to guard the exit. And while he didn't recognise either one of them, instinctively he knew they had to be the two Metalgant prison guards who had recently suffered a limbo of their own.

But how skilled are they in the technique of using Iquique?

His mind fractured back, his skill had to be learned over a series of time at Lake Gardenia. And while the prison guards hadn't subscribed to the same length of time he had, they had one advantage; they'd witnessed him fight Skada earlier and claim the Braska sword in the blue hue, maybe even learned a strike or two for themselves…

Rhuand knew what he had to do. Just as Erasmus had stated before they separated company, his and Salt's weakness was for each other. Therefore Female Munrah had calculated to separate them yet again, recognising together they were stronger than when they were apart. He had to alert Salt to prepare for conflict –

Swiftly he transformed the steel threads from his slate coloured overcoat into several gleaming warfare missiles. Aware of feeling his now tattered coat fall were it touched round him, Rhuand shouted her name out wildly, then expertly threw a gleaming curved silver weapon into the air, it drove into and through the semicircle coloured glass window. The glass shattering, falling down the exterior of the building –

Then he heard the curved missile re-enter the building as it spun with force through the remaining coloured glass that was obscured from his sight. Acutely he listened for any giveaway signals to prove his gut instinct right – and then, there is was, the sound he'd been listening for, as he pinpointed the smashed fragments of glass hit the floor inside the building behind the partitioned false wall, and he knew for certain Salt must be there – he willed her through his mind to reach out and catch the defence object, and transform the steel missile through her power of Iquique into a weapon of choice against Skada.

:

#DanceBeforeDeath – Taken by a forceful hand movement from behind and the Earthlet was sent reeling through a retracting panelled doorway within a false wall. Before she could yell out alarm to Rhuand, the door smoothly closed and she found herself being hauled backwards by her bountiful hair.

"No point screaming, Earthlet. By the time Rhuand Mezarron discovers this hidden room you'll already be dead!" the assailant chillingly whispered into her ear from behind, causing her heightened senses to rack through her mind who the man was...

The sibilant voice resumed softly – "May I suggest, you save your energy and instead put up some degree of fight against me? I do love a fight. Even a suggestion of a struggle is better than a surrender, especially from you, my favourite Earthlet."

She felt his body vibrate with laughter against hers and in that split moment she knew who he was – Skada!

In awakening anger and burning rage, Salt knew by bitter experience, a well laid plan can be rudely disrupted by surprise, simple preventative measures and effective release techniques – so before he could pull her down backwards by her hair, she quickly grasped his wrist with both hands while keeping his hand as tight as she could against her head, then crossing her right foot over her left, she forcefully pivoted to face him. Deliberately leaning away from him, she knew this would lock his wrist and strain it. Her self-defence action stretched him upwards, by the pressure of her need to survive, Salt Delray kneed him as hard as she could in the groin – but there was nowhere to run – they were closeted behind closed walls.

Bent doubled, Skada fell heavily to his knees, his face distorted in pure agony as he clutched and groped his groin. "Insufferable!" he spat. "Little Earthlet bitch! Bitch! Bitch!" he gasped, inaudible words followed by almost unrecognised cursing expletives which did not bruise her mind.

Self-preservation was utmost to her and at the same time she thought – *There are few things so discouraging as to make a special effort and to find your attacker, mysteriously, still at the same distance.*

Nevertheless, she edged her way along the false wall in order to survey him more clearly, while at the same time desperately looking for the outlet.

"Oh, you're a smart little objector aren't you? But in the end, we both know how this is going to turn out!" He rose unsteadily to his feet, and for the first time she noticed his grip on a steel axe in the other hand. Seeing his grip tightened.

Clearly thankful, she told herself, Skada had no knowledge that she now possessed from Rhuand a level of Iquique. Yes, unbeknownst to him, he had been saved from a reverberating shock to his bodily system by the fact he had held onto the steel axe, and she wore the Regard brooch. Without these buffers of foreign metal, Skada would now be convulsing uncontrollably across the floor in further torturous agony.

Salt tried to be polite as well as grave. She was good at that, she knew. "Nothing should be taken for granted, Skada as well you know." She had escaped from him before, and planned to do so again. But Salt held back from aggravating his ego, she had been taught, never to use provocation which could needlessly escalate an armed threat, into an armed attack. She needed him to go along with her approach, not anger him into unpredicted action.

He snarled, "You're simply delicious. I think, no… I know, I'm going to take real pleasure in each and every private moment with you… until, you take your last ever falter of breath." With renewed agility he began to ghost dance round her with skilled intimidating movements. "How do you suppose we take it from here, hmm, Earthlet? Do tell me, as I'm sure you will."

He was a sadist. How could she appeal to him without arresting any suspicion of her acquired Iquique? What she had to do was separate him from the axe – but how? She knew she'd have to play along with him to gain the first part of this objective. Her approach must appear believable to him. "Before I die I'd like to make one request that's, of course, if you're able to permit it without asking the permission of Female Munrah?" She simply couldn't stop herself from a measured provoke at his Metalgant ego, after all, it was common knowledge, no wise Metalgant would deviate away from strict instructions given by their tyrannical leader. "I'd love to dance for one last time, before..." She submissively lowered her head. "Before the fatal outcome you speak of."

"A dance before death?" He smiled but the smile did not reach his eyes. "Yes, I believe I could warm to such a request."

Salt removed her sacred Regard brooch, and placed it on the floor in an engaging and graceful manner. "Let's not have anything between us. Body to body." She flashed him a professional smile which hid a multitude of thoughts.

His ridicule movements of mimicry dance stopped abruptly. He narrowed his cold glittering eyes suspiciously upon her and his mouth curled into a cruel shape.

Sensing she was about to lose his confidence in her, she had to appeal to him directly. "It's highly unlikely I can physically overpower a strong male like you." She cajoled him, her speech was soft, soothing almost. "And one cannot truly dance from the heart while carrying a weapon in hand, and we both know, the male must lead the dance – unless we dance separately." Salt held his callous eyes, unthreateningly. "I've seen the way you've looked at me in the past, Skada. Now you have your time to dance with me. Alone. Take the invitation with both hands while it is here. For this is a one and only opportunity, never to arise again as you so rightly point out." She smiled appealingly, aware he knew a hopeful look, and would take full enjoyment of slowly destroying it.

He continued to stare at her, hard-faced. She was unable to read anything into his outlook, then, all of a sudden he dropped the weapon to the ground, and in a brusque manner waved her well away from it. She obediently followed him to the other side of the divided room.

If only he knew – she thought grimly – *how much of a disservice he was doing to himself by moving further and yet further away from the axe.*

"That's no big askance." His voice resounded with deceptive mildness. "I'll take one dance with you and it will be the last memory engrained in your Earthlet mind before I turn your life-light out." His sadistic smile twisted cruelly across his face as he slinked his way across to her.

The Earthlet graciously curtsied, and he mockingly nodded his acceptance to partner her. She held out her hands to meet his in a pose of dance, all the while visualising her current of energy clashing with his life-form to cause a violent electrical shock to his body of sinister flesh.

In his overconfident moment of over-shared contact, his body began to shake involuntary. She held onto him, tightly, determined not to break the circuit of electro-current passing through her and into him. She cupped her hands steadfastly round his thicken hands, feeling her own strength of power grow. He juddered backwards, her body persistently followed his. She couldn't let him go, not now, for if she allowed him to breakaway, he would undoubtedly attack back. She had to see this phenomenon of energy force through to the bitter end. Death by electrocution.

Skada let out a guttural cry, pleading pity for her to cease the current of excruciating pain. She steadfastly refused to adhere to his pathos wish, knowing if the shoe was on the other foot, he wouldn't show her the slightest glimmer of mercy. No, he would take an attentive and mind twisted delight in this. And that was the bold truth.

Without warning she heard her name shouted. Salt looked into Skada's contorted, facial features.

No. It hadn't come from his mouth!

She was certain. Promptly from this flicker of knowledge she heard a violent smashing of glass.

In swiftness, she turned to face the direction of the shattering noise and sighted a steel missile whipping through the air from the semicircle window of coloured glass. It was heading towards them.

Rhuand, she thought, and instantly pushed Skada away. He hurtled backwards within a fit of vicious shocks which continued to possess his entire body. Within a heartbeat, Salt visualised catching the steel missile in her grasp and transforming it into a deadly dagger.

Darting lithely into the stale air, she extended her arm and caught the object with effortless precision, and found herself holding a shiny steel dagger in her hand. With cold and calculating intention, she walked towards the brutal Metalgant, who had now fallen, thrashing about on the sandsomme stone floor. He lurched forward. "You... don't... have it... in you, Earthlet!" he taunted, in-between catches of laboured breath and dripping saliva down his chest.

"Words are merely lip-service without action." Salt bent down to retrieve the Regard brooch from where she had left it. And with surmounting deliberation, she pinned the jewellery back onto her turquoise garment. "Badbye, Skada." She knew she must take the opportunity while it was here, for he would forever seek his revenge on her and Rhuand while he remained alive. And while dying here in this alternative dimension would mean he would enter limbo-form, at least it would gain her some time. For he had to be stopped now! She couldn't plan for the future – that would take care of itself.

Mercilessly, she threw the steel dagger through the air, it cut through his flesh and embedded deep into his chest. Slowly, his convulsions subsided in their regularity, along with his gurgling breath, to the final death rattle.

She turned her back on him.

Done with him!

Now, Salt's thoughts sparked instantly to Rhuand. She traced her fingers along the dividing wall, hoping to find the hidden door she had been forced through. It was so expertly concealed she was at a loss.

In desperation, her eyes looked upwards to the shattered semicircle glass window, and it occurred it her, this could be her exit from here and her entrance to him, all she had to do was follow the path of the curved steel missile.

Recalling Erasmus, the foreteller's advice – visualise. Resourcefully, Salt picked up the axe, and using her new found practice, visualised a long, flexible steel rope, and quickly she felt the axe change from its designed shape and bend to her mind. With no time to marvel at her newly found mind-power, she lassoed the fine steel rope upwards to coil round the remaining bowed lead frame that had held each pane of glass in place.

Affirming, she pulled and strained to gain a feel of the rope before allowing it to take her weight. In fleetness, she began to climb upwards, using her feet to push against the inner wall and stabilise herself from swinging out uncontrollably as she placed one hand directly above the other, and in turn with metrical movement, heave herself upwards along the transformed steel weapon.

A welcoming enchantment of fresh warm air traced her face and hands as she came near the top. And as she looked out into the magnificent reddening sky, she was filled with an added resolve to fight on and locate Rhuand the warrior. Her hero.

Alerted, hearing dulled voices and darkening screams of sufferance, carefully, Salt stepped among the large broken pieces of glass on the broad windowsill, feeling vertigo beginning to waver over her as she looked down.

Must get a grip of myself! She told herself sternly.

Now is not the time of times to be dizzy in the head.

She breathed in a long breath, centring herself with the new strength of Iquique. She had to forge ahead. She had to see this through and walk alongside Rhuand into the stunning reddening colour of his salvation.

Uncoiling the steel rope, Salt swung her body across to reach the other side of the semicircle window, and as she peered down through and between the remaining jagged edges of coloured glass, what she saw taking place below within the building sent a chill through her Earthlet system… witnessing, Female Munrah stepping over *The Hound's* convulsing body. He appeared to have taken a sizeable electric shock from Rhuand's state of Iquique, frothing profusely from the mouth.

"Expendable goods!" spat Female Munrah, seemingly undeterred by the architect's pending death. "He's served his purpose by redesigning this gateway building, and I estimate the Earthlet will have taken her last breath on the other side of this wall of incarceration. Now, however, it's your turn, Rhuand Mezarron to be challenged. I will happily promote another Metalgant to Head Kielter just as soon as we're through here. Don't think for one moment you were unique to my establishment. You are, but one of many..." Wielding an axe she headed closer towards Rhuand. "Now, let's see the real extent of your strength against one of your own." She sounded almost conversational. Then, just as quickly, her mood changed – "Guard!" she shouted harshly across to the male stood in front of the sandsomme stone entrance, "I call on you, to do your very best of worst to this traitor of Metalgants."

Loyally the guard began to stride with even, deliberate steps across the stone floor towards Rhuand. And while Salt didn't recognise the male dressed in a fitted metallic suit with blackened shades, she knew he had to be one of the Metalgant prison guards who had been assigned to supervise her in the Irongate prison all that time ago, and who shadowed her and Rhuand through the Rainbow of causeway colours – only now this guard had risen to the same level as Rhuand – a spirit in limbo.

Silently watching from her elevated outlook, she sensed no-one had sighted her silhouette against the reddened skies inside the broken window, as fretfully she observed Rhuand and the guard moving, circling, keeping equal distance from each other in a clockwise direction. And with a burden of anxious intensity, not knowing who would commence the first strike, she willed Rhuand on, and – as if he'd picked up her vibe of willed strength, the former Head Kielter lashed out with a curved missile that audibly whipped and cut through the air to strike the limbo guard's steel face. The guard's head jolted to one side from the hit, the weapon clanged to the floor.

Quickly, Rhuand hurled several more curved missiles at him, but the forceful ambush didn't in anyway appear to prevent him from striving onwards with purpose to carry out Female Munrah's ruthless order, his only response was vocalised through an utterance of gruesome grunts following each violent crack delivery.

"It must be like looking in the mirror…" Female Munrah laughed raucously. "Tell me, how does it feel to finally meet your equal, hmm? Debilitating, humiliating, or simply the way it was always meant to be?"

Rhuand held his countenance. Salt knew he was super-sensual at that.

"My advice – save what little dignity you have left, Rhuand Mezarron by accepting you'll never achieve anything of distinction here! You're merely a traitor!"

Suddenly, the guard in limbo charged straight for Rhuand, forcing his back to hit a large stone pillar, and in retaliation the former Metalgant Kielter hit the guard square on the jaw, causing his shades to fly off. Visibly startled, the guard veered off to the side, stumbling to regain his balance.

In that instant of reprieve, Rhuand's eyes looked up to meet Salt's fretful stare, and a sickening feeling of emotion churned wildly in her stomach, for she had no indication as to how the clash between limbo verses limbo would end. But Female Munrah was right – it was like looking in a mirror, an exemplar mirror of strength. And as his attention moved from her to fervently fix back on the rapidly recovering guard who commenced an attack of equally strong metal fists onto Rhuand, who retaliated back likewise, the Earthlet's attention left the fighting Metalgants in limbo, seeing Female Munrah move closer towards Rhuand and begin to raise her axe vertically.

Instantaneously, Salt launched one end of the steel rope from her precarious position through the air, with the aim to strike Female Munrah and knock her off balance.

Contact!

Surprise!

Withdraw!

Speedily, Salt recoiled the rope back to herself while Female Munrah let out a torrid scream of pain as she involuntary released the axe from her grip. The axe fell heavily downwards, its blade sliced deep into her flesh and severed through the ankle joint to dismember her foot well above her stiletto footwear.

It flashed across Salt's mind, was this the same metal stiletto heel that had smashed with deliberate force into the frozen Gardenia Lake all that time ago, causing a momentous crack to appear in the ice and consequently leaving Salt to fight for her life, and Rhuand to lose his?

The Earthlet felt a cold and controlled rage settle within her, and with velocity, she began rapidly to scale down the vertical face of the internal wall from the broken window using the steel rope – landing lithesome onto the floor.

Feeling no guilt at sighting dark crimson blood pouring

profusely from the amputated foot, Salt let out a prolonged gut wrenching scream – causing both Rhuand and the guard to halt in their bombardment of steel fisted punches.

"Get herrrr!" shouted Female Munrah to the second guard through a growing realisation her severed foot, encased in a bloody stiletto shoe lay obscurely on the sandsomme stone floor. "Get them both! End this treacherous betrayal!"

And as the Earthlet prepared herself to demobilise the second guard, if only for a matter of moments, by planning to project out and whip the steel rope round his body-of-spirit – something extraordinary happened right there in-front of Salt's eyes – the second guard's outward appearance began to change, and seeing her stunned reaction, promptly he looked down at himself. Recognition spread across his face as he became aware he was changing from a silver spirit to a whitening transparency that rippled in its degree of clarity. Instantly he ceased in his forceful pursuit towards the Earthlet as his eyes quivered and dulled with a dread beyond explaining. He lifted his trembling pupils directly in alignment with Rhuand, then Salt, and whispered, "I'm afraid!"

"Something terrifying is happening!" cried Salt. She stared wide-eyed from him to Female Munrah who was now unsteadily leaning her weight against a stone pillar. Moving her gaze onto Rhuand, and following his penetrating stare, Salt saw the same occurrence taking hold of the first guard too, and in these startling moments of awareness, she felt a tremor of vibration begin to move up from beneath the floor of the colossus building, as the construction and everyone in it began to shake...

"The Ark of the Okarpi," shouted Rhuand, amidst the advancement of violent rumbling. "It has to be because neither of the guards have walked out into the red hue – and yet they appear to be transcending!"

Salt looked back at Rhuand. Yes, he must be right as the vibration felt different to those they had experienced from Tervanous. And Tervanous had been destroyed. Therefore something else was indeed happening and causing this powerful vibration. She searched for any like-for-like signs within his appearance to the guards changing states, but as yet, thankfully she saw none. Nothing had changed about him.

She felt choked with emotions.

But oh, please, her silence begged, *how much longer did she have left with him before he would feel his own personal transcendence?*

"Salt, we must get out of here! This entire building's about to collapse."

"Don't speak of the impossible!" yelled Female Munrah insanely. "Okarpi is hidden from sight, and will remain so. I, attended to that myself..."

And as she spoke, a pressure crack appeared at one end of the floor, and with tremendous speed it cut through to the other side, widening as it sped passed *The Hound*, now laid lifeless on the floor. Salt couldn't help feel a sense of overpowering relief. He too had met his life-demise, like Skada. Then her perceptive eyes locked onto the evil dictator, and she surprised herself by realising she had unknowingly developed a sadistic streak within her make-up. She spoke with relish – "While you strove to hunt us down, a great plan had been devised in your absence from the home planet. Friends and comrades from different element backgrounds joined together to help bring the Ark of the Okarpi back into the light, from where you darkly chose to conceal it, forever. A change is taking place, Female Munrah and you shall hold no formidable part in it, no dominance. The old regard will be reinstated to equalise all five elements–"

"Guards! Guarrrds…" The dictator panted in vain for more commanding words. But neither guard moved, still fixed in their position of transparency.

Female Munrah hobbled forward on her amputated ankle while her other foot still wearing her high heeled stiletto, scrapped irksomely across the sandsomme stone floor. But the damning tremors caught her off balance and forcefully she lurched forward, unable to save her downfall, she collided with the unforgiving hard floor. Gasping for breath, her mouth wide-open in uncontrollable destructive rage. "You mark my Metalgant words, Earthlet when I say – I'll see to you! This is not over, consider that my solemn promise! My ultimate pledge."

Before Salt could respond above the grating sounds of vibrations, the large sandsomme column closest to the injured tyrant began to move, dislodging from the ceiling as the building disintegrated round them.

And in the knowing of future knowledge – they only had moments to escape – a strong, steel, arm closed round her waist, ushering her forcefully away from danger and causing the Regard brooch to blossom – like a jewel of the new dawn.

And as they raced towards the exit door, deathly resonance screams could be heard, followed by an almighty crash full of resounding noises. And a great plume of yellow dust rose and shrouded upon them, screening their vision as they looked back –

Salt knew –

Female Munrah was dead!

:

#Relumine – With an overwhelming sense of survival, hands locked together, Rhuand and Salt raced towards the distant sandsomme stone exit door, stretched out, stretching the backs of their knees to their utmost limits, each step an age; like dreamers who mistake a nightmare for truth; unable to dissolve the edge of unconsciousness and escape –

He turned toward her, agile as a viper, feeling more so perhaps than ever before that he'd never be free from her presence. "Hold on tight."

She smiled bravely, and he felt her hand grip tighten, both unafraid to show fright, yet fighting – both seeing the recumbent walls shaking violently, while leaning dangerously inwards – hearing the criss-cross of discordant noises of the dislodging stones crashing to the floor, strewing the floor with fallen debris.

"These buildings have always been a place of refuge!" shouted Rhuand, hauling Salt at arm's length behind himself.

"If we don't escape it'll be my burial place!" she answered in a high clear voice that she understood his meaning. They leaned towards each other like fighters, and he could see her large beautiful eyes shining brilliantly in defiance, more perfectly understood to him now, than the rules of the Metalgant establishment.

"Run like the wind, Salt Delray!" he shouted. His face felt for a moment both sinewy and exultant. Then he laughed and she laughed in the face of danger, gathering speed, their fleeing feet kicked up the yellowish-red grinded particles which scoured them down like harsh sand-paper as they triumphantly pushed open with all their might, the last sandsomme stone exit door and rushed out into the reddening causeway colour, hearing unyielding thunderous noises as the building collapsed in on itself, crashing to the hardened ground.

Instinctively they stopped at the same time and glanced back to witness the building's final destruction. "It is a loss – such a beautiful building, gone!" she said with feeling.

"Better a loss we can gain from, than the loss of each other." They slowly turned to face each other and he felt a shared victory pass between them.

"This is it, then. We've made it as far as the red causeway colour." She sounded and looked as relieved as he felt.

He wound his steel arms round her slim, taut body and pulled her close to him, feeling her mouth kiss his neck and lead all the way to his eager lips. She stopped and gave an exquisite sigh. And he thought, *Salt Delray, you are beautiful… you are magnificent… you are… mine.*

"It's all thanks to you. You made it possible, I couldn't have taken this route through limbo alone..." He paused, too full of emotion. The silence between them was in this way busy, not awkward, yet familiar. "And neither would I have wanted to."

She began to pull away from him.

"What is it, Salt? What's the matter?" He waited painfully for her agreement, now he needed her reassurance.

"It's happening." She smiled, but the smile did not reflect in her amber eyes, and a travail of tears slowly appeared in them. "You're beginning to change. Just like the alteration that happened to the Metalgant guards earlier. You're changing from a state of limbo and entering the transcendent stage." He heard her sharp intake of breath while looking at him with increased attention, and when she spoke again, her voice was quiet but tentative, "The whole area round you seems to palpitate with white waves of illumination that attends upon you like a misty infatuation."

He felt the dire urge to push back the hair from her flushed cheeks, but he didn't want to let go of her hands, as though their contact together was in some way sacred and held the very essence into his movement of transcendence.

"Hold onto me," he said. "Don't let go." She nodded her agreement, and he felt an increasing ripple of magnificent warmth begin to travel throughout his spiritual light, and the ripple projected from him and into the Earthlet through their palm of connection. "Can you feel that? Can you feel the difference?"

"Yes!" She inclined her head in a beautiful gesture. "You always were written in the palm of my hand."

"And you in mine. Only now, this isn't a rehearsal, this is all there is. It's official."

Her eyes narrowed as she held onto him. "I can see glimpses of how you used to look when alive, as well as echoes of your limbo appearance – it's as though the two sides of you are morphing into one – and the connection between the two should not be questioned."

Then, curiously, as though he had suddenly remembered he had forgotten something, Rhuand became silent, concentrating on the abstract feeling – searching to pick up a corner of it and bring it into full focus – to gain a known knowledge.

He looked deep into the Earthlet's eyes, and as if sensing his necessity to be still, she too became silent, but watchful to his change.

Then, as if a door was instantly unlocked, his mind was flooded with hidden answers to recent questions. And Rhuand Mezarron recognised, he, like all individual souls across the five elements knew the answer to every possible question. They had just learnt how to forget them while on the home planet.

For to know all outcomes and possibilities would mean never being truly free to live a life away from the end result. Destiny. Instead one would be so consumed with planning for the future, and by its very nature, would hinder a life in the present. For this one gift of liberty had been given freely to all souls on the home planet by the infinite parent spirit of all elements who exists in the place of salvation.

But this gift of freedom had been twisted against all life-form elements through displacing the Ark of the Okarpi and keeping it hidden from majority sight to be almost forgotten, and in doing so, this had upset the balance of harmony across all five elements. And in its place, a deliberately misleading teaching had been created in the aim to benefit the few... creating a class-system with Metalgants at the element head. But the balance of harmony could never be substituted by worshiping false figurines and self-made dictating leaders, this, and so much more, Rhuand Mezarron now knew, and the knowledge reverberated through his whole soul.

Filled with a devotement of happiness, Rhuand parted his lips to speak, "Salt," he said softly. "Will you come with me?"

"Come with you? But I don't know if it's possible to go where you are going..." Sadness deepened her voice and squeezed it tight.

He could not, would not be separated from this beautiful female. They had strived together through thick and thin, through grave darkness and the occasional glimpse of brilliant light. And now he knew for certain, they could build a freeform existence of hope and love away from all echoes of sinister forces. "I remember, Lapis mentioning to me in the orange desert that the transcendent stage takes nothing away from the individual, it only adds. And now I am just beginning to know and really appreciate what those words actually mean…"

"Rhu," she interrupted gently. "I dare not allow myself to acknowledge what you're trying to say. But it is a word of optimism. Yes?" He felt the intensity of her lovely eyes possess him, willing him to clarify the whereto.

"My transference of Iquique to you is a veiled gateway, abridging your life-form to my spirit and so connecting you to both sides as it were – the home planet and a spiritual salvation with me."

"Are you saying, we will forever be connected as there is a part of you within me?"

"Yes. And from this gateway, you may enter the sunset of red along with me from this transcending stage and into the eternal levity of salvation. The part of you which remains life-form will enable you to exit through the red particles of sky, back to the home planet at any time you so wish. And from there, any red sky during night or day will carry you from the home planet back to me. You are free to go where you wish."

"Free…" Her voice lingered over the one word. "I have never thought that one word could apply to me, an Earthlet–"

"Yes, Salt!" he assured. "You, and I are without twisted restrictions, spiritual or otherwise."

"And as our bodies connected through life, so have our souls through the causeway of colours," she spoke softly. "That is agreeable and comforting to an Earthlet of belief."

"Indeed. That's the key, Salt Delray. There is a place for us both, together, if you agree. You have the freedom to remain with me in salvation, and return to the home planet if and when you so choose..." As he looked down at his once steel hands, he noticed for the first time his own energy of sparkling particles, and spirit slowly displaced through the process of transcendence.

"I do," she said joyfully. "I agree implicitly."

"It *was* and *is* our bond that has kept us strong, held us together, it can never be taken away, only added too."

She nodded. "Just as Lapis-Lazuli indicated..." She threw her arms round his displacing spirit and sank her face into him. "No more twisted Metalgant rules. No more brutal Metalgant boundaries. Just us."

'Just us.' Her words echoed in his mind and to his spiritual light. For that was what he'd always longed for from the first sighting of her on the home planet.

She was his beginning.

His ending.

And everything in-between.

"Walk with me, into the reddening sunset and embrace what is to come – breath of new dawn."

"B. o. n. d." She laughed generously, and he felt his energy lift as she moved and refocused on him. "Now that's an acronym to carry us forward."

And with her life-being of pure happiness and death-defying love for him that shone out from her into a sphere, mirroring his own eternal feelings for her, that's exactly what they did. Together.

#DecreeOfFate – *"Together..." I close my eyes, but as I reopen them everything has changed – blackness at the centre thread of a single candle flame; to an encompassing mauve; to a transparent yellow which edges the translucent tongue of flame disparaging darkness in the room. My, room. My, cell?!*

I look down, in my hands, the book titled: **Prisoner Of The Past: Salt Delray**. *And a sudden feeling solemns me, a feeling without namesake, but it is known to me, and I to it – for I have fallen out of the future. And I am reduced to a promise, while keeping hold of the words:* **If you sit very still, you can hear the sun move**.

THE END

:

Thank you for reading #Entrangement

Where Colours Don't Bleed

By the same author

#GirlRogues:
braggadocio

"They're dangerous to love, more dangerous to ignore –
which girl are you?"

Zizzi Bonah's collection of phem phant noir short stories and verses are for those with minds as broad as braggadocio, and nerves hard enough to rival a diamond from the first water.

There's the writer who murders words that press upon her page, and serves up a word-corspe poem... There's the optician who extracts salt crystals from her clients' tears, and dashes them on her fish and chips... Not forgetting, the lady who blinks a truth-moment into a picture, she is a living camera...

Health warning: This book is rather like surviving your renegade's cooking, and should therefore be taken in small bites. For that reason, it comes with no letter of recommendation!

paperback ISBN: 978-0-9935527-6-2
eBook ISBN: 978-0-9935527-7-9

ZizziBonah.net

About the author

Zizzi Bonah is a 5ft 3" lass born of Yorkshire parents. She spent seven dedicated years; three busking her self-penned songs on Bridlington, Scarborough and York streets, to then gigging pubs and clubs in and around the North of England, gaining airplay on BBC Radio York and Humberside using her birth name, Ida Barker.

A change is as good as a reply, (a line taken from one of Ida's eclectic-electric songs). With this in mind, she chose a new direction – to become a fiction author.

Zizzi's innovating, dangerous warrior characters are influenced by: wood, fire, earth, metal and water – all sources of dire changes and perilous reactions while having the power to control and/or destroy each other. Yet capable of creating the element that follows in the continuing cycle of existence – for better or bad!

Look out for Zizzi's other releases

:

Alice Returns Through The Looking-Glass

"For children of all ages"

A story where every goodbye isn't gone and every eye closed isn't sleep, Alice must find the answer to the Looking-glass question; much to the rage of infamous book reviewer, Paige Turner who threatens to jeopardise Alice's writing career in Authorland.

Hoodlemania descends, and together Alice and her predatory blonde alter-ego, Miss Penopause walk the Critical Path to set forerunning hazards and high-jinks in motion in a bid to make Paige Turner eat her words and silence the damning book review before publication – but at what cost? For as Alice learns; it is far easier to get forgiveness than it is permission to get Paige Turner!

eBook ISBN: 978-0-9957479-1-3

paperback ISBN: 978-0-9957479-0-6

>> audio book see website

This original story by Zizzi is also available as a screenplay and a stage play: both formats are adapted by Zizzi Bonah; script editor Gwen Hullah.

Alice Returns Through The Looking-Glass: A Musical Vaudeville Screenplay, eBook ISBN: 978-0-9957479-3-7 and paperback ISBN: 978-0-9957479-2-0

Alice Returns Through The Looking-Glass: A Musical Vaudeville Stage Play, eBook ISBN: 978-0-9957479-5-1 and paperback ISBN: 978-0-9957479-4-4

zizziology.com

www.ingramcontent.com/pod-product-compliance
Lightning Source LLC
Chambersburg PA
CBHW020957120726
47905CB00009B/2741